DEREK VITATOE

DEACON'S CIRCLE

— SEQUEL TO —

WITH THESE HANDS

Nyack **Books**

The Soul of Urban Literature

Published by Nyack Books
P.O. Box 980586
Ypsilanti, MI 48198

www.nyackbooks.com

Editor: Dennis Billuni

Cover Design: Latanya Orr
                               lterrydesign@comcast.net

Interior Book Design: Shawna A. Grundy
                               sag@shawnagrundy.com

Library of Congress: 2007908771

ISBN: 978-0-9769426-1-0

ACKNOWLEDGEMENTS

Again, I thank God for his many blessings and for being the force behind my ability to express myself through writing. It is through His glory that I am able to share this creative gift.

To Amiya and Makayla, know that I love you dearly. The sacrifices that I make now will be understood later. My heart shadows you at all times. You are truly a blessing. I miss you terribly when we are apart. Autumn, you are a terrific mother. Thank you for the abundance of love that you give to the girls.

To my mother, words can't express how grateful I am for the affection you shower on each of us. From grandkids, to your very own, you always find a way to share the unique qualities that makes you this amazing woman. You are an inspiration and a mentor to me. Without your guidance, teaching, and believing, none of this would be possible. There are two types of people in this world...those who learn how to be leaders, and those who are born leaders. I speak respectfully in saying you have been a leader to many. Brother Billy, you are a terrific husband to my mother. There's not a day that goes by that I worry about her. Thank you for the world of knowledge that you have bestowed upon me.

Jay, I will always appreciate you. Monnie, love you big brah. Thanks for allowing a little pesty, annoying, bothersome little brother hang on your coat tail. It's not often that I express my indebtedness to you. You have done more than you'll ever know. Gerald, thanks for everything. God has a plan for all of us. Stay focused on your objectives and goals. Thanks for being my tutor of manhood. AJ and William, miss you cousins. Wish we were all close and down the street like many years ago. Although distant, we still share love. Aunt Bev, you are survivor. I knew that you would not be defeated. You have all the courage I wish I had. Keep going. You can do it. You have done it. And I'm so proud of you! To my family in NOLA and New Iberia, love you all. We must get together soon.

To the families that have been so encouraging and kind (The Lawrence, The Samuels, and The Metters) thanks for everything and providing me with friendships that will last for many years.

My little brother Maurice, I know you would do anything for me. Know that I'll return the favor, tenfold. Thanks to all my other family: Quincy Lejay and the rest of the H.L. Crew, keep grinding. The brotherhood…#2, #3, barber-brother, thanks for hearing the complaints and providing sound advice. Cliff and Kenny, I appreciate you. Rush, P-Will, Beef, B.C, A.B, Ron Rice and the rest of the Eagles, thanks for your support.

Those with the keen eye who helped me shape this book: Pamela Artis, L-Boogie (church girl), Dawn, and Dennis Billuni, I thank you. LaTanya Orr, thanks for the design and many other services you provided.

Kwan, you have helped me tremendously. I mean it when I say that I'm grateful for your sharing the ins-and-outs of this challenging industry. You've been real from the jump.

To everyone I have left out, I apologize, but I still got love for you!

PROLOGUE

She thought the world of him. He had rescued her from an abusive relationship with her father, taken her from the dismal private school where she was enrolled back home, and most important, he had treated her like a lady, something Nizama had not experienced in her tender years of courtship. She now had a new love.

For the past three days, though, it seemed like something had been on his mind, and when she questioned him about it, he snapped at her. Their intimacy had waned, going from stimulating to demoralizing rather quickly. In her mind, he was so into pleasing himself that at times, he would tigerishly bang at her youthful pussy until he came, completely oblivious to the fact that he was ravaging her insides. Now, as she sat across from him at the Big Boy restaurant in the suburban city of Royal Oak, the nonchalant look on his face said it all. She thought about calling home.

"Maybe I should just call to let them know I'm all right," she said. "They got to be worried sick by now."

"I don't suggest that," Manuel said, blowing her off. "Hurry up and eat so we can get back."

"Seriously, I think I better call," she insisted. "Even if it's just for a second. I'll tell them not to worry."

"No!" he snarled. "You'll call some other time. Now hush up and finish what's on your plate."

Never had she heard him use that tone before. The feeling made her uneasy, and she couldn't help but express it.

"You're scaring me," she said, gripping her butter knife in the palm of her hand. "I think you should just take me back. Better yet, drop me off of at the police station. I won't tell them a thing, I promise."

He ignored her.

"Manuel," she spoke out, irritated by his sudden volatile behavior. "Do you hear me? I said that I'm ready to go home now. I've been away long enough. We can still keep in touch, right now, I need to get back."

As she stood to leave, Nizama felt his callused hand grip her tiny wrist. She stopped in her tracks, casting him a surprised look.

"Okay, I'm sorry," he caved in, releasing her wrist. "I'll take you back, Miami is hours away. There's no way I'll be able to take you until Friday."

"That's three days away," Nizama said, snatching her arm back. "Just drop me off at the bus station then. I'll worry about getting home myself."

Hurrying to pay the check, Manuel pulled out a crumpled wad of bills and placed some on the table. He grabbed his keys and hurried to catch Nizama, who had left in a rush. He followed her out the door and into the foggy parking lot, quickly deciding that if he was going to do it, now was the time.

"I'll take you," he said, grabbing her from behind to embrace her. "I'm just gonna miss what we had. The last few days have been amazing."

"Oh, Manuel, I'm gonna miss you too," she said, returning his hug. "I've just been gone too long. I love my parents. Even though they can be assholes at times, I still love them. You do understand?"

"Of course," he replied. "When will I ever see you again?"

"I don't know," she told him. "We're going to have to take a break from each other. Just for a little while. Everyone's been looking for us, and the last thing I wanna do is get you in trouble."

"I understand," he conceded, moving in closer. "One last kiss?"

"Sure," she said. "One last kiss."

They locked lips in the middle of the dark parking lot, passionately trading tongues. When they separated, Manuel became the impatient one.

"Let's go then," he said. "I'll drop you off."

It was only seconds later when Manuel was walking Nizama to her side of the car that a solid thump caught her on the side of the face and knocked her to the ground. Struggling to lift her into the car, Manuel closed the door, ran around to the driver's side, and hopped in.

An hour later, Nizama opened her eyes in pitch blackness. The cold basement where she found herself trapped reeked of mildew and aging drywall. When the lights suddenly came on, she was shocked to see six other girls tied together sitting near the furnace, their faces all with signs of having been badly beaten. Manuel stood at the top of the stairwell with dinner plates in his hands, then he began his journey down, glancing into Nizama's eyes with a smug look as he walked past. His expression told her that he had planned this well in advance.

CHAPTER ONE

The lead story of the *Detroit Free Press* read, "Four Detroit Teens Shockingly Acquitted of Rape Charges."

Sitting at the dining room table with a tall cup of steaming coffee in her hand, Theresa Gaines woke up early that morning to get the paper from the driveway, knowing that her son would likely be on the front page.

It had been a grueling two weeks of testimony. Theresa had endured listening to the victim's family and friends along with prosecuting attorneys denounce her only son, Ali. The victim, Elena Sanders, a promiscuous, well-developed teen, played the pity card so well when she testified that Theresa wasn't quite sure if the ten-man jury would side with her son or sympathize with the girl and send him upstate. Nervous about Ali's chances, Theresa had closed her eyes and begun to pray, until finally, the court clerk read the overwhelming not guilty verdict.

Theresa smoothed the paper onto the sturdy mahogany coffee table and read every word of field reporter Shane O' Bryan's column, then closely examined the picture of her son jumping for joy after the verdict. She sat with a refreshed look on her face and recalled watching the reaction of the Sanders family, all in complete disbelief that the final teen to be tried had also gotten off. If any of the four boys were to be convicted, they wanted it to be Ali, since they felt he was the instigator of the entire scheme.

With the burden finally lifted from Theresa's shoulders, she was ready to pick up her son from Booking and Release, stop at her church for prayer and to thank supporters, then hopefully resume an anonymous, normal life. Involved in the neighborhood church, she had gathered with the pastor and the church's faithful every night during the trial, begging and pleading with God to somehow get her son off, and they would never miss a Sunday morning service again. When her prayers were answered by the ten-man jury of Wayne County's Fifth District Court, Theresa Gaines immediately began preparing a homecoming celebration for Ali and his three childhood friends, Eric, Stanford, and Chris. Even though all four teens would celebrate their freedom on March 15, what truly occurred seven months ago on the hottest day in fifteen years, told another story.

*   *   *

It was one of those hot and humid Fridays in August when household fans blew out an agonizing heat, pulling in the warmth from outdoors and dispensing the roasting temperatures throughout every room in the house. Theresa Gaines was running late for work as usual and contemplated calling in for an unpaid day. With no more sick or vacation time available, the thought of working in her office under the slow fans management had pur-chased gave her second thoughts about going in. She wiped the sweat from her face and calculated certain expenses in her head to determine whether she could afford to take the day off. Sorting through the piles of junk mail on the table, she ran across an unopened phone bill. She took a deep breath, tore the envelope from one end to the other, and pulled out the statement. The past due amount printed in red ink convinced her to grab her keys and head out.

Ali Gaines had been planning Junior Ditch Day for the last month. Fully aware of his mother's work schedule, he called her at random times throughout the days prior to assure that she was where she was scheduled to be—work! An employee in the Customer Service division of DTE Energy for the past fifteen years, Theresa had a good work record, and Ali didn't remember a time when she went home during her thirty-minute lunch break. Just to make sure, he called home and heard the answering machine pick up. He decided to dial his mother's direct work extension, assuming she was there after her voice mail picked up. Worry-free now, Ali informed his select group of juniors of the ditching time. The only thing remaining now was to execute.

The welcome-back-to-school rally was scheduled to start at ten-thirty that morning. Whoever planned to go to the ditch party was to attend the two morning classes first, the back-to-school rally next, then break from their class line at the conclusion of the assembly. The sixteen expected ditchers would hide behind the tennis courts adjacent to the gymnasium, then once all was clear and before the janitors arrived, they would flee into the student parking lot. The majority of the school's campus security was expected to be in the center of the campus quad monitoring the behaviors of several hundred students leaving the rally, allowing the rebelling students to run through the parking lot undetected to the dirt trail that led to Ali Gaines' home.

In total, fifteen juniors had decided to participate, ten guys and five girls. One of the teens had chickened out at the last minute, frightened at his chances of being caught. Deciding he'd lay down the law at once, Ali made clear the rules of his house.

First, he informed everyone that no one was allowed to go upstairs or into the bedrooms unless accompanied by him, Eric, Stanford, or Chris. Secondly, no one was allowed to raid the kitchen, cupboards, or cabinets; he planned on taking up a collection for pizza and pop, so there was no need for anyone to go searching for food. Third, there was no stinking up the house with smoke. Anyone with the urge to smoke a cigarette or a joint had to take it to the porch. Next, there was to be no leftover alcohol bottles or empty beer cans. Everyone was expected to clean up behind himself and not leave any empty containers for his mother to find when she came home later that evening. Lastly, in the case of a disagreement, he advised everyone that the backyard was big enough to host any thumping. He didn't expect there to be any, but just in case, he instructed everyone to take any fighting or horseplay out back.

With every detail covered, a confident Ali bravely strolled over to his mother's newly bought home theater sound system, turned on some groovin' music, and began dancing the best way he knew how.

Hours passed without a glitch, and the beautiful rays of sunshine beaming through the windows slowly began to fade. The ditching party was a success. Everyone had a good time playing cards, slamming dominoes on the kitchen table, and throwing craps on the hardwood floor of the foyer. Several of the teens had made what's called a beer run earlier in the day, when underage youth set out to the store for liquor regardless. While one teen waits in the car as a getaway driver, the others invade the store, grabbing and running with any beverages they can carry, often a case of beer since the merchants display it near the front entrance. The thieving teens would run back to the car and speed off with cases of booze.

Elena Sanders was depressed. Three ex-boyfriends had dumped her in the last two months with her most recent, Anthony Kramer, calling it quits after a week. They were the typical boys who were after one thing and one thing only, what was between her legs. After achieving that in a short time span, they would kick her to the curb shortly after. They had all heard how easy Elena was to get in bed. Anthony had conversed with her over the phone for just a week before she was intimate with him. He dumped her soon after. She was given the nickname, "The Blunt," because like a joint was shared from one person to the next, so was Elena, and she had a track record of allowing numerous guys to *hit it*.

Suffering tremendously in school, Elena could care less about her 1.0 grade point average. Half-Filipina and half-African-American, Elena once had long, beautiful, curly hair that hung to her mid-back, until she cut it off after being dumped by a boyfriend she really liked. A slender girl who normally weighed about 115 pounds, Elena was dropping pounds faster than a spokesperson for the South Beach Diet. At her current weight of 107, her meatless bones showed the weight discrepancy. Why did Elena choose to attend the ditch party? She certainly wasn't in the mood to sit in a classroom and the mere thought of ditching must have been much more enticing.

Three o'clock rolled around, and the majority of the ditchers had left, except for Ali, his friends, and two of the girls. The school's first football game of the year was soon to start, and most of the ditchers chose to go home and sleep off their buzz before their parents arrived home from work. Eric, Stanford, and Chris had planned to crash at Ali's house and would leave at five thirty, the same time Ali was expected to meet with the football team in the school cafeteria. His mother worked a lot of overtime, and he didn't expect her till well after six.

Elena and her friend were the only two girls who decided to stay at the party, and given that Jessica had already had a bit too much to drink, she was laid out on the sofa next to a loud speaker. The boys were in the kitchen cleaning up when the discussion about Elena jumped off.

"What's up with Elena and the drunk girl?" Stanford asked. "What are they still doing here?"

"She's waiting on Ali to go over there and talk to her," Eric spoke up, shooting a disappointed look at Ali. "He keeps avoiding her like the plague."

Hours earlier, Elena had expressed interest in Ali to Eric. Just like a true friend would, he advised Ali of Elena's fascination. Ali, more concerned with safe-guarding his house, found the conversation at the time uninteresting.

"Who is she interested in?" Ali asked as he placed dirty silverware in the dishwasher. "How can she be interested in me? I thought she had a boyfriend."

"She did," Eric replied. "They broke up a few days ago. Why else you think she's been downin' those beers like that? Look at her over there, three cans in front of her and another in her hand."

Looking her way, the boys couldn't tell if she was drunk, tipsy, or sober. When she stood up to go to the restroom and stumbled into the fireplace mantle, all uncertainty vanished.

"You need some help?" Ali rushed to her assistance, grabbing her left arm and wrapping it around his muscular neck.

"I just need to get to the bathroom," Elena answered slowly. "Can you tell me where it is, Honey?" Sloppily kissing Ali on the cheek, Elena left a wet blotch on his face for him to wipe off. He pointed down the hallway.

"It's down the hall to your right," he told her with a smile. "You sure you don't need any help?"

"I can get there by m—myself," she stuttered, snatching her arm away from him. "Why haven't you talked to me all day? I've been waiting for you to come over here. Didn't Eric tell you that I like you?"

"Yeah, he told me," Ali replied. "Look, I'm sorry. I've had to play police all day and make sure nobody fucked up my mom's crib."

"Well, I'm going to the bathroom," she said after picking up her expensive handbag from the side of the couch. "I'll give you one last chance to come and talk to me. If you don't, I'm leaving."

She zigzagged her way into the bathroom, and Ali rejoined his eavesdropping friends in the kitchen.

"What are you doing coming back in here?" Eric asked eagerly. "That was the sign for you to follow her. Go in there and get some. This is it! It's time for you to become a man now."

The boys considered losing their virginity a sign of manhood, something they always talked about. The first thing they did when they became teenagers was make a pact that after each week passed, whoever was still a virgin had to put a dollar into the jar they kept hidden in Chris's basement. For the last year, Ali had been the only one still donating. They all had experiences to share except for Ali, and the others often ridiculed him about how much he was missing. As a result, now he felt the peer pressure thicken like cold soup. Ali silenced himself and picked up another plate to wipe off.

"Don't get scared on us now," Eric warned, taking the plate from Ali's hands. "Go back there and see what's up. She didn't have to use the bathroom. She said it to get you back there. What you waitin' on?"

"How do you know that's what she wanted?" Ali faltered. "With all she drank, she could be in there throwing up."

"Ali, her nickname is The Blunt," Eric insisted. He moved in closer, lowering his voice to a whisper. "You know what that means? She's been around the block and back, man. It doesn't get any easier than this. You'll be able to save up all those dollars for something else now."

"I didn't know her nickname was The Blunt," Chris jumped in. "That completely changes things."

"What do you mean, changes things?" Stanford asked with a look of concern.

"Well, have any of you ever heard of the saying, *Running the Bustos*?" Chris asked. He was familiar with the slogan from hearing his older brother talk about different girls that he and his friends would screw, one after the other. He overheard them once brag about a girl that the three of them tag-teamed one night. They called it, *Running the Bustos*. "Come closer, and I'll tell you what it means."

*   *   *

Walking past Jessica, who lay peacefully in a deep sleep, Ali inched into the hallway and tiptoed around the soft spots in the wooden floor until he was standing next to the bathroom door. He tapped gently.

"Elena, you all right?" he asked, clearly concerned. "You've been in there for a while now." He waited a second for a response, but there was none. He looked back at his meddling friends and shrugged his shoulders. He called out to her again.

"Elena," he spoke even louder. "Elena, open up. It's me, Ali." He slowly turned the doorknob and stretched his long neck into an empty bathroom. He closed the door and ran back down the hallway to his friends.

"She's not in there," Ali screamed. "Where did she go? She couldn't have left or we would've heard her.

And she didn't go out the back door." He looked into the backyard.

"She's gotta be in here," Chris added. "If she's not down here, the only other place she could be is upstairs."

They searched the house like little kids on an Easter egg hunt. The boys checked the downstairs closets, the foyer, behind couches and curtains until, after every inch of downstairs had been checked, Ali scaled the stairway that led to the upstairs bedrooms. When he looked inside the upstairs bathroom, Elena wasn't there. He checked the guest bedroom, and she wasn't there either. He decided to rejoin his friends downstairs and made it to the top of the stairwell when the struggling moans coming from his mother's bedroom led him to Elena, facedown on the comforter.

Playing hidden underneath the thick European blankets, Elena had messed up the perfectly made bedspread that Theresa was so particular about keeping in order. Ali glanced to his left and saw that Elena had already thrown her pants in the corner. Shocked to see the rest of her clothes balled up in a pile, Ali slowly advanced to the headboard.

He pulled the covers from off her head and watched the facial expressions Elena was making to keep from regurgitating the drinks she'd consumed. Without warning, Elena snatched Ali onto his mother's cot. Before he had a chance to get back to his feet, Elena's thick, wet lips engaged his. The quick strikes of her tongue back and forth in his mouth caught him off guard, and the strong taste of malt liquor made him feel queasy. It was after she slithered her hourglass figure on top of him like a snake that he wanted to stop and wait for another day to enter into manhood. He wanted his first act of intimacy to be special. Never did he envision losing his innocence to a girl so liquored up that she could barely stay conscious. But when he glanced at the bedroom door and saw all the eyes watching his every move, Ali knew it was impossible to stop.

Her scent was potent, like the smell inside of a world-class brewery. As the strong odor of malt liquor seeped through her skin, the funk made it near impossible for him to get into the mood. And when she kissed him, the remains of saliva in his ear forced him to change positions. Elena pulled up Ali's shirt and licked his "six pack" of abdominal muscles, and like any man or boy, the slight brushing of her tongue near his pelvis made him rise faster than a flagpole. When she felt the stiffening bulge in his pants, she lowered herself towards his belt buckle.

She unbuttoned his pants with her mouth and granted him his first breathtaking encounter with oral sex. The boys at the door watched in awe and envy, yearning for their chance to be in Ali's shoes. The foreplay was like nothing he had ever felt before. The warm sensation inside Elena's mouth was too much to handle, and as he grabbed the back of her long curly hair, the back-and-forth bobbing motion of her head forced a load of semen to spurt from the tip of his shaft. The thick, white, bleach-smelling semen slowly oozed out of the corners of Elena's mouth. For the very first time in his life, Ali Gaines experienced what it felt like to cum. It wasn't long until Elena had him erect again and prepared to experience another first.

She slowly rose to her feet and undressed, captivating him with her balloon-sized breasts. Ali agreed that the nude magazines he had collected up until that point couldn't compare to the real thing. As she seductively undulated her naked body like a pole-hugging stripper, she didn't bother asking him for protection. She reached down into her own pocketbook and pulled out a spermicidal condom. After she tore it open with her teeth, she contemplated whether or not she really wanted to roll the prophylactic onto his rock-hard penis and made an impulsive decision to toss it aside.

This young dick she was about to devour needed no protection.

Fighting cobwebs that had invaded her head, Elena was soon on top and riding him, engulfing his inexperienced dick with an overpowering passion that made her smell like roses instead of aging ale. Her spinning head caused her to pause for a brief second, long enough to prevent Ali from climaxing so soon. She quickly regrouped and continued drowning his unbending phallus, moving, popping, and steering her hips like a video vixen competing for the lead role in a porn movie. Although Ali ditched class earlier in the day, the heated intercourse he learned in his mother's bedroom was a lesson ten times better than any classroom instruction.

Feeling as if she was sitting at the peak of the Millennium, the most thrilling rollercoaster ride at an amusement park in Ohio, Elena suddenly became dizzy. Her mouth moistened with mucus traveling upstream, and she climbed off Ali in time to heave the gritty rummage from her stomach into the toilet. For the next twenty minutes, she emptied out everything in her system until only bile remained. After she finished, she sat nearly gagging to death, laying her head against the cold ceramic bowl and passed out on the floor next to the toilet.

*   *   *

The intense pain was too much for her to sleep through. Elena's vagina throbbed in agony, a pain so great that she could only surrender herself to the culprit assaulting her. Using her body one after another, the boys played a game of sexual musical chairs. As one jumped off, another hopped on. Trying desperately to wake herself, Elena couldn't, nearly deathlike from the vast amount of alcohol she had consumed.

The pain was inconceivable, like that of a ten year-old girl having had her innocence brutally taken by a sexual predator. Elena felt that same ache. Someone was violating her, had violated her, and she couldn't shake them off. She could only lie like she was, arms and legs spread-eagled. At the beginning of the day, Elena had only wanted to miss school and grieve peacefully over the boyfriend she had lost. But now, as different guys were jumping on and off her like an Amtrak train, she hoped it was all a dream. Was the sharing of her body with a different guy just a nightmare? She wished. When Jessica burst into the room, screaming and yelling, Elena could only reach for her best friend's hand and murmur a soft cry for help.

*   *   *

School didn't miss a beat, and all seemed normal. The school's football team had a perfect 7-0 record, and the glass jar hidden in Chris's basement hadn't collected any dues lately. In fact, they had much more to talk about now that they were all men. Ali had actually entered manhood twice. Days after his encounter with Elena, he was so destined to find another chick to have sex with that he had coerced a college student into going back to her place, having met her at a party that his crew was privileged to attend with Chris's older brother. Ali had lied about his age, telling the girl that he was eighteen. After socializing for a bit, they went to her apartment, where he seduced his way into her bed.

"Was it truly this easy?" Ali had to ask himself once he finished and was staring at her bedroom ceiling. It was the million-dollar question that eventually would be his undoing.

The fifth game of the season was against cross town rivals, the Detroit King High School Crusaders, who went into that night's game competing for first place in the division. The bleachers were filled to capacity five minutes prior to kickoff and there was standing room only. The biggest game each year was between the Detroit Cass Technicians and the Detroit King Crusaders. As was the case that year, when those two teams got together, scouts from major Division One universities attended to evaluate prospective athletes. While a freshman, Ali had been highly recruited after starting as a cornerback on the varsity squad. During mid-season of his sophomore year, he switched to wide receiver, where he helped lead the Technicians to the third round of the state playoffs. But the team's expectations for this year were different. They were anticipating exceeding last year's berth and competing for the state championship. With Ali's phenomenal talent, Cass Tech's goals seemed very realistic.

The game was tied at fourteen with a minute and thirty-five seconds left in the half when the Technicians took over at the Crusader's twenty-yard line. Knowing that the offense would have to go the length of the field to score, the coach decided to run a no-huddle, two-minute offense. Down the field the team marched, play after play. Ali had already caught eight passes, three during that particular drive. It was on third down when he made a remarkable catch for twenty yards to keep the drive alive.

The quarterback had dropped back five steps and heaved the ball towards the nearest sideline. Out of nowhere, Ali stretched out with one hand to catch the ball, tight roping the sideline and keeping both feet in bounds until he was knocked out of bounds by a ferocious blow from the opposition's free safety. When the sideline's visiting coach from the University of Michigan, Lloyd Carr, helped Ali to his feet and whispered, "Nice catch, son. I expect the same from you in a couple of years," Ali could only gleam with appreciation. He sprinted back to the huddle.

At halftime, the score was still tied at fourteen. The Technicians had fumbled seconds before the end of the half, ending their threat of scoring. In the locker room, the head coach chewed the team out for playing so passively.

"What the hell are you guys doing out there?" the coach scolded them. "Nobody's gonna give it to you. You have to take it. Do you want to go home now and forget all the shit you had to do to get here?"

"No sir!" the team yelled in unison.

"Then I expect to see the same team next half that I've coached the past nine weeks and not some Cinderella team with dreams of making it to the next round."

The coach left the room shortly after and allowed the team to focus amongst themselves. Ali rose to his feet first and began the team's chants to try and get everyone riled up. Once everyone seemed ready, they lined up at the tunnel, hyped and ready to exit onto the field. Surprisingly, it was the wide receivers coach who tapped Ali on his shoulder pads, signaling him to break away from his teammates. A short, stubby police officer with a head full of gray hairs was standing next to the head coach. Ali walked over to the two of them.

"Ali Gaines?" the hefty, gray-haired officer said.

"Yes sir, I'm Ali Gaines."

"Place your hands behind your back for me, son. You're under arrest for the rape of Elena Sanders." The officer pushed Ali face first against the wall. He slid his armbands off his forearms and tore the tape away from his wrists, then fastened the handcuffs around Ali's wrists.

"Wait just a second!" Ali's head coach screamed at the officer. "You can't do this now, midway during a football game. What's going on here? Let him go!"

The coach moved towards the officer.

"I'd suggest you stay right there." The officer grabbed the butt of his baton with his free hand and spoke into the receptor on his shoulder, asking for backup. As the other fifty-six confused team members looked on, the officer began to read Ali his rights.

"Wait and let's discuss this," the coach pleaded for Ali's release. "Ali, what's this all about? What have you done?"

"I haven't done shit, Coach." Ali tried jerking his wrists free. "Let me go!" He squirmed, trying to maneuver himself from the clinch. The officer kept a firm elbow in his back, preventing Ali's sudden surge of struggle.

"Stop resisting, son! It's only going to make things worst." The officer wrestled Ali to the ground. His back-up support arrived and assisted with the restraint. The head coach advised the team captains and assistant coaches to take the team onto the field. Ali was taken out of the backdoor of the locker room and placed into a police van next to the other detainees, Eric, Stanford, and Chris.

*   *   *

It was considered the trial of the decade. A stellar athlete and his three friends were being tried for rape, a possible term of twenty-five years to life in prison if found guilty.

Ali was placed on home studies until the conclusion of the court proceedings. His mother felt that with all the hype surrounding her son's possible conviction, it would be best to keep him out of the public's eye and preserve his image of the ideal athlete. Recruitment letters had begun to diminish from the mailbox, and the constant phone calls from the nation's top universities had come to a standstill. When the allegations of his accuser surfaced, most of Ali's bandwagon supporters and entourage tapered off. Still, with the few people in his corner, Ali remained optimistic that he would not be found guilty of the charges brought against him.

Months passed, and the trials of his three best friends had concluded. Each was found not guilty of rape, and in the process, the victim had been completely exposed. Defense attorneys had done a phenomenal job of bringing in various men Elena Sanders had slept with, shredding her credibility. By the time Ali's case rolled around, a total of eight guys had testified, seven of them admitting they had been sexually involved with Elena within a week of meeting her. The prosecutors objected to the witnesses, stating that past occurrences had no bearing on the case, but the defense's rebuttal claimed that past relations were acceptable and that having a track record weighed heavily on the emotional stability of a victim. The magistrate agreed, and the defense later showed that the victim had an addiction to sex.

Although never convicted of that crime, Ali's mom made him go to church faithfully. He had to sit in the front row and take notes on the lesson taught each week. At the end of the morning service, she would quiz him. If he didn't know the answers, she would force him to sit through the same evening service later in the day. She was heavy into her belief and felt as though God would help her family weather the storm and find Ali, like his best friends, not guilty of the rape charges. At last, Ali was found not guilty on all counts, and every night thereafter, Theresa dropped to her knees to thank God for His wondrous blessing.

CHAPTER TWO

Naveen Majhi roamed the squalid streets of Mumbai, India, ashamed of himself. The fact that he would have to face his family for the third consecutive night with no food in hand tormented him, and he was nervous. He worked from sunup to sundown and barely made enough to pay the street merchant for the shelter provided to his loved ones. As he circled the block once more, he dragged his feet through the dirt, collecting all of his thoughts before finally deciding to head home.

Met at the door by his youngest child, Naveen quickly walked past the energetic boy, who seldom spoke of the schooling that his friends received during daytime hours. He kissed his other children on their foreheads, then walked into the loving arms of his wife, who could tell by the distraught look on his face that again she would have to get creative and make a meal out of nothing just to feed the hungry stomachs of their children.

It was later that night after the children were asleep when Naveen cried. What kind of man was he that he couldn't feed his family? His wife didn't mind. She loved him regardless. But for the last four months she had noticed as her husband's pride slowly declined to the breaking point. Never had she seen him cry before. And while he wept on her shoulder for the remainder of the night, she could only stroke his head gently, assuring him in a whisper that everything would be all right.

Poverty and deprivation were common in the crowded city of Mumbai. It wasn't shocking to walk into a restaurant or a grocery store and be greeted by an eight-year-old boy working for a small monetary gain to help provide for his family. The girls of that city occupied most of the jobs in homes, washing clothes, cleaning floors, and caring for babies. At the tender age of five, the girls had better be ready, for they never knew when their doorbell would ring and a job offer would be made to go and work in the home of a complete stranger.

The worst of Naveen's frustration was when he had to look his daughter, Seema, in the eye every night. The fact that she wasn't enrolled in school, had very little clothing to cover her body, and had one hell of a disturbing hygiene problem, was unsettling and enough incentive to finally make the decision. His boys were in the same boat, but at least he could coach and guide them towards making the best of the poverty they lived in. Realizing that he had to do something, anything, to give his daughter a fair chance in a world of such uncertainty, Naveen called his sister, Ketaki, who had moved to America and to the city of Detroit, Michigan, in hopes of prosperity and a better lifestyle.

It was three weeks later when Seema's aunt came for her, taking her away with the promise that she'd receive adequate schooling and a job making enough money to provide for herself as well as a little extra to send small change back home. Naveen was ecstatic at the fact that his daughter would be taken care of. From a financial standpoint he could do it no longer. Plus, to him, taking care of four kids as opposed to five would alleviate a heavy burden.

"Why didn't I think of this years ago?" he asked himself as he cried blissfully at the thought of his little girl's future, watching her climb into the back seat of his sister's car. He looked at Seema proudly, confident that this was the best decision he had ever made.

Unfortunately, that would be the last time he would ever see his daughter again, and if he had known of the journey she was about to undertake, he never would have let her go.

*   *   *

On a Saturday afternoon in mid-July, the wedding of Madeline Harris and Johnny Baker was about to begin. It was a perfect autumn-like day with a warm gentle wind playing music through the orange-colored trees. Wiping the dripping sweat from her face, Madeline looked behind her to make sure her helper held the train to her wedding gown high in the air. With every eye soon to be on her, she couldn't afford to trip like the man she saw on television the night before when he hurriedly ran up the steps to receive an award. Smiling at the remaining flower girl in her wedding party, Madeline's soon-to-be niece had the confidence to walk down by herself and join the others. It was only afterwards that the doors flung open and everyone standing saw the most beautiful woman in Michigan prepared to meet her prince at the other end of the aisle.

A swift breeze from the ocean waters abruptly chilled her smiling face, and Madeline woke from her dream to the sun retiring from its days work. The cold white sand trickled between her toes. It was her afternoon ritual for the past two days. No worries, no problems, no issues, it was all-inclusive. Amber was in the second grade now and needed only minimal supervision. Anyways, she was under the care of the tour guide, who participated in snorkeling classes with her. As Madeline relaxed in her beach chair on the sunny shores, she couldn't think of a better way to spend her seven-day vacation than being away from the changing temperatures in Michigan and in the steady warm climate of Aruba.

"Another drink, ma'am?" the shirtless islander asked as he carried a tray around to all of the adults wearing a bracelet. Those who paid for the holiday package, including drinks, were given green bracelets to wear.

Madeline had booked the vacation destination after a year in the Homicide Division where she had worked on the Infection Man case. Until now, she had been unable to afford the time off even after a near-fatal incident.

It was just a year ago when Madeline was confronted by an ex-boyfriend who wound up being the brother of a criminal she was investigating. When Michael attacked her and threw her into the entertainment system, Madeline's whole life flashed before her eyes. All she could think about was her daughter and the fact that Amber's father had already been killed by a random act of violence. Amber needed her mother, so as Madeline groaned in pain on top of a pile of scattered books, she could see from the corner of her eye as Michael Washington pulled his .25 from his pocket. *She had to get to hers first.* As she began heaving books at his head like flying saucers, Madeline was able to outfox him and reach her own pistol. She double-tapped the trigger, firing two hollow-tip bullets deep into Michael's chest. When a little white poodle broke free from its owner and raced up the driveway to the sound of the gunfire, Madeline realized that her worst nightmare had come to a screeching halt. She would live to see another day.

Months after taking the life of Michael Washington, Madeline was accepted into the Homicide Division. She didn't know how her counterparts would react if she had requested time off right away. After all, she was a diligent worker and didn't want the stigma of being labeled a part-timer attached to her. She had caught up on her paperwork, and there weren't any pressing cases requiring her attention, so she was able to break away for a relaxing vacation.

"Yes, I'll take another one," she said and took another coconut filled to the rim. She was on her third drink and feeling good. After finishing off the beverage, she decided to join the dancers doing the salsa near the bar. She would have kept going all night if it weren't for Amber returning from her snorkeling excursion.

Amber's tour guide's name was Reynolds, known as Sparky on the island. Sparky handed the girl off to Madeline and informed them that he would be returning in the morning for a full day of horseback riding. Amber was exhausted. Deciding they would lie together on the beach until the sun finished setting, they sat in their beach chairs watching the beautiful reflections glistening on the ocean. Amber fell asleep soon after. With Madeline feeling a little tipsy herself, she asked the waiter to call Sparky back to help carry Amber to their room.

With Amber sound asleep on the queen-sized bed, Madeline decided to make the most of her expensive suite and take a jet stream bath. She undressed and turned on the bathroom television before easing into the bubbling water, leaning her head back against one of the cushioned tub pillows.

What a vacation!

Drifting off into never-never land, her moment of calm was interrupted by a vibrating noise. Madeline stepped out of the tub, went into the other room, and found her purse shaking ever so lightly, which made her relaxed eyelids tighten instantly.

Everyone knows I'm on vacation, so why would they call me?

She grabbed her three hundred dollar Louis Vuitton bag and pulled out her phone. Three missed calls. Scrolling through the numbers, she came upon 313-506-7700—*Zucal*.

Zucal had been Madeline's "Nigerian-American" partner for nearly a year now. "Nigerian-American" was a race Madeline had come up with just for him, primarily due to his remarkable African appearance. He was much darker than anyone she had ever known; coated with two tones of darkness—black—and extra black. Growing up in the inner city, Zucal's parents accepted a job on the Southside of Chicago, an area heavily populated by black folks. He was submerged in the community from high school until the time his law enforcement career began. In his fifteen years in the Homicide Division of the Detroit Police Department, he hadn't respected any of his partners the way he did Madeline, becoming quite fond of the way she performed when called upon. Many opportunities had come his way to move upward within the department, but he took pleasure in piecing together clues and helping solve murder crimes. He enjoyed helping victims' families vindicate the death of loved ones. For him, it wasn't just a job, it was his life. He loved his work, especially for the last year. He finally had a partner as dedicated to the job as he was, and both were committed to apprehending killers.

Madeline decided to call back, knowing she had better make it quick because of the roaming charges her cell phone company was going to charge for making a call from another country. She pressed redial on her new picture phone and waited for an answer.

"Zucal," her partner said on the other end.

"Hey," Madeline said with a frown. "I see you tried to call. What's up?"

"How are you enjoying your break, Madeline? You gulping down some of those Long Islands for me?"

"I'm trying to," she barked at him. "You called three times in a row. So quit the bullshit. Before I left I told you not to call unless you absolutely had to. And you did. So go ahead and give it to me."

"Well, Madeline, I'm afraid I got some bad news," he said with a sigh. "Cromwell told me to give you a ring to see if you could end your vacation a little early, like today-early. There's been a homicide that's caused an uproar. I can't work it 'cause I'm still on the school shooting out in Plymouth, and everybody else's hands are tied. You're the only one available. With all the controversy that's started already, Cromwell wants you back ASAP."

Vincent Cromwell was the Deputy Chief overseeing the Homicide Division of the Detroit Police Department. He had been giving Madeline fits ever since she transferred from the Sex Crimes Unit. His division was normally staffed with old heads about ready to take an early retirement package. With Madeline a part of the new era of baby-boomers, she was brought into the division to revitalize it with some youthful energy. At first, the chief wasn't very receptive and put her on some of the most complicated cases. But her work spoke for itself, and he was forced to acknowledge her ability to handle the bizarre. He grew to tolerate her although she would never hear him admit it. She had the personality that you loved to hate and even if you hated it, being around her long enough would eventually make you love her. But the chief would never admit it, and because of that, he stayed strict with her at all times.

"You've gotta be shittin' me, Zucal!" she yelled at him. "What do you mean, get back? I'm on vacation, for God's sake."

"I know, Madeline," he said with regret. "I'm just the messenger. The chief says he needs you to catch the next flight back so that you can start on this case."

"Fuck that!" Madeline spat. "Can't they find anyone else to put in some overtime or cover till I get back? This is bullshit!"

"I know it is, Madeline. That's why I was afraid to call. But an order is an order, and the chief said to get back. Sorry."

"Yeah, well, so am I."

Madeline threw the phone against the wall, shattering it. For the next twenty minutes she sat on the bed, fuming with anger, then she started to pack their belongings. They would catch the 9:23 flight out in the morning.

*   *   *

After Madeline's call about the time, flight number, and gate information, Charles Monahan was waiting at the terminal with open arms. He took the day off work, showing his dedication to Madeline by rearranging his tight schedule. Once he picked up Amber and lunged her over his shoulder, he began filling Madeline in on the latest about the recent homicide. Although Monahan was still part of the Sex Crimes Unit, when Madeline made the transition to Homicide, he took a keen interest in the division and began monitoring her work the same way an over-protective father would audit his daughter's schoolwork. Careful not to leak out too many details with Amber in the car, Monahan gave just enough for Madeline to have an idea about the phenomenon she had to face. After they dropped Amber off at Rosemary's, they headed to the Brighton truck stop.

Construction barriers had been set up as a roadblock to cars exiting the freeway. Madeline held her badge up to the patrol officer, and he allowed the vehicle to enter the grounds. Several vehicles were already parked with a huddle of people near the bathrooms. After Monahan pulled to a stop, they got out to see what all the chatter was about.

"Look who finally decided to show up," Zucal said, greeting Madeline with a plastic bag filled with lipstick, eyeliner, and a hair brush. He greeted Monahan with a firm shake. "Sorry I had to call you back to duty, Maddie, but bossman wanted us on this one at once."

"Thought you were working the school shootings," Madeline said. "If this one's mine, why are you barking down my side of the street?"

"I had to say something to get you to come back," Zucal confessed, his face reddening with his dishonesty. "If I would've just said the Chief wants you back, you never would've come."

"You jerk!" Madeline blasted off, punching him in the shoulder. "You gonna at least pay me back for changing my ticket." Madeline took her shades off and stuffed them in her purse before continuing.

"Oh, the hell with it," she said. "So, what do we got, anyways?"

"Are you sure that you're ready for this one?" Zucal asked her, looking over at Monahan to hint that he was about to drop a bombshell.

"Come with it," Madeline urged.

"Well, we haven't been able to ID her yet, but from what they're saying, she couldn't have been more than sixteen years old."

"Don't tell me someone killed another baby!" Madeline said, taking her coat off and flinging it into the arms of a colleague passing by. "Where is she?"

Zucal led them around a park bench and into the women's restroom, where several officers were collecting evidence. At Madeline's request, they left at once.

Her body had already begun to rot. Even after a year in Homicide, Madeline still wasn't accustomed to the smell of dead carcass. As she knelt over this one, she couldn't help but shake her head at the innocent little life that some lowlife had the audacity to take.

She was a beautiful little girl with long wavy hair and curly bangs hanging down her forehead. Madeline was amazed by the exotic look. A petite, narrow shaped face, it was evident that the girl wore way too much makeup, probably to age herself a bit, but Madeline wasn't buying the coverup. At first glance, she was able to come to her own conclusion.

"This girl isn't older than twelve," she said just loud enough for Zucal and Monahan to hear.

They didn't challenge her opinion, knowing Madeline had her own child to use for an age comparison. She grabbed the girl's wrist and inspected her arm. The bruises covering her entire left arm were signs of physical abuse. And if that wasn't enough, when Madeline lifted the girl's short shirt, her entire torso was black and blue, and on the right side of the girl's neckline were four finger imprints.

"What the hell did they do to her?" Madeline said in frustration. "She's bruised everywhere. What kind of animal would do such a thing?"

It was when she lowered the white sheet covering the child's body that Madeline's jaw dropped. Surprisingly, the child had on a dingy pair of torn underwear.

"My dear God!" Madeline breathed. The girl had been sexually abused, as the dried blotches of semen on her inner thighs made evident. "How could anyone do this to a little girl?"

An officer in a tight-fitting blue uniform burst into the bathroom.

"Detective Harris," the rookie officer stammered. "They sent me for you. I think you had better follow me."

He took them around the back of the building and into a wooded area, tracking through the mud for nearly a half-mile. While the young policeman led the way, Madeline followed on his heels, anxious to see where he was taking them. When they arrived, the girl was sitting on one of the picnic tables, her head in her hands, and she was sobbing.

She had a bruise circling her right eye. A Hispanic girl with long brown hair, she was skinny. If it weren't for her extreme thinness, the girl was pretty enough to be sisters with Shakira, the Colombian pop star. But something about the way she was shivering wasn't right. As Madeline inched closer, her eyes widened at the sight of the little girl's busted mouth and bloody nose. Madeline sat on the bench next to her.

"Good luck with her, Harris," grumbled Detective Grady from Sex Crimes. "I've been trying for the last ten minutes, but all she does is sit there and look like that."

He pointed in her face, and Madeline grabbed his hand, lowering it. "Maybe you need to try a different approach and not give in so easily."

She wrapped her arm around the girl's shoulders. "It's okay, sweetie. No one is going to hurt you anymore. I promise. Can you tell me what happened to you?"

The girl remained silent. Madeline looked at Monahan and Zucal for suggestions and they both shrugged their shoulders.

"When we found her she was laying face down in the leaves," Grady told them, gently wiping the twigs and dirt off the little girl's back.

"Do you have a name?" Madeline asked the girl, who continued to sit there and look spaced-out. Her eyelids were fat, red, and puffy. "Sweetie, you're going have to come with us if you're not going to talk. But as I said, there's nothing to worry about, you're safe now."

Madeline held the girl's hand and they stood to leave. It was literally moments later when Deputy Chief Cromwell walked up with a lady tightly holding onto his arm. The woman, clearly distraught and disturbed by the girl's appearance, snatched her arm away and ran towards her. The chief ordered them both be taken to the precinct for questioning.

In a room the size of a Manhattan studio apartment, the woman and girl sat silently, only glancing at each other for a brief moment before the girl averted her eyes. When Madeline walked in, it was like a ghost had entered and sudden relief shone on the girl's face as she smiled. Madeline opted to sit next to her. Establishing a feeling of easiness before getting down to business was important.

"How old are you, pretty?" Madeline asked the girl as she examined her bruised neck.

"She's fourteen years old," the woman answered. "Her name is Nizama, and I take care of her. I was so happy when I heard you had found her."

The woman looked at Nizama before continuing, "She ran away days ago with her friend. She's dead now, huh?"

"Yes, she is," Madeline answered her coldly, wondering why this woman was so quick to speak up for this girl. "Did you know the other little girl as well?"

"I did and I didn't," the woman replied. "I run a girls' home. For the last month, she's been like a sister to my Nizama. They played well together. Don't know where she lives. She always would come over at night and leave in the morning."

Madeline asked the girl, "Where did you go when you ran away, and who were you with?"

The girl looked up at the ceiling. Madeline couldn't tell whether or not she understood the question or if she was too scared to even answer. When the woman began speaking a different language to the little girl, Madeline knew it could be a little of both. The girl took a moment before replying, speaking only to the woman.

"She says they hitched a ride trying to get out of town but was picked up by three madmen in a truck," the woman answered. Realizing she wasn't being clear enough, she leaned towards the girl and asked her another question. "They were taken to the place you found them. They both were forced to have sex a lot of times."

"With the men at the truck stop?" Madeline asked her, stunned.

"Yes," the woman answered for the little girl.

At that moment, Madeline chose to take a five-minute break from the questioning to see if she could hunt down her own interpreter to come into the room. It wasn't that she didn't trust the woman's translation, but this was police business, and she had to make sure the questioning wasn't tainted with any bullshit. When she returned with Officer Patesh, the first female Indian officer to wear a uniform for the DPD, questioning resumed.

"Did they pay you to have sex?" Madeline asked the little girl with the assistance of her colleague.

"She said they didn't," Officer Patesh replied after the girl answered in her native language. "She says they were all very mean to her. They hit her, spit on her, even pissed on her. She's lucky to be alive."

"What happened to your friend?" Madeline asked, waiting patiently for an answer.

"She doesn't know," the officer replied. "She managed to run away the night before you found her. They didn't bother to chase her when she ran, so she just went far enough to where she felt safe. When she saw all the police cars the next morning, she began making noises. That's when officers found her."

"Does she remember what the men looked like?"

"Vaguely," the officer said. "She counted how many times she had to have sex in her head, and she lost count after the tenth guy."

For the next fifteen minutes, Madeline continued questioning the little girl. She scribbled notes down on the notepad but when scanning back over them, they proved useless. Trying to get the girl to open up was like pulling teeth from a lion. Then again, most of the questions were answered by the other woman, who made Madeline about ready to throw in the towel, but she had one more question to ask first.

"Where is it that you say you're from?" Madeline asked, questioning whether or not the girl was even from the States. Even those raised in a foreign-based community would be able to speak a little English. This girl appeared to understand none.

"Something's happened. She's turned mute," the translating officer said. She asked the question again. For a second time, the girl turned her head and folded her arms. "She refuses to answer for some reason."

"Ask her how she got here?" Madeline remained persistent, looking over at the woman whose eyes were on the girl in an intimidating manner. "She has to know."

Once the officer asked the question, the girl looked at the woman, and after that, she shut down and wouldn't answer another question for the remainder of the session.

"Tell her there's nothing to be afraid of," Madeline said, her patience wearing thin. She snapped her head around and cast an evil look at the woman, who clearly held the trump card. *Whoever this woman was had this girl scared to death!*

"Won't answer. She's suddenly gone blank," the officer said after giving it a last shot.

"Let her know that we thank her for helping. We'll contact her later if we have any more questions."

Madeline stalked out of the room, recognizing she had no choice other than to release the girl back to the custody of her guardian.

The woman sped down the busy city street, anxious to get back to her place of business, a massage parlor on the Southwest side of Detroit. At the time, the Southwest side had a large Mexican population, approximately ninety percent, occupying most homes in a ten-mile radius. For women, it was easy to get lost in the culture if you had brown skin and straight hair. All of the girls they used fit the description. When they finally pulled into the parking lot, the woman looked around to see if anybody was watching, then, out of the blue, she back-handed the little girl across her face.

"You stupid ass!" the woman yelled. "What are you trying to do to me, huh? If you think you can make it out here on your own, you're a stupid little bitch, Nizama."

The woman grabbed the girl by her hair and slammed her head against the car's dashboard.

"You idiot!" the woman shouted again, attacking the little girl like they were in a street fight. She pounded her over and over again until her tirade was over, then she leaned across the seat and hugged the beaten girl.

"I love you, Nizama," the woman cooed, holding onto the girl until she stopped crying. "You make me too upset sometimes. All I want is for you to never try and run away again. You see what happened to Sumati, huh? Seven days you were gone. Could've been you that was dead." The woman broke the embrace and peered into the girl's eyes.

"Don't do it again. You understand?" she held onto the girl until she nodded. "Now you know that you still have to face Papa, right?"

The girl continued to shake her head while tears raced down her cheeks.

"Good, now fix your face, and let's go back inside. The others will be glad to see you. Plus, there's someone I'd like you to meet."

The parlor was a spacious privately owned business containing several rooms with long padded tables for guests to lie on while being given a massage. There was a long walkway to get to the back of the shop, where sleeping in a chair was a short, stubby man wearing beige colored khakis and a white T-shirt. When the women walked by he opened his eyes and jumped all over Nizama, hitting her constantly like an attacking animal.

"Stupid bitch!" he yelled, pounding her with a bruising blow. "You think I'm dumb?"

He grabbed a handful of her hair and flung her to the ground. Kicking her like a ball, he measured her up and lashed out. The thump of his shoe against her jaw ricocheted off the walls. "You disloyal tramp! Run away from here again, and I'll beat you to death." *He wanted to make sure that she'd think twice the next time.*

While she lay on the ground in pain, he reached over to the coat rack and grabbed an iron hanger. He beat her senselessly, battering her young body until her skin was covered in blood. For the next twenty minutes, he let her have it, brutally beating and cursing the girl to the point where she truly believed she was every foul name he'd called her.

After two devastating bashings within an hour, the girl was finally able to go down into the basement of the massage parlor to join the others.

They looked like her, Hispanic or Indian, from Mexico and India, brought to America with prayers that they would someday return to their country with enough money to support their families. After being told that they needed to repay the debts for being smuggled into the country, all six of the girls had to live in this brick basement with no windows. When Nizama was finally shoved down the steps to join the others, there was one new face and one girl in particular that she knew was from the same country, India, as she was. Nizama immediately drifted her way.

The next day, Nizama and Seema talked to each other for most of the morning, isolating themselves from the others. They were both from Mumbai, and their English was surprisingly decent. While the other foreigners struggled to follow the English language they spoke, Nizama and Seema talked to each other of the broken promises made to them of happiness and a solid education, that if they worked hard on a daily basis they would live an affluent lifestyle. But where was the money going that was promised to them? They surely hadn't seen any of it. And if either complained she would be beaten. The only motivating factors were the high hopes and dreams of a prosperous future promised to them, believing they would be given the opportunity to live their dream. That in itself was enough inspiration for them both to continue and do whatever it took for the chance to get ahead.

Two weeks later, Nizama was staring at the clock on the wall, hoping that time would freeze. She had grown use to her new job, knowing that it was something she had to do in order to pay her Auntie back for bringing her to America. The travel ticket, cab fare, fees to others for helping smuggle her into Miami, then into Detroit, all came with a price. The problem was, Nizama hadn't seen her aunt the last few days and was no longer getting paid the three dollars a day she once received when she had first started. *Why did her aunt just disappear on her without saying anything?* It was a question that Nizama was mulling over right before the basement door opened and the man who was now so familiar, stood at the top of the stairway and yelled, "Let's go, now! And hurry it up. Time is money."

Nizama rushed through the hallway and into a room near the front entrance.

"You better be good tonight," the man shouted at her before closing the door.

Nizama sat on the edge of the stool and waited, thinking of her father and wondering if he would be proud of the work that he sent his daughter off to do. Knowing that she couldn't disappoint him, nor withstand another beating that night, Nizama slowly lifted her shirt over her head and tossed it aside.

As soon as the door to the room opened, Nizama knew that her night would be like living in hell.

He was a young man with straight, shoulder-length hair. He wore a crumpled hat and dark sunshades. His beard was thick, his mustache the same. A tight black T-shirt tightly gripping his stomach showcased his washboard stomach, and he was wasted. Stumbling over and onto the table, he slowly lifted his head and licked his lips after looking at Nizama's young body from head to toe.

"Come here, pretty one," the man said once he was able to roll himself over onto his back. It was after he began to lower his pants that Nizama inched her way onto the table with him.

As she tried to kiss him on his mouth, he pushed Nizama away, and she realized that the routine she often used with other patrons wasn't going to work with this one. She tried lowering herself to his waist, but he wouldn't allow that either. When she looked at him like a deer caught in headlights, the man stood up and began to dance. He held her closely, and for the next five minutes the drunken man moved to his own beat.

In fulfilling this crazed man's fantasy, she was able to keep up with his lousy moves. He wrapped his hairy arms around her and kissed her neck. After two-stepping in the center of the room for nearly ten minutes, the man began to perspire heavily, forcing Nizama to detach herself from his wet embrace. Why she did this, who knows?

He slapped her face so hard that his shades went flying across the room. Nizama stumbled against the table, dazed and surprised by the man's sudden hostility. Quickly following behind her, the man bear hugged her and threw her onto the hard floor. That gave him just enough time to remove his pants, and he did just that. Hovering over her like a boxer who had just knocked his opponent down, the man began to stroke himself. Looking at Nizama in a submissive position was a turn on, and his dick began to harden in the palm of his hand.

Yanking her off the ground, the man tugged on Nizama's pants until they were down to her ankles. He spun her around and pinned her face onto the cushioned table, wanting to enter her doggy-style; it was his fetish. He spit a wad of saliva into his hand and rubbed it into her tight, adolescent pussy, then he forced his dick in, banging and pounding against her until he had himself all the way in. After nearly ten minutes of cramming his thick salami-like dick into her, he came, and the satisfied look on his face was pure delight. He had just had some young ass, and at that very moment there was no feeling greater in the world. In tears, Nizama ran back down the hallway and into the basement with her clothes in her hand, and the man gleefully walked towards the front of the parlor.

"Thanks for the wonderful massage," the man said as he handed the broker a roll of money and walked through the front door. "I'll be sure to tell my buddies about this one."

He laughed to himself and hopped into his red F-150, dialing his best friend on his cell. He couldn't wait for him to answer so he could share the experience with him.

"Hey," he said, bragging when his buddy finally answered the phone. "Guess what the hell I just did tonight?"

CHAPTER THREE

He pulled into the empty parking lot behind the grocery store, dimmed his lights, and looked at his watch. 4:25 a.m. "Where is he?" he griped as he reclined in his seat. He couldn't afford for anyone to see him, not even the young boy who had just exited to dump a huge bag of trash into the dumpster. He waited for the youngster to go back inside, and once it was clear, he flicked his lights three times. A man appeared from behind the recycling bin and made his way towards the parked car. He couldn't tell whether or not the man was the same person—though the description he was given of an elderly man, mid-fifties, surely fit the bill. It was too late to speculate as the man was at his driver's side window. Fidgeting and nervous, Ali Gaines pulled out two stacks—three thousand dollars—and handed the money over in a brown paper bag. Shaking with nervousness, he studied the man's wrinkled face before driving off, looking for any signs of a possible setup. He eventually made it to the main street and was soon on the road headed back home.

*   *   *

Tuesday morning started off hot, wet, and extremely humid. With the sticky weather not expected to clear out until late afternoon, Ali sat fanning himself, grinning widely at the thought of next Tuesday's festivities.

It should be his best party yet. A veteran at throwing off-the-wall celebrations, Ali had prepared well in advance. *Shrimp, checked; Dungeness Crab, checked; cheese and wine, check.* While he sat on the park bench with his pen and pad marking off the remaining entrée items, a young man on a mountain bike rolled up the hill and came to a screeching halt.

"Hey, what's up, Ali?" the sweaty bicycler said once he hopped off his bike. "Long time no see."

Ali looked at the man strangely. The face was familiar, but he couldn't quite put a name to it.

"Come on, man. It's me, Reggie!" he said with joy, waiting for Ali to reciprocate the same excitement. "Remember, from high school? I was on the varsity team with you. You were a senior when I was a freshman."

The light bulb suddenly flicked on inside of Ali's head, and he remembered his friendly teammate.

"Earthquake?" he called out the man's nickname. It was a name given to him by one of his teammates because of his weight. Reggie was much bigger than anyone in his class, let alone Ali's own.

Mesmerized by his slim physique, Ali continued.

"It's been years," he said with a firm handshake and a hug. "Damn, you look good. What you been up to, man?"

"Working out," the man said, flexing his biceps. "Two hours a day and a hundred pushups. You look good yourself. What are you doing nowadays?"

Ali looked around as if he had a secret to tell. "I'm a deacon at a church," he whispered just loud enough for the man to hear. Back in the day, he'd been like the Godfather to the underclassmen. Admitting that he was a deacon now would have been too embarrassing.

"A deacon?" the man asked, laughing at the perceived joke. "Don't tell me you had some life changing run-in with death and are now holier than thou?"

"Not hardly," Ali retorted. "I'm still that ruthless mothafucker from way back when. Don't let the cover of a book fool you. It's all in the game. Some playas make their money selling drugs and by lying on their tax returns. I make mine hustling a church."

"That's what I'm talking about," the man said, exchanging high-fives. "That's why I had to stop. I heard the rumors and had to check it out for myself. You sure don't seem stiff to me."

"Hell naw, I'm not stiff," Ali countered the put-down. "I'm looser than wet pussy, man. Like I said, it's just a hustle." The two men doubled over in laugher.

"You probably don't know this," Reggie said, looking away bashfully, "but there was a time I wanted to be just like you. You had all the girls, a nice whip, and was straight ridiculous on the football field."

The praise was heartfelt, and Ali admired the man's willingness to admit that. *"A role model? Wow!"* Ali realized that at least one other person thought highly of him.

"So, what are you up to these days?" Ali asked while he checked out the man's sporty mountain bike. "Looks like you're trying to become the next Lance Armstrong. You know, they don't let black folks compete in the *Tour de France*."

"Naw, this is just recreational," the man admitted. "Gotta do something with all these fast food joints popping up all over the place."

"I hear that," Ali agreed with him.

Reggie abruptly changed topics. "Look, I'm glad I bumped into you," he said. "I don't normally ride this route, but I heard that you're often out here in the mornings."

Ali's right eyebrow rose on his forehead. "What's up?" he asked, curiously.

"Well, do you remember Little Daryl, who played linebacker your senior year?"

"How can I forget," Ali said bitterly. "He took the scholarship from the University of Michigan that I was supposed to get. What about him?"

"Well, I wasn't going to say nothing, but he told me about this party you're having on Tuesday night," the man said, licking his lips. "What do I have to do to get a ticket? I heard your parties be off da hook."

Ali nodded. "It's not public knowledge," he said, irritated by Reggie's knowing. "Wasn't nobody supposed to know unless they were invited."

"I know that," Reggie admitted. "All I'm asking is that you make room for one more. Please. I swear I won't tell anyone. Technician's word!"

"You got it, man," Ali caved in, "but you better not tell a soul. And what goes down Tuesday had better stay between us."

"I gotcha back," he raised his right hand. "I promise."

Ali was expecting that to be the end of the discussion, but from out of nowhere came another curveball.

"So, did you hear?" Reggie asked in a calm voice.

"Hear about what?"

"About Elena."

"Elena Sanders?" Ali asked.

"Yeah." He came closer. "She was found dead in her apartment. They say she killed herself."

"She killed herself?" Ali shouted, surprised by the news. "No way!"

"It's true," he confirmed. "She was suffering from depression and decided to take her life. It's a shame. She was such a sweet girl."

"Yeah, a shame," Ali replied, completely lost in thought now. Although Elena was a childhood nemesis, he would never wish death on anyone. As the late rapper,

Biggie Smalls, once said, "There's no coming back from death."

"All right, let me get outta here," Reggie said, remounting his bike. "I'll see you Tuesday night. Thanks again for the invite, *Deacon Ali Gaines*."

As the man vanished up the hill, he chuckled at the thought of Ali claiming to be a deacon. And for the next hour or so, Ali sat in dismay at the piece of information he was handed down.

"Elena Sanders dead?"

*   *   *

THAT SUNDAY: "God is good all the time," said the pastor. "All the time God is good," repeated the church's congregation. Minutes earlier, the pastor had concluded his sermon titled, "Walking in the Shoes of Jesus." It was a forty-five minute lecture on the stringent effort to live one's life as God would live his. He was so convincing and motivating that six churchgoers decided to unleash a new start on life and turn their lives over to God.

Christopher Spellman, known as "Little Man" on the streets, was leader of Play-Time Posse, a Crip gang on the Eastside of Detroit. He was visiting with his mother when the Holy Ghost struck and swayed him from the life of guns and murder to a life of righteousness.

Bobby James was another well-known street thug who decided enough was enough and took the extended hand of a church member, who, in turn, escorted him to the front of the altar. Bobby had been living a life of evil, in and out of prison, doing and selling every drug known to man. He had a history of assault on females with two assault cases weighing heavily on his criminal record.

Sweet little Chrissie Valentine was far from sweet outside of the church home. A teenage call girl on the streets, she had made quite a few visits to homes in the Metro-Detroit area. Her reasoning was, since it was mainly doctors, lawyers, and councilmen and not the lower class citizens that she visited, then just maybe it wouldn't be so bad if her family and friends were to ever find out. If they did find out, at least she would get the attention she desired. With her father being gone twenty-four hours a day and a mother so focused on church that she had no idea her daughter was a street freak, Chrissie was making good money and making it fast. But she, like the five others who gave their personal testimony that day, knowing their lives of sin were over, made a commitment to live free of evil.

After the doors to the church opened and the pastor extended the invitation to join the place of worship, the soft melody of the twenty-voice choir serenaded the worshippers. "You Can't Beat God's Giving, No Matter How You Try" was the song selection and perfect groundwork for the tithes and offering. The pastor made an effort to harp on the scriptural reading of Malachi 3:10. *Bring all the tithes into the storehouse that there may be food in My house and prove Me now, says the Lord of hosts, if I will not open for you the windows of heaven and pour out for you such blessing that there will not be room enough to receive it.*

When finished with his address, the pastor had scared nearly everyone into not holding back on their offering. The repercussion of holding out was believed to outweigh any justification. The ushers continued going up and down the aisles handing out the deep, straw-woven, offertory baskets to each church member.

Sister Sheila was as faithful a believer as any. Her belief in God was so strong that she just knew the new job she had received as principal of Hartley Elementary was due to her faithfulness in paying her expected tithe every month. When the basket filled with dollar bills, change, and envelopes reached her, she didn't hesitate to drop in her precise ten percent offering check: five hundred eighty three dollars and thirty cents.

Brother Altman, Human Resources Manager for Dobe Enterprises, wasn't quite sure about the Lord's return blessings and couldn't muster up enough conviction to salvage a huge chunk of his monthly paycheck. Ten percent of his monthly check would've been twelve hundred dollars and he believed that since he couldn't see God, then God couldn't see what he had stashed in his wallet. Still, he was generous enough to write out a check for three hundred dollars.

In and out of the aisles the baskets were passed, collecting dues from every member in the church. After everyone had placed their offerings into the baskets, they were quickly retrieved by the ushers and brought to the front of the church for blessing. The pastor then asked for every head bowed and every eye closed. He prayed over the monies given to the church and for those who were incapable of giving. The baskets then went to the deacons, who scurried out of the sanctuary and into the back conference room with the counters. The pastor ended the worship with the benediction prayer and excused everyone for the day. In the back room of the church was where the counting began.

Brother Ali Gaines had been an active member in the church for eight years. In his early years as an associate, he started helping out as an usher, then progressively began attending Sunday and Bible schools. He joined the men's choir for a year and became spiritually and personally connected with the pastor. After extensive tutoring and lessons from his reading, Ali soon became a deacon, overseeing several responsibilities. Initially, he was in charge of reviewing the weekly program and making sure the information in it was written accurately. Then he became in charge of the church's special programs: youth circle, plays, church concerts, etc. For the last year, he had undertaken the assignment of counting the offering, securing the monies, and reporting the totals. He was the only deacon truly overseeing the church money. Two other members of the church joined in on the counting, Sister Teague and Sister Douglass, who had over fifty years of commitment to the church between the two of them.

"Today was a good day," Sister Teague said as she counted from her basket. Each person had two baskets full of money to count. "God is good."

"All the time," Sister Douglass finished the idiom. "And all the time God is good." Sister Douglass was an old head with a lot of wisdom. Every Sunday she would wear an authentic fruit basket-like hat on top of her head, symbolic of the years of fertile insight received and given to other churchgoers. Whenever a fruit would fall from the collage on her hat, she would replace it with a new one from what she called her "Garden of Eden" and claim that God had fully ripened another soul with the spiritual testimonies she shined upon others. Although the one soul she struggled in helping was her own beloved daughter, Chrissie's, she felt relieved in having her in church that day. Sister Douglass had been a money counter for twelve years, and with each year that passed, she seemed to count slower and slower. Many times she would have to recount because somewhere, something went wrong, and she would forget the exact amount. Although others may have believed that age was a contributing factor, she begged to differ and knew that the calculations she reported every Sunday weren't the same amounts being deposited into the church's bank account each week. Sister Douglass became more and more suspicious that God's people were being cheated out of their offering, and she made a promise to herself that she would get to the root of the enigma of the missing money. If someone was stealing, they should be damned to Hell, no exceptions. Embezzling money from everyday hardworking people was in her eyes a huge sin and shouldn't be tolerated. She had her suspicions but would wait until she could gather enough evidence to back her opinion.

"Four hundred and five, six, seven, and eight," Sister Douglass wearily counted out loud. She picked up her pen and jotted down some figures, not wanting to lose her count. She added up the calculation already scribbled and announced her totals, "Three thousand seven hundred dollars and fifty-nine cents."

Each of the three shared their totals and boasted their excitement about the day's collections. They stuffed the money into a large duffle bag. Ali hugged his helpers, then excused himself, carrying the sack out of the room. He was supposed to deposit the money into the church's bank account first thing Tuesday morning, prior to heading to the Deacon's Men of Praise annual retreat.

*   *   *

Since its commencement five years ago, the day-long retreat was held at the Grand Ball Room, a conference room located at a resort in the city of Taylor, Michigan. Twelve to fifteen promising church members attended every year with each sharing a condo, two per room. Ali was excited. He hadn't seen or talked to his old pals for weeks. He had invited Chris, Eric, and Stanford to come up and share his condo with him. Although many believed Ali had changed his lifestyle after the near-disastrous encounter with Elena Sanders, his best friends knew better. Ali had never given up his old tricks.

About a month after the final court case, Theresa Gaines had invited Ali's friends to visit their church on a particular Sunday as special guests. She didn't know the impact the pastor's lesson would have on the troubled youth. It was so unreal, like a spellbinding trance had been cast upon all of them. Eric rose to his feet first and decided to surrender his life to God. Initially, the others were hesitant and watched closely as he walked towards the welcoming arms of the pastor.

With the spirit being as strong as it was that day, the pastor decided to alter his morning service, knowing the troubled lifestyle that Eric was living. Fully up to speed with the recent information that the media reported, the pastor had followed the outcome of the court cases and kept up to date with all of the post-trial reactions, as had nearly everyone in the community. Overjoyed when Eric stood up, the pastor knelt down on his knees and began to pray while Eric slowly reached the front of the church.

Pleading passionately to God, the pastor began weeping during his invocation. After anointing Eric's head with a bottle of oil he kept in his pocket, the pastor signaled the ushers to take him into the back to change. When he returned from the back dressed in a white robe and black flip-flops, the orchestra began playing the soft angelic tune, "Take Me to the Waters." Eric Thompson followed the pastor to the baptistery, where he was dunked into the Holy Waters and cleansed of all his sins.

The pressure was building on the other three boys since the pastor had made Eric the model person living an imperfect life, who made the choice to denounce that lifestyle of sin. He had the church in a frenzied uproar, applauding and celebrating with Eric his choice to turn around his life of evil. Then it happened. The pastor turned and gracefully walked up the aisle toward the other three. He stood directly over them.

"My brothers, are you ready? The choice is now. Jesus is here today and is prepared to shower down his love."

Each of the boys lowered his head, ashamed and humiliated by the pastor's unsettling comments. He continued with his moralizing.

"He understands your mistakes, He understands your sins. He knows! Come with me, my brothers, for God is real. Don't be left behind on Judgment Day! Make sure that your name is called when it's time to enter those pearly gates of Heaven!"

The excited congregation stood to their feet, every eye fixed on the three teens. Feeling like the walls were caving in faster than a trash compactor, Chris stood and faced the pastor first. The pastor placed the wide palm of his hand on Chris's forehead, screaming and crying for the boy's salvation. Chris had seen enough gospel shows on the cable network to know what the fill-in actors did once the pastors placed holy hands on them, and he decided to emulate them. Since he was nearest to the aisle, he stretched out to allow himself more room. With the pastor's sweaty palms gripping his head like he was passing some mysterious power, Chris fell out on his side onto the floor. Church members rushed to his aid in glory, fanning him and thanking God for his anointing. The pastor looked directly at Ali and Stanford.

Theresa had been frantic to get Ali to turn his life over to God, believing He was the reason for Ali's successes in the classroom and on the football field. So when Ali stood with his friend Stanford to pretend like they were turning in their keys of wrongdoing, Theresa took off running, sprinting up and down the aisles with her hands held high in triumph over her son's so-called pronouncement. So overcome with joy, it took four to five church members to settle her excitement.

Months passed and the group of friends grew closer than ever. They enjoyed indulging in the benefits of the church. In the beginning, it was difficult for them to devote their time, but as they became more and more actively involved, they didn't mind it in the least. The pastor was relatively young at, thirty-eight, so he was able to share all of his experiences and relate to the crew. When the pastor talked, the boys listened. He was more than a mentor to them; he was someone they looked up to. But like a person majoring in physical education forced to sit through a boring accounting class, when the pastor began to harp on forsaking the womanizing life-style, he quickly lost the boys' attention. They coveted the free activities sponsored on behalf of the church such as the basketball leagues, picnics, and the free trips with the ladies, especially the "Single and Mingle Worship Cruise," a riverboat cruise around Mackinac Island for single young adults. They were cheating the church and stealing all of the perks that came with membership. Eventually, all three of Ali's friends began to feel guilty for betraying God and had to back off a bit, but not Ali. His craving for the gratuities landed him in the Baptist Church of Ministry School in Sebring, Florida.

After four excruciating years of study, Ali graduated with a degree in Ministry. The conspiracy was just about perfected. Months following the direction of the pastor, Ali was designated a deacon. The mastermind plan had worked. Now, he was in a position powerful enough to immediately begin masquerading as a servant of God.

They were all back together again. For one full day, they would attend seminars and lectures in the morning then set aside time for extensive prayer during the midday. After the early afternoon two-hour reading from the book of Psalms, their brains would normally be fried like an egg. Expecting that to happen, the meeting organizers had typically scheduled a ceremonial dinner around five o'clock in the evening, allowing the attendees to formally meet and greet with each other and still have enough time to recuperate before nightfall. That was where Ali Gaines met an interesting gentleman, who seemed way out of his league.

He was Brother Paul Fisher from Mt. Zion Christian Church of Faith in Washington, D.C. Ali was impressed with his knowledge of the entire King James version of the Bible. In less than ten minutes of conversation, Ali excused himself from the scholarly chat and proceeded into the banquet room where dinner was being served, and a less complex discussion was taking place.

Throughout dinner Ali struggled to remain poised, knowing that in just a few hours the private party he had planned would be jumping off. Thus far, everything had fallen into place. The food and wine were already in the suite, brought precisely at the time Ali had excused himself earlier and discretely ran up to the room to receive the delicacies. He had already made the phone call confirming the evening's special guest. He was so overjoyed with that year's entertainment that he had to keep running back and forth to the restroom just not to pee in his pants. The gathering would be like nothing he had ever planned before. Everything was set. Realizing that he would soon be throwing the party of the decade, Ali could only stare down at his dinner plate and count the seconds slowly tick in his head. While church members from far and abroad showed their genuine interest in the invited keynote speaker, it was Ali who was thankful when they were finally excused for the evening.

Three hours later, the four friends were in the party room. Earlier that day, Ali had paid the nominal fee in order to change the room location to the fifth floor and towards the back of the complex where not much traffic was expected. He wanted to separate his room from the other deacons, who had a row of rooms next to each other on the first floor. Now that Ali, Eric, Stanford, and Chris were out of harm's way, Ali changed out of his suit and put on some leisure clothes.

They had not been in touch with each other lately. In fact, the only person Ali had spoken with over the last two weeks was Chris. And that was only because they had happened to bump into each other at the gas station. Once they were done catching up on each other's latest indiscretions, they decided to kick-start the night by having a pre-party of their own.

Ali walked over to the door and opened it, placing the Do Not Disturb sign on the doorknob. Chris opened the overhead counters and pulled out four small glasses, Eric exited from the bedroom wearing a wife-beater and jeans, and in his hand, held high above his head, he waved a hundred-fifty dollar bottle of cognac. He walked over to where Ali sat.

"Deacon Gaines!" Eric exclaimed. "Bless this bottle with thy holy hand."

"To tonight!" Ali responded by tapping the bottom of the bottle with his right fist. As the bottle passed hands, each person made sure to tap once on the bottom, a tradition that had started during their childhood years.

For the next hour, they played Texas poker and drank fine cognac, making high bets on each hand. Wasn't a need to bluff as though they had a good hand when they didn't; they could afford to lose the free money they played with, stolen from Ali's church bank account.

His plan upon return from Ministry School had been perfected. He had gradually become the right hand man of the pastor at his church, regaining the respect of other church members by participating and getting more involved in services. Ali began filling in as the alternate speaker on Sundays when the pastor was called away. Soon it seemed nearly everyone had forgotten about the shameful incident from years prior. Taking more trustworthy assignments within his church, Ali was soon appointed an usher, seating worshippers and preparing offertory baskets. Scheming even further, he soon obtained the position of deacon, and for the past three years his church paid for his attendance at the conference, where he gratefully splurged with the money that he stole from the hands of the church's faithful.

Ali pushed out a stack of bills to cover his hand.

"I'm in," he said with a smile wider than Batman's Joker.

When Stanford scooped all of the money off the table with the winning hand, Ali chuckled at losing a huge chunk of that year's monopoly money.

Later that evening, others began to show up in spurts. When all the guests had finally arrived, Ali discussed the rules of engagement, informing everyone about the private event. He trusted everyone there, but he still made sure to clear the air, just in case. There was one person in particular he wasn't quite sure about, Earthquake. But with the thrilled look of a youngster begging his owner for a treat, all Ali had to do in order to keep him quiet, was invite him to another get-together.

A knock at the door interrupted the gambling session.

"Who is it?" Ali yelled out.

"It's the police," a soft spoken voice answered. "Open up at once!"

When Ali opened the door, he stood pleasantly surprised.

"Welcome," he graciously said as three women sidestepped their way into the suite. A man wearing a violet pimp hat with a feather followed.

All the men began howling and cheering. Ali had to calm them, especially if he didn't want to get kicked out, or even worse, arrested for solicitation.

"Shut up!" he demanded. "Act like you got some damn sense, would you?"

The men muffled their excitement. Ali approached the man who had arrived with the women and handed him a wad of money.

"Good to see you again, my friend," Ali said, watching as The Broker counted his money slowly. "It's all there."

"Always gotta be sure, Ali," The Broker said with a friendly hug and pat on Ali's back. "The pleasure is mine. So, how do you want to do this?"

Minutes later, Ali was in the bedroom of the suite, kissing and groping one of the girls as if he hadn't had sex in years. Once he had her undressed, he was fucking her wildly on the bed, while the others watched. When Ali finished with her, he tossed her aside like a piece of meat and gave someone else a turn.

Eric volunteered to be next, taking one girl's hand and walking her to the bed. Ten minutes later, he was done. For the duration of the night, the rotation continued like clockwork until everyone had a chance to be with a girl; some girls ended up going twice.

The Broker allowed Ali to have one more crack at it, and him only. It was a gift to Ali for coordinating the expensive sex party. As he began to close the door to give Ali his privacy, the jealousy of the others showed because they weren't able to watch.

"What the heck?" Ali heard Eric exclaim as the door closed shut. "How you gonna close up shop now?"

The girl was much younger than Ali's earlier one, and he was curious enough to ask her age.

"How old are you?" he asked as he began to undress. She didn't respond.

"Ohhh, a quiet one," Ali said. "You can tell me. It won't change anything."

"Old enough," she whispered. She had been told she was not allowed to talk with the customers about her age, so she made sure to keep her voice down.

Ali looked at her hour-glass body and wondered.

"Why do you do this?" he asked her, temporarily stopping her from going down on him. "I'm sure there's something better out there than this, isn't there?"

She looked at him coldly. If only Ali could see the fear that weighed heavily in her eyes, he would understand.

"You're such a beautiful girl," he said, running his hands roughly through her curly hair. He didn't intend to spark a conversation with her, but he couldn't help it. "Tell me your name."

Oddly enough, she felt more comfortable with Ali than she had with any other customer before.

"Nizama," she muttered.

"That's pretty," he said. "I take it you're not from this side of the world?"

She shook her head no. "I'm not," she told him. "I come from Mumbai."

"India?" he said. "You speak good English. What's up with that?"

"In my country we begin learning the language of the Americans early."

"So, how exactly did they get you here?"

It was a question she wanted to answer, but the trepidation that ran through her was overwhelming, especially when The Broker peeked his head inside and told them to hurry up.

The sex was invigorating to Ali. As an active partaker in the sex trade, he had slept with several girls already. He had his pick of the litter, but that one led the pack. When Ali finally came inside of her, he collapsed on top of her from the powerful ejaculation. The Broker, keeping a close eye on them both, told them when time was up.

When the night was over, the four friends were the remaining bodies left. Everyone else had gone for the evening. The party was huge, as expected, and all of the guests left pleased and sworn to secrecy. With everyone else laid out on the floor, too stoned to climb into bed or pull out the sofa bed, Chris decided to call home and check in on his wife and kid. Before punching in the digits, he looked at the service charge for long distance calls. Not wanting to pay the expensive fees, he decided to take the long trip to his car to use his cell phone. Enduring ten minutes in rainy weather was wiser to him than paying a service fee.

He staggered up the walkway, stopping for a second to rest because he felt like hurling the liquor out of his system. Although nothing came up, his mouth watered at the mere thought. He collected himself and continued on his journey.

In the near distance he saw a man and woman, arms interlocked, walking his way. They were hugging and kissing, much too busy to mind him. Not wanting to ruin their late night rendezvous, Chris crept past, and continued down the darkened path.

Approaching slowly, a white man was oddly dressed in a long, black trench coat. As the stranger neared, Chris tried to correct his sluggish walk, and the dark-clothed man slowed his pace. Chris became frightened by the undertaker look-alike and picked up his pace, receiving an alarming stare from the man as he passed.

He made it to his car and grabbed the cellular phone from the glove compartment, choosing to make the call on his way back so the fellas wouldn't wake from their sleep. He dialed home.

"Hey, you," he addressed his wife, Terri. "You not sleeping yet, are you?"

"What do you mean, I'm not sleeping yet? Of course I'm not asleep!" she yelled at him. "You haven't called all afternoon. I've been worried sick about you."

"Why? You know that the guys get together at night and do something. We haven't seen each other in a while. We've just been catching up."

Terri's insecurities had been a problem for quite some time. It was the one thing that irritated Chris the most.

"I thought that by spending the entire day there you would've been fully caught up by now," she commented. "You usually call at least to check on us. And why do you sound like that?"

"Like what?" he struggled to cover up his slurred speech. "It's my phone. The reception's not good out here. How are the kids?"

"The kids are fine. Why are you calling me from your cell phone? And why are you still out at this time of night?" she asked suspiciously.

"I just decided to take a walk, all right? I'm about to go. It's cold and dark out here. Let me hurry up and get back to my room."

"Chris," she said, clearly worried. "Are you sure you're okay?"

"Yeah, I'm fine," he griped, annoyed. "I'll call you tomorrow when I get up."

The phone call ended, and Chris picked up his pace, trotting up the dark hill. Suddenly, a shadow appeared about fifty yards away. Was that the same person from earlier? If so, he looked even more bizarre this time with gloves on his hands and a hood covering his head.

What the hell?

When he came within arm's reach of the man, he contemplated jolting past the guy in an all-out sprint back to the room. But running past him would have been suspicious, and he didn't want anyone to find out he had been drinking, especially the other individuals at the conference. He tried to remain calm and inch his way past, taking a giant step, then another, until finally he was past the man and continuing up the pathway.

His hands were feeling the cold, so he stuck them deep into his pockets, and that's when his cell phone fell onto the pavement. Camouflaged by the color of night, the black Motorola phone was gone. He tried to retrace his last steps, but the limited lighting proved useless. Down on all fours, he began sweeping the ground like a blind man searching for an object in front of him. Just before he stood and gave up all hopes of retrieving it, his left foot struck the phone's antenna. He grabbed it and stuck it in his back pocket.

He hadn't had a chance to get to his feet when a fiery stab in his side caused a sharp pain to constrict the muscles of his guts. Another sting made him gasp for air as he felt the metal blade pierce his skin again. He called for help, but his cries went unheard. When his assailant sliced his throat, Chris moaned. He felt his cheeks swelling, his tongue drying. The attacker bent over Chris and looped a thin rope around his throat. Unable to loosen the tight noose, Chris began to zone out. Whoever was attacking him was strong. With thundering force, his executioner pulled back on the rope the same way a jockey pulls the reins of his stallion, snapping Chris's head backwards. Sadly, Chris never had the chance to see the face of his attacker, nor was he given the chance to fight for his life. He had planned to give up all unlawful activity in his current lifestyle and live the All-American family life with a family who loved him dearly. Asking the Lord for forgiveness and to cleanse his soul was in his plan, but thanks to his killer, Chris wouldn't have that opportunity. As all the nerves in his body began to weaken, he gasped his last few breaths of air.

When the half-lit moon hid behind the thick patches of clouds at the end of the night, the only thing in the middle of the darkened walkway was a desecrated body and the question of whether Chris's soul was going to Heaven or to Hell.

CHAPTER FOUR

"Johnny, I give you this ring. Wear it with love and joy. I choose you to be my husband, to have and to hold, from this day forward. For better, for worse, for richer for poorer, in sickness and in health, to have and to cherish, as long as we both shall live."

Struggling to contain her tears, Madeline spoke her wedding vows with enthusiasm and fervor, realizing that Johnny was soon to be her husband and overseer. Looking deep into his eyes, Madeline's tears were carefully caught by the maid of honor who had rushed to blot the streaming flow from ruining her mascara. When Johnny placed the two-carat princess-cut diamond ring on her finger, overpowering emotions took control of her, and she began whimpering more and more. Reaching with her lips, Madeline waited for Johnny's soft, electrifying lips to meet hers. After all, the pastor had already blessed the ceremony instructing the newlywed lovers to kiss.

*   *   *

With the slight touch of her earlobe in the puddle of drool on the pillow, Madeline awoke from her sleep. Slipping into her work uniform, she rushed to get Amber ready for school.

Maneuvering in and out of traffic, Madeline rushed to work in her new Volkswagen Beetle, purchased with the extra money she had saved from surviving spouse benefits, the department having sent her a check for $20,000 in the accidental death insurance settlement. Now, after already setting aside money in a college fund account and purchasing a new wardrobe for Amber, Madeline had finally bought herself something, a new whip. And while she broke in the flashy two-door vehicle, swerving, tightly cutting corners like she was driving at the Daytona 500, onlookers stared at the early-morning yellow speedster racing down the Walter Reuther Expressway. Madeline pulled into the Detroit Police Department's parking lot and finished dressing in the car, preparing for the day in Homicide.

Homicide was much different from the Sex Crimes Unit. For the past few years, Madeline had grown accustomed to deskwork and piecing together clues at a central location, rarely seeing the sunlight. But now, Homicide presented her with a different challenge. She was out and about and on the streets, interviewing witnesses and apprehending the more sadistic criminals. Sitting at her desk, Madeline decided to browse the top stories on the net before the eight o'clock briefing.

One story in the headlines was out of Mumbai, India. A twelve-year-old teen had been reported missing and was believed to have been smuggled into the greater Detroit area. Seema Majhi, a well-developed Indian girl with shoulder length hair, was last seen with her aunt at an airport fifty miles west of Montreal, Canada. Surveillance video inside of the airport captured the drop-off between the aunt and a man wearing a ball cap and tinted sunglasses. He has since been identified as Manuel Llanos, AKA "The Broker."

Madeline continued reading the story: *Manuel Llanos, a registered Michigan sex offender, is believed to have driven his white 1989 Honda Accord to the Canadian city to meet Ketaki in what is now being considered as a sex trafficking scandal.* Familiar with the last name, Llanos, Madeline decided to dial Monahan's direct extension.

"Sex Crimes," he answered after looking at the caller ID. "If you need good sex, I'm your man. How can I help you?"

"Stop playing, Mono," Madeline said, staring at the picture of the alleged abductor. "You remember the name Llanos? He was part of a raid about three years ago."

"You mean Manuel Llanos?" Monahan asked, opening a file drawer containing archive records. "Hell yeah, I remember that asshole. What about him? Last I remember he was doing five to ten for the prostitution ring he was running at that strip club down on Verner."

"Yeah, well he's back on the streets. He's believed to have taken some little girl from Mumbai now."

"Where the hell is that?" Monahan asked.

"It's a place in India, and she was brought here to Detroit."

"That slimeball!" Monahan screeched, pulling out Llanos's file, the thickest in the drawer. "I remember him like it was yesterday. He had seven or eight girls working for him. I shouldn't even say the word work. He was pimpin' the shit out of those poor girls."

"I remember him too," Madeline claimed, scrolling her mouse down the page to the little girl's picture. "And she's such a pretty girl at that. There's no telling what this asshole is gonna do to her. Have you guys been assigned the case yet?"

"Not yet. You know, kidnapping's all over this. We won't get it for about a week at least."

"That doesn't make any sense," Madeline huffed. She knew that every wasted minute was valuable. "If the creep's a known sex offender, doesn't that establish enough cause for you guys to have it?"

"In a normal world, yes. But you know it has to go through the proper channels first," Monahan reminded her. "We'll be assigned to it pretty quick, though."

He continued to flip through the paperwork in Llanos's file. "Look at this shit." Monahan pulled out charge after charge. "Assault and battery, C.S.C., solicitation of a prostitute! It's a wonder how they would let a bum like this back on the streets."

Monahan took out his reading glasses before continuing, "Remember Victoria Weathers?" he asked. "Listen to her statement of facts from years ago after we had brought her in for questioning."

"There were eight of us. I was the leader, forcing these young girls to do it. I'd threaten them, beat them, I'd even molest them. Whatever I had to do to strike fear in their heart is what I did. I had no choice. If I didn't do it, it would've happened to me, and The Broker would have made sure I'd suffer ten times worse.

"There was one girl in particular who was forced to grow up super fast. She was a favorite, and the youngest, eleven at the time. Everybody wanted a piece of her. But The Broker was picky with who he allowed her to entertain. If he liked you, you went unharmed, and he liked her. That's until she crossed him and ran away. You would have thought she was Bin Laden the way he had his team searching for her. But she escaped successfully. And as a result we had to pay the price. Ever since, whenever he would think any of us were planning to escape, we'd get beat, just because."

Stuffing the paperwork back into the manila folder, Monahan closed the drawer.

"A true sucker," he said. "How can anyone force a person into doing something against their will?"

"I don't know," Madeline replied, shaking her head from side to side. "I'm just afraid that if you don't get him soon, there will be plenty of other girls forced into doing things, including Seema."

"I'll work on getting it in a hurry, Maddie. Trust me, I want this asshole buried deep," Monahan said. "Look at you. If I didn't know any better, I'd think you were beginning to miss being in Sex Crimes."

"Not hardly," Madeline denied the truth. "I just find certain cases interesting, especially since I worked this one before. Curiosity has set in, that's all."

"Well, I'll be sure to keep you in the loop," Monahan told her, "but I have a new partner now. And she's just as good as you were, if not better."

Madeline knew Monahan was teasing her. For the last year he had done nothing but try to influence her to return as his partner.

"We both know that isn't true," Madeline said with conceit. "She's just a temporary fill. I'm like…your first love. Regardless of how hard you try to get rid of them, some people you just can't do without."

Shutting down the computer, Madeline grabbed her pen and pad, deciding she'd get to the conference room early to chat with other detectives before her scheduled meeting. When she entered Conference Room C, it was filled with detectives from different units. Madeline sat next to two already holding a discussion.

"Morning," Madeline said, interrupting the ladies' gossip. "Any of you happen to catch the story of the girl stolen from Mumbai? They say she could be here in Detroit."

"Yeah, that's mine," Detective Rusco said, scooting her chair closer to Madeline. "Did they happen to release more information this morning? These damn news crews are gonna be the death of me. Whenever they start releasing false info, it just makes our jobs that much harder."

"Well, now they're saying she left with Manuel Llanos. This guy is notorious for forcing little girls into child prostitution," Madeline told her. "He was part of this sex ring I helped break up a few years ago. He was forcing eight teenage girls to work as sex slaves in his strip club."

"Sure did," Officer Rusco agreed. "You did good work on that case. Harris, right?"

The woman stuck out her hand towards Madeline. Reluctantly, she shook it. "Yes, how'd you know?"

"Captain gave me the file. We got this case earlier this morning. I briefly glanced through it and saw your name mentioned, along with my new partner's."

"Your partner?" Madeline asked, knowing from firsthand experience the officers who teamed together in Sex Crimes.

"Yes, my partner, Monahan. I was promoted into Sex Crimes probably about a month ago," Officer Rusco said as if she had a small chip on her shoulder. "When Grady accepted the position with Postal, I took his spot. Now I have the chance to work with one of the department's finest. And girl, I do mean fine, in every way."

Even though Madeline could tell that Rusco was trying to be an asshole, she wouldn't allow her facetious comments to piss her off.

"Yeah, Monahan is a great partner to have." Madeline tried to remain respectful to her indirect colleague. "Hopefully you'll have the chance to learn all the intangibles about the job that I did. Sex Crimes is an interesting unit. You'll learn for yourself that a prostitution ring is no joke."

"It sounds to me like it was their fault anyways," Rusco snapped. "Anytime you choose to sell your body on the streets, you risk the chance of some pimp coming along and controlling you. Sounds like the same thing happened here."

"That's not true," Madeline retorted. "These girls were kidnapped and forced into it. And when I say forced, I mean forced. They were beaten, threatened, and beaten again, until they had to accept the fact that they weren't going anywhere. They believed that opening their legs was the thing to do."

"That's just horrible," said Detective Anderson, the other officer sitting at the table. A victim of child molestation herself, she knew exactly how the girls must have felt. "Those poor girls, they were probably so afraid that they wouldn't run or tell anyone what was happening."

"You got it," Madeline said. "And now this freak is back on the streets. This time he's getting them from other countries."

"And what makes you say that?" Rusco asked. "Couldn't it just be a coincidence that this one is a foreigner? You do know that the Canadian border is less than twenty minutes from here?"

Madeline was getting even more angered by Rusco's stupidity. "No, it's not a coincidence," she said, handing over a copy of the little girl's picture that she had printed off of the computer. "My experience is, once you're a sex predator, you're always a predator, regardless of where you recruit your prey."

"Well, let's be glad that you're using your experience in Homicide and not Sex Crimes," Rusco said, snatching the picture out of Madeline's hand. "Thanks for the picture, but I had already printed this exact one earlier."

Seconds later, the Chief of the Homicide Division entered the room, followed by a rush of other officers taking their seats. A hefty black man, the Chief was the type to shop at Big and Tall stores, places where XXXL clothing was sold. With a face full of hair, he resembled a professional hoop player from the early '70s, when blacks in the NBA sported the universal shag.

Discussing past and new developments, the Chief brought the team up to date on several recent homicides. Exhorting them to keep an eye open, he presented pictures of wanted criminals as their faces flashed across the projection screen.

The newest addition to make the list was Manuel Llanos AKA "The Broker", a middle-aged Mexican-American male weighing approximately 165 pounds. At 5'6 with a flabby physique, Madeline wasn't quite sure how a man of his make-up was able to intimidate anyone, let alone eight girls. After giving the necessary leads, the Chief advanced to the next slide. It was then that Madeline and Zucal both sat up in their seats.

A woman known as Ketaki Majhi appeared in grand fashion wearing a long dress and open toed sandals. She looked elegant, yet tough as nails. A medium-built woman, Ketaki looked like she could scam a person into doing anything she wanted. Madeline was mesmerized by her professional demeanor, and if she hadn't known better she would say that Ketaki was damn good at what she did. What was surprising was the fact that Ketaki had just been brought in for questioning and was released along with the girl from the truck stop.

If only this was presented to us two weeks earlier.

Madeline looked over at Zucal, who seemed to be registering the same thoughts. The chief informed the group of the information passed down from Sex Crimes. Since a homicide was involved, both units were now required to work in conjunction, sharing leads and information to hopefully solve the case.

"It is believed that she has a network of people helping her," the Chief said, moving to the next slide.

"How we think they're pulling it off is, Ketaki, who owns a successful business and a travel agency, is able to fly in and out of the country at will. She goes to towns where poverty is a way of life and recruits young girls to come to the States in hope of a better lifestyle."

"Then she sells the poor girls after she gets them here," Madeline spoke up for the Chief, familiar with the art of sex trafficking, having completed her master's thesis on the same exact subject.

"And because these girls are sold and forced into hard labor, they have one of two options, live with it or run away."

"You got it, Harris" the Chief agreed with her. "Why don't you tell us what happens when they run away?"

"Well, they turn to the streets," Madeline advised the team. "Because they have no family or support system, they end up getting picked up by pimps who promise to take care of them. A long story short, they count on them for support and end up having sex for money. It's a settlement clause. The pimps save them from the streets, and they reap the benefits when the girls sell their bodies."

"Bingo," the Chief said, admiring Madeline's awareness. "Then I guess you understand now how these two individuals link together."

It took Madeline a moment to put the pieces together. Like the brilliant cop she was, she came to her own conclusion.

"I got it," Madeline said, confident that she knew the connection. "When Ketaki returns, The Broker is the one who the exchange is made with. That's how he runs his prostitution ring so smoothly."

"Right again, Harris."

"But, Chief, what I don't understand is why did he decide to recruit here in the states? How would Samantha

Cater benefit him more than maintaining a group of girls from foreign countries?"

"Don't know, Harris," the Chief answered over the sudden side discussion that had broken out amongst the officers. "That's why we pay you the big bucks. It's your case, and it's information that you will need to find out."

Madeline looked fiercely at the Chief until he was finished with the briefing. Once he was done, he asked both Zucal and Madeline to stay after. As the other detectives left to work on their respective cases, the Chief strolled over and took a seat next to Madeline.

What could he possibly want now? Everything gets put on me. He expects me to fail!

"So, Madeline," the Chief started, "it's been a gorgeous past few days here, hasn't it?"

"Sure has," Madeline said, nodding, "and it's supposed to continue through the weekend too. No chance of rain in the forecast."

"Yeah, I just love these types of days. A few years from now I'll have it year round. Could be sooner if the city decides to bring back incentives."

Last year, the City of Detroit decided to offer early retirement packages to those who were nearing retirement. The Chief had missed the cutoff by one year, but now if it were to come back again, he'd be on the first train out.

"So, what's the deal, Chief?" Madeline said, growing impatient. She knew when someone was blowing smoke up her ass and when someone was holding a genuine conversation, and it just seemed as though at any moment the chief would crisp like bacon if he continued rambling. "Give it to me straight. Is there a problem with the way the case is being handled?"

"No, there's no problem. Not a problem at all," the Chief said, cynically. "A little girl is dead, others are probably getting raped as we speak, we have no suspects in mind, and no arrests have been made. No, Detective Harris, everything's just peachy."

"Well, I've only been back for two weeks," Madeline defended herself. "I haven't even had the chance to get my feet wet."

"And neither have I," Zucal spoke up now. "You just pulled me off the school shootings case to work this one fulltime."

"Yeah, and I've been finishing up the paperwork on the Yates case too," Madeline reminded him. "Then you also gave me last Thursday off. Remember that?"

"Both of you stop with the damn excuses!" the Chief said, pounding his fist on the table. "I put the two of you on this because you're the best I have. All I wanna hear is that you have a suspect in custody. That's it. Don't give me this shit of how long you've been on the case. Each day costs if this animal isn't caught. I'd hate to put Pratt and Kline on it, but I'll do what I have to do if you two can't get it done."

"But Chief," Madeline muttered.

"But nothing," he cut her off mid-sentence. "Get out there and find me a suspect. Case closed. I'm giving you guys till the end of the week to have somebody in custody. I don't care what it takes, just get it done. I make myself clear?"

"Sir, yes sir." Madeline and Zucal said, simultaneously.

Silence took over the room before the Chief continued.

"Look, I know it's hard," he told them, "but I believe you two can crack it. It's been one battle after the other with this trafficking bullshit. It started overseas but now it seems to have made its way to the states, primarily here in Detroit. And I won't stand for it. Not in my city.

Our little girls have enough shit to deal with growing up in fucked-up homes. "

The Chief looked out the window. Across the street stood a row of abandoned homes.

"Look at that shit," he said with a scowl. "It's gonna take years to turn this city around. It once was a beautiful piece of land, but I won't tolerate slave sex regardless, even if we do live in fucked-up conditions. I don't care if I have to hit the streets myself. I won't stand for it."

"We'll get them," Madeline assured him, looking over at Zucal, who seemed to be somewhere in space. "This one is personal. I have a daughter and couldn't imagine if—"

"I know, Harris," the Chief interrupted. "Just get out there and do the job that I know you can."

Even though at times he was required to light a fire under their asses, the Chief did believe that if anyone could get the job done, Zucal and Madeline could. Threatening to take their case away was strategic. He had no true intention of doing such, but the Chief, like any other good coach, utilized tactics and knew that threatening to take your star player's position would only motivate him to play harder.

"I have something that might help build your case," the Chief said with a grin. "The annual fireworks will be downtown at Hart Plaza this Saturday."

"Wait a minute," Zucal cut in. "You're not about to ask us what I think you are?"

"Look, it's only for a couple of hours. You can get there, stay for a little, and just keep your eyes open for a few hours afterwards."

"I don't think I can get anybody to watch Amber." Madeline tried justifying her pre-excused absence. "That's why you print the month's schedule ahead of time, so mommas like me can find babysitters and those sorts of things."

"Already taken care of," the Chief stayed persistent. "Rosemary will be at your house around eight."

How the heck does he even know Rosemary? She's new!

"No way," Zucal said in disbelief. "That's for street patrol to handle. You have more than enough officers on hand for that."

"Look, all I'm asking is that the two of you get lost in the crowd, and once the event is over, see what you see. This is one of the biggest events of the year. Girls who are on the run are guaranteed to flock to this. They think they may be lucky enough to find someone to take care of them."

Chief cleared his throat before going on. "Sad to say, the predators will be there as well, those same animals that prey on young girls with low self-esteem."

By the way the Chief expressed such emotion, Madeline could tell he took that one, if none other, personally. She continued listening.

"They'll sweet-talk them into anything, including selling their bodies. The girls look at it as a positive. A shelter, a few dollars, and food, for just opening their legs, they're in a win-win situation. With a million or two expected to be downtown, they could easily get lost in the shuffle. They know exactly who they're looking for, and vice versa. Having you out there is a perfect way to see if anything looks suspicious."

"But Chief, I was supposed to have a movie night with my girlfriend," Madeline said, fearful that she would have to let down Simone again. Since her transfer to the Homicide Division, Madeline could count on one hand how many times she and Simone had spent time together. "Can't you find someone else just this once?"

"Maybe next time," the Chief denied her request. "This one you need to work. Go out there and enjoy yourself. They've invested a lot of money into those explosives. The least you can do is make it worth it."

Realizing that the Chief was set in his decision, Madeline and Zucal rose to their feet, departing with a baffled look on their faces, as if the school teacher had just punished them with detention.

CHAPTER FIVE

I sing because I'm happy and I sing because I'm free.
His eye is on the sparrow and I know he watches me.

Sitting in the front row with her son, Theresa Bailey couldn't stall the tears falling from her swollen eyes, mourning the loss of her husband while the beautiful voice of Karen Clark Sheard soothed the other mourners.

The three days planning her husband's funeral had been challenging due to his notoriety in the community, position on the board of trustees, and affiliation with Detroit's first YMCA. Thanks to Chris's friendships, Theresa had entertained in her home the likes of the city's mayor, Detroit's police chief, and the governor. Her deceased husband also played a role in the expansion of Fruit for Life Church of God in Christ. From a small building on the corner of one of the most rugged neighborhoods in Detroit, Fruit for Life started from the ground up with only fifteen members and grew into a million-dollar complex with members well into the thousands, thanks largely to her husband's commitment to bring the slum off the streets and into the Lord's house of worship. With hundreds of mourners from far and near coming to pay their respects to Theresa and her family, she reflected on the good times that they'd shared, and on the very first time that she and Chris had met.

Sweethearts since childhood, Terri Johnson and Chris Bailey were the couple voted Most Likely To Get Married by nearly every student at Cass Tech High School. When Chris wasn't with the crew, he was with Terri, and if he wasn't with her, they were talking on the phone. A lovable couple, Chris and Terri lit up a room when they walked in, and everyone enjoyed their company. But things weren't always what they seemed, and when Elena Sanders brought rape charges, they ended up parting ways. However, relentlessly pursuing Terri eventually won her over, and she accepted Chris' invitation to join in on a lifelong commitment.

Terri didn't care for any of Chris's friends and wouldn't shed a tear if any one of them fell off the face of the earth. Even though they each tried to earn her liking, they were never able to penetrate that defensive wall she held up that prevented their acceptance. She always felt they were no good for her husband, and after the episode with Elena Sanders, she surely wasn't going to accept them at that point. She believed Elena's story and was an expert at telling when Chris, her boyfriend at the time, lied. When she questioned him about the incident, the slight stutter in his answers was all the proof she needed. Given that he was never man enough to confess, and since the testimonies from the prosecution's witnesses seemed too reliable, she never completely forgave him and grew to despise Chris, along with his closest friends, Ali, Eric, and Stanford.

They sat in the second row behind Terri and her immediate family, and when it came time to view the body, the three friends stood together and walked over to the open casket. Chris's pampered face was just how they remembered him last, at ease and with a smile. Ali was first to kiss Chris on his cold forehead, then the others followed. Moments later, they circled as a group and prayed over his stiffened body. Finished with their prayer, they opened their eyes to the swollen face of a livid woman standing in front of them. Terri had decided to confront them at that time.

"What did you do?" she cried out. "Look what you've done to my husband. What did you do?" She began pounding on Ali's chest.

"We didn't do it, Terri," Ali said, grabbing her flying fists. "We didn't have anything to do with it. It's gonna be okay. We know. God has it all taken care of now, and it'll be all right."

Breaking free, Terri ran towards Eric and with every fiber of strength in her, slapped him, leaving a five-finger indentation on the left side of his face.

"I hate you!" Terri screamed. "All of you. I can't stand none of you!" She spat at Eric, luckily only hitting him on the shoulder. Falling to her knees, she began crying hysterically. "Why'd you have to take him, dear Lord, why?"

As she got back to her feet, Terri went fiercely for Ali but was restrained by several family members and rushed out of the church. The three friends paid their final respects, deciding it would be best to skip the burial.

*   *   *

The killer was always timely, and that morning was no different. He had woken up early enough to steam press his shirt and jeans. It was his forte, always dress comfortably before a killing. With a soft cloth he wiped the dust off his Kenneth Coles and examined himself for the last time. Appearance was everything to him.

He grabbed his .45 off the counter and clipped it onto his belt. Seconds after exiting through the back door, he was sitting in his Explorer with the music pumping through the speakers. Like an athlete ramps up to music before going out onto the field, the killer found that same excitement prior to facing his opposition. He threw the car into reverse and pulled out from his driveway, determined to continue his perfect record.

He crept up slowly to the four-way stop and looked both ways before continuing. When he pulled into the intersection, he was suddenly forced to slam down hard on his brake pedal, jamming his upper torso into the steering column. After shaking the sudden rush of adrenaline, the killer looked to his right at the front grill of a Honda Civic, inches away from his passenger's side door. Behind the wheel, a short Chinese lady was still moving her mouth like a minimum-wage receptionist, too busy talking on her cell phone to notice that she had just nearly caused a collision.

"Watch where you're going!" the killer yelled at the short, stubby woman who was tightly holding the steering wheel at the ten and two position like she was still in driver's training. "Learn to drive before coming over here."

The woman, not backing down, took both hands off the steering wheel and gave him a double *fuck you* with both middle fingers.

He couldn't believe she had the audacity to do that. The Chinese bitch had really pissed him off, causing his blood pressure to race to a dangerously high level. Not only did he not care for *her people*, but he had just been completely disrespected by one. While she passively continued about her way, the killer made a sharp left turn and began following her.

He could see her look in her rear view mirror and suddenly tense up. She tried to drive faster but couldn't control the small car at top speeds. When she almost spun out, the killer chuckled out loud.

"Stupid fucker!" he blurted out before choosing to end the cat-and-mouse chase. Deciding there was no need to prolong it any further and chance the police coming to her rescue, the killer zoomed up next to her. The look on her face was complete confusion.

Is Michigan road rage really this bad?

Before she had the chance to stomp on the brake pedal, the killer had already lowered his window and had the barrel of his automatic pointed at her back tire. A single shot caused her to swerve off the road and crash head first into a tree. The killer snapped his head around, just in time to see the woman's car go up in smoke. He pressed on the accelerator and slumped back in his seat. Raising the volume of his radio to the max, he was pumped up again and ready to take on his next victim.

Twenty minutes later he was parked outside a house on the Eastside of Detroit. The neighborhood was in bad shape. The street thugs occupied every corner, claiming their block similar to a particular Blood gang in Los Angeles, who claimed a street called The Jungle, a ruthless cul-de-sac that catered to no stranger. As the killer waited patiently for his next victim to come outside, three teens approached his car, eager to see who the hell was that posted on their street. One of the teens banged on the driver's side window, startling the killer.

"What's the deal, man?" He stood with his hands in his pocket. "Don't you know better than to come on the block without permission first? Who you looking for anyways?"

The killer lowered his window halfway and flicked out a cigarette butt that landed on the youngster's throwback football jersey. He quickly raised the window.

"Ohhh no you didn't!" the teenager responded after wiping the ashes off his expensive clothing. One of his friends decided to bang his fist against the car door.

"Fool, open up, and get your ass out the car!"

Once again, the killer lowered his window, flashing his gun at the three juiced-up kids. Like the helpless babies they were, all of them quickly lost the tough-guy image they proclaimed to have and transformed themselves into pathetic soft-spoken punks.

"All right man," one of the teens squealed higher than a mouse, throwing his hands up. "We were just trying to see who you were, that's it."

"Yeah, that's all, buddy," another added. "Put the gun down. We were just playing with you."

Their cowardly responses were good enough for the killer. He waved the gun before them.

"Get the hell away from me!" he hollered at them. "Now, before I put one in each of you. Get the fuck outta here!"

The intimidated kids took off running down the block. When they were finally out of his sight, the killer turned his focus back on the house. About five minutes later, Theresa Gaines's garage door began to open, and the killer started his engine, prepared to follow Ali to his church.

That time the route had been oddly changed. The past three Sunday mornings, he had followed Ali as he traveled southbound on the I-75 expressway. But that day, he had passed the Livernois Ave. on-ramp and was heading north.

Where the fuck is he going now? The killer cursed under his breath, realizing that regardless, he had to keep his promise. As Ali merged his black Mercury Sable into the flow of traffic, the killer had to floor it just to keep pace, still remaining at a safe enough distance behind him.

*   *   *

Easter Sunday at Mt. Sinai Methodist Church was no normal Sunday, attracting members normally reluctant to wake up for church and bringing them into the house of worship for praise and celebration. This year's early sunrise service, as well as the ten-thirty service, expected to fill to maximum capacity. An exclusive four o'clock evening service was added to accommodate those who didn't mind waiting in order to avoid the crowd.

Tenise Sheldon hadn't been to church in years, but she had chosen Easter Sunday for her return. Dressed in her Sunday's finest—a long-sleeved lilac jacket, matching pleated skirt, and skinny, leather, strappy slide-ons—she looked as classy as a businesswoman going for an interview with Donald Trump. While most women took hours prepping themselves, Tenise made looking good effortless. And as she smiled at the complete package standing in front of her long vanity mirror, her cheerful expression said it all. She grabbed her Coach purse and hurried to get a decent seat.

Thirty minutes later, as predicted, the church's parking lot was jam-packed. Standing behind a long line, Tenise waited in disbelief at the growing crowd forming around her when a clean-shaven man, dressed in an all-white suit and a pink and blue striped necktie, approached her.

"Morning," the man said. A stocky middle-aged man, he wore a Tuscan beige cowboy hat that complimented his tie and gray hair. "You mind if I cut?"

"I would," Tenise said, "and probably so would the hundred folks waiting patiently behind me."

"Come on, Ms. Lady. I'm just trying to get a close enough seat. I have a serious case of hearing loss. If I don't get a decent seat I won't be able to understand what the pastor is saying."

I can't believe this man is actually running game at church.

"Sir, I think you better goon back," she said calmly, pointing towards the end of the line. "There will be plenty of seats inside."

"Really," the man said, pulling out his digital hearing instrument, "I truly do have a disability."

"Oh, I'm sorry," Tenise said in embarrassment. "Sure you can cut in front of me. How silly am I?"

Stepping aside, Tenise let the hearing-impaired man stand in front of her until the doors opened and like a massive day-after-Thanksgiving sale, the crowd hurried to get the best seats. Tenise secured a place in the fourth row and was finally able to loosen up, taking her jacket off and laying it across her lap. As the choir sang "Jesus, The Light Of The World," Tenise stood with the other members and sang along, joyfully welcoming all into the house of worship.

Midway through the service, Tenise began preparing for the altar prayer. It was finally the time for complete tranquility. Stressed lately over her job security and financial burdens, Tenise had a tremendous amount of affliction to pray about, not to mention a mother who received weekly chemotherapy treatments for her recently-diagnosed cancer. For the next fifteen minutes, Tenise let it all hang loose, calling upon the heavenly powers to minimize some of the burdens that had unexpectedly invaded her life. Once she finished crying and had returned to her seat, Tenise sat in the pew with the Holy Bible on her lap, softly rubbing it, deciding that something essential had been missing from her life, and that something or someone had been God.

When the guest speaker finally concluded his elongated morning sermon, the doors to the church opened, welcoming the non-believers and those without a church home to join the Mt. Sinai family. Given that Tenise was only seven when she had first been baptized, she had done a lot of sinning since. For that reason and many others, she was first to rise to her feet. With the assistance of ushers, she made her way to the front of the church where, with the blessing of Deacon Ali Gaines—the guest speaker for the special Easter Sunday service—she was born again and cleansed of her sins.

"The Lord has brought you here today for a reason," Ali said, taking Tenise from the arms of his helpers. "You realize that a change is needed in order to prosper in this world where it's so easy to fall victim to the evils that lurk outside them doors. Well, I'm here to tell you, Sistah, asking the Lord for forgiveness is not easy. Although you may feel like your back is already against the wall, it's the step forward you've made today that will draw you nearer to the Lord."

Cries of "Amen" and "Yes, Lord" rang throughout the cathedral as Ali continued.

"What is your name, Sistah?" he asked, motioning for the choir director to lower the soft playing music.

"Tenise. Tenise Sheldon."

"No need to be afraid, Tenise. Don't be scared. God is with you. He is with us all. What brings you here today?"

"I'm just tired of living life the way I've been living it for the past five years. I need a change before it's too late." She began to weep. "I can't go on like this. I just can't. Please help me."

"Jesus is our Savior. He is here to help." Ali wrapped his arms around her.

"I know he is," Tenise replied, "but this is something that I should've done a long time ago. It's not too late, is it?"

"The Lord has no timetable," he told her. "He's the magnificent, the highest, and whenever you call upon Him, He answers."

Again, the church rang with echoes of, "Yes, Lord." Ali knew exactly what to say in order to arouse them.

"But I've done some really bad things," Tenise said, dropping her head. "I don't know if He'd be so willing to forgive me."

"Of course He would," Ali reassured her. "Look around you. You think all of God's children have lived perfect lives?"

Tenise briefly gazed the room.

"Of course not," Tenise said. "I'm ready to do whatever I need to do in order to rid my wrongs. Can you help me?"

"Of course I can. All you need to do is believe, and God will handle the rest." Ali slowly lifted his hands high into the air. Soon after, the five hundred plus worshippers in the house rose to their feet.

After a short prayer, Tenise was rushed into the back by ushers who formally welcomed her to the church, exchanged some church information with her, and invited her back for the New Member Orientations that occurred each Wednesday. Tenise then came back into the sanctuary, where she was well received with smiles and looks of acceptance from many members.

Ten minutes later, Ali brought everyone back to their feet for the benediction, and the church doors opened again. Ali gleefully strolled towards the exit, greeting and shaking hands with members, while the drummer gently tapped the pleasant tune of "Blest Be The Tie That Binds." When Ali began to officially thank those in attendance, the crash of breaking glass made everyone suddenly scuttle to their safety.

Latching onto whatever was in its path, the burst of flames engulfed the church's main lobby like a California wildfire. The thick smoke forced the majority of people back inside. Once a second and third smoke bomb penetrated the tall glass window and landed next to the wall, the thick curtains ignited quickly. Members rushed towards the back while the flames exploded. Soon after the wooden pews caught fire, everything was ablaze. Mothers and fathers carried their children in their arms, but several were trampled in the midst of the hysteria.

Sister McGill was in the choir stand when the bombs came crashing in. At the sight of the flames, she leaped over the banisters like a champion hurdler, snatching a little boy whose back had caught fire and ferociously taking him to the ground. Rolling twice, the flames that had caught his gray suit were put out.

Sister Fisher wasn't so lucky. In the midst of the disturbance, her old, weakened legs weren't able to move as fast as they used to and she fell to the floor. Luckily, the young drummer saw her go down and was courageous enough to help her, placing himself in imminent danger and succeeding in getting them both out of harm's way.

Opening the back doors, the ushers directed the majority of individuals into the parking lot where Ali made the rounds to ensure family members were safe. Crying hysterically, Sandy White had lost her son during the commotion and was about to collapse, until little Gregory ran up to her from behind and wrapped his arms around her legs.

After the smoke cleared, the estimated damage to the building was several hundred thousand dollars. The damage to the morale of the church's people was even worse, especially with the deaths of two children who were unfortunately trampled in the panic, and one adult, Tenise Sheldon, who died from smoke inhalation.

*   *   *

He sat on the porch with his head cocked, counting the stars in the sky. Despite the cool temperature of the night, he took out a harmonica and began to play. After twenty minutes, he decided to turn in for the night and flopped onto the worn couch. He turned on the television and began flicking through the channels, desperately looking for a late-night thriller. Frustrated with each channel airing the same story, he sat upright to see what the buzz was about.

The news of the church fire blared from every station as though it were presidential election time. He hadn't seen a story receive that much hype since the Oklahoma school bombings years ago, but he remembered reading an article about that church in particular. It was one of the most attended churches in the city and home to an array of Detroit celebrities. With Thomas Hearns and Anita Baker being interviewed, he went to the rosewood wine cabinet, pulled out a bottle of Tequila and a shot glass, and watched in disbelief as the "Hitman" was talking with a news reporter.

A simple fire gets this much play. He tossed a shot of Cuervo to the back of his throat.

It was after the announcement of the three dead bodies that he began to lose it, slamming his glass down so hard, he nearly broke it. His plan of burning the church down had backfired. He hadn't wanted anyone to die, not that time. What started as a mere scare tactic had resulted in three fatalities, and he would have to claim the deaths of someone else's kids. Slapping his wide hand against his forehead, it wasn't until he looked towards the fireplace and at the pictures hanging over the mantle that he felt instant gratification from what he had done. He would eventually come to grips with himself, realizing that more work was required.

*   *   *

Weeks later, during a friendly game of dominoes in Eric's basement, Ali decided to share his thoughts with the others.

"Do either of you find it ironic that Chris gets killed, and months later the church that I'm in is bombed?" He looked at the other two, who suddenly lowered their heads, covering their faces with their dominoes. "Well, do you?"

"It's just a small coincidence," Stanford finally spoke up. "Besides, we're in Detroit. Church bombings happen all the time here. It's what they call hate crimes."

"You know good 'n' well this was no hate crime," Ali said. "Otherwise there would've been some type of message left. There was nothing like that. The church was targeted for a reason."

"And what reason would that be?" Eric asked with a look of concern. "I agree with Stanford. It was probably just a hate crime."

"You sound foolish. Tell me, how could it be a hate crime? Detroit's ninety percent black folk. You both know race played no part in this one."

"City of Howell is right next door, and it's ninety percent white folk," Eric said. "The city just had a KKK rally a few months ago where they auctioned off a white robe. Why wouldn't the Klan burn a church down? Everyone knows the best way to launch an attack on a group of black folks is to get them at a morning service.

It's the only place where we can get together and not kill each other ourselves. A church is the perfect plot."

"That's a racist thing to say," Stanford admitted, even though he knew the truth behind the statement. All he had to do was turn on the nightly news, and one of the stories out of Detroit would mention a fight that escalated outside of some club that led to a shooting. "The Klan would burn down a church in a heartbeat. You're right about that one."

"Come on!" Ali shouted, standing up and throwing in his hand of dominoes. "The shit's coming back to haunt us now. We're doomed, and it's just a matter of time." Ali opened the window to let in some cool air.

"Stop talking stupid!" Eric shouted and went for Ali. Stanford grabbed him.

"All right, both of y'all need to calm down 'cause neither of you is getting shit accomplished," Stanford said, leading Ali and Eric back to their seats.

They always tended to disagree with each other, and at times tempers flared. This was just another example of one of their typical arguments.

"I'm just saying, it's mighty strange how things are happening," Ali said. "I don't mean to be a punk, but I thought I'd say what's been eating me. All the things we've done are coming back to haunt us now."

"These were two completely separate incidents," Eric said. He picked up the deck of cards to shuffle before going on. "Let's just say that the bombing was meant for somebody. The church is filled with heathens who think just by going to service once a year they'll be safe. It don't happen that way. If I owed one of these crackheads some money, he'd shoot up whatever building I'm in to get it. That goes for a church too! I could be standing behind the cross of Jesus himself, and he'd still shoot at me. Criminals are criminals, and they don't care about shit, let alone a church."

"Forget I ever said anything," Ali said. He refused to debate with Eric so he simply gave up, knowing from childhood that there were some things Eric refused to agree upon once his mind was made up. He could say rain was coming on the sunniest of days, and would actually believe it.

Topics changed, and they began mulling over plans for the upcoming church picnic. Days ago, Ali had convinced his pastor that a picnic would be a strong morale booster and a chance for members of other churches to meet one another at Elizabeth Park in two months. After taking the lead as the event planner, Ali called his friends to help with the activity planning. As they sipped on Hangar 1 Vodka, they discussed how to keep the picnic under a twenty-thousand-dollar budget. Working through most of the night, Ali managed to forge expense report after expense report, miscalculating all associated costs. In the morning, he was prepared to pull the twenty grand from the bank and only use half for the picnic.

They had just finished working on the picnic planning for August 13, when Ali heard a gurgling noise and smelled gasoline. Someone was trying to burn down the house!

The killer struggled to light the match in the intense wind.

Bursting through the basement door like Federal agents, the three friends ran through the kitchen to the front door. When Ali swung open the door and exited onto the porch, he was the first to see the perpetrator running down Barclay Parkway.

And the foot chase was on from there.

CHAPTER SIX

Seema knew exactly what she had to do later that night—11:00 p.m.—but how could she do something she had never done before? Having sex? With a man? The anticipation invaded her mind like an army of ants. She felt confused, guilty, and scared.

For the next hour or so, she sat with a dejected look on her face, counting the cracks on the basement floor. The thought of someone sticking something in her besides a needle at a doctor's office was driving her nuts. She clasped her inner thighs together.

"Will it be too painful and hurt me?" A complete wreck, she began quivering uncontrollably. Nizama inched her way over to embrace Seema.

"What's with the long face?" Nizama asked, pulling Seema's head to her shoulder, running her fingers through her long curly hair. "You're gonna have to toughen up. You can't show them any fear."

Seema wiped the tears that had suddenly stormed into her eyes. "I don't care anymore," she said. "Anything's better than this place. I don't want to be here. I miss home. I miss my family."

"You can't think about them no more." Nizama raised Seema's chin and looked her in the eyes. "You hear me? No more! We're your family now. That's it. I don't want to hear any more shit about your family. You understand?"

Seema nodded.

"Good. Now, what is it that you're afraid of?" Nizama asked in an attempt to downplay the circumstances. "Listen to me, just do as they say and keep them happy. That way you make things a lot easier for yourself."

Nizama, noticing that Seema wasn't getting any more relaxed, slapped her across the face.

"You snap out of it, hear me?" Nizama demanded. "Wipe them tears off your eyes and straighten your face. You know what you have to do, so why cry? I don't have time for you showing any sign of weakness."

Seema couldn't understand why Nizama had been so cold lately. For the past few weeks she seemed so demanding and aggressive. At times she got into it with the other girls when they would talk about being unhappy. *Didn't she feel the same way too? Nobody could truly ever get use to what they were all being forced into doing. Could they?*

"I'll be fine," Seema finally said, hoping Nizama would leave her to herself. "Trust me. I'm okay now."

"Good," Nizama replied and began to help Seema with her makeup. "I know you can do it. Just stay focused and remember that the sooner you pay The Broker back, the quicker this will be over with."

*   *   *

"Do you think she's ready?" The Broker asked Nizama as they sat outside on the porch, waiting for time to pass.

"I think she is," Nizama told him. "She's like anyone starting out; she's a little scared. Don't know what to expect, that's all. I think she'll be fine, though."

"Are you sure? You know how I feel about this. If she's not ready, you need to tell me."

"She'll be okay," Nizama reassured him. "I had a talk with her, and she knows what to do. She's a little different from the others."

Nizama looked out into the fading sun, something she frequently did as the only privileged one out of the bunch to step outside.

"What do you mean by different?" The Broker asked.

"She just seems smarter than the others, that's all," Nizama said, nearly breaking her neck to read the writing on a huge tire that stood above every other sculpture.

"For her sake, I hope so," The Broker told her. He reached over and touched Nizama's stomach. "She take you to get it taken care of yet?"

"Not yet," Nizama said, dropping her head to stare at her belly. She slowly lifted her eyes back to his level. "I would like to keep it. I feel like I know him already. It's a boy, I'm sure."

"Don't be silly," he scolded. "We don't allow the girls to keep the babies. And that goes for you too. Why do you think I put you in charge of the others? Besides, how would you be able to make up all that money you owe?"

"But I would take care of him," Nizama promised, becoming overly anxious. "I would have him help out around here. He can cook and clean. Whatever you want, I can train him to do."

"Enough!" The Broker shouted. "The answer is no and will always be no! Tomorrow you will go to the doctor and get it taken care of, or else I'll do it myself."

And that was it. The Broker sent the crying Nizama back into the house and waited patiently for the pearl white Lincoln Navigator to pull into the driveway.

*   *   *

To him, Seema's body was hypnotizing. As she walked past, he licked his lips in anticipation. How could a young girl's legs appear so thin, long, and smooth? Visualizing her knockout figure through the tight, blue-faded jeans made him excited, and he couldn't wait for the opportunity to introduce himself.

A victim of a collapsing relationship, the man was in desperate need of time away from both his demanding job and his attention-needy wife, who, because of her sudden demands had caused him hardship in their marriage. *Come straight home after work, no hanging out with the guys on the weekend, I need you now.* That's all he heard from her, and he had been seeking a way out of the marriage for months. After all, he was on the road quite a lot as a truck driver, stopping and visiting different cities throughout the U.S. *Why should he put up with any of his wife's crap when he could have women in several different states?*

Behind closed doors she appeared even lovelier than she looked before. As he reached over to kiss her, grabbing Seema by the chin, he disregarded the tiny pimples huddled beneath her thick make-up. Her big lips and strong tongue fought him back as they engaged each other's mouths like suction cups. Soon after, he moved in for the front of her neck and began sucking on it until a huge hickey appeared. Once he advanced to Seema's earlobe, he played with it like it was a rubber band, pulling gently with his lips. The tickly sensation made her restless, and she backed away.

"Take off your clothes," the man instructed when she broke free of his clinch. "I wanna see you naked."

"Naked?" Seema seemed surprised. "Completely?"

That's when he looked at her oddly. "Are you serious?" he asked her. "What kinda fucking question is that?"

She tried to shut him up by coming to him and kissing his mouth, but he pushed her backwards.

"I said to take your fucking clothes off," he swore, struggling to control his temper. "What in the hell is wrong with you?"

She knew that the advice the other girls often shared on how to please a man would need to come into play then more than ever, but she couldn't get rid of the voice that constantly rang in her head.

But I'm just not ready to have sex. Her subconscious mind continued to torment her. *I thought I could, but I was wrong. Oh, God, get me out of this.*

At least she was good at stroking egos. It was the one trade she had learned that could help diffuse nearly any hostile situation. Making a man feel special was an added bonus and a tactic worth trying.

"Let me touch it," she finally said, pointing towards the front of his jeans. "I want to see how big it is."

"I don't think you'll be disappointed," he boasted, with a smile on his face as he stood and grabbed his crotch. "Not disappointed at all."

"Oh, baby," she said, "let me see what you got. If all of that's yours, I'm not sure I can handle you."

Those were the words that put a smile on his face. He liked to be complimented, and the slight mention of what he was packing in his pants was more than flattering.

He pulled down his boxer shorts and grabbed her hand, placing it on his rock-hard penis. Taking it in her palm, Seema dropped to her knees. *Maybe this will satisfy him, and I won't have to have sex.* She skillfully inserted a good three-quarter of his pole down her throat. Her accomplished oral sex caused him to rest his hands on his hips until she finished, and he stood there like Superman after a well-fought victory.

What next? Kiss him goodbye. She rose to her feet and was able to kiss him on the mouth. *How could he refuse to kiss her after that blowjob?* The foreplay minutes ago had been much more than his wife had done lately and more spontaneous than any Vegas ranch whore could offer. When he lay back on the table and rested his head against one of the pillows, the delighted smile on his face said it all. Seeing his satisfied expression, Seema thought she was finished and sat down on the chair. She grabbed a towel from under the small stand to wipe her mouth. She had pulled it off!

"Turn the lights off," he suddenly instructed Seema. She sat in the chair, motionless. *What now?*

Seeing her delayed reaction, the man yelled, "I said, turn the lights off! You don't listen very well, do you?"

She couldn't say a single word. Fearful, she rose to her feet and walked over to the light switch. She heard the flicker of what sounded like a lighter. When she turned back around, she saw that he had lit the two aromatherapy candles used for guests during massage sessions.

While the flames swayed, and the wicks burned with a soft crackle, the man took a moment to admire Seema's figure. An enthusiast of little hardbodies, he loved himself a young girl with womanly features. Physically, Seema was much more mature than her age.

"You're drop-dead gorgeous," he said, peering at her teenage body. "Come here and let me take a closer look."

Seema stayed pinned against the wall.

"Get your ass over here!" he ordered. "What is it about you? Are you deaf?"

Slowly, Seema inched toward him, careful not to piss off her customer any more than he already was. She had heard the horror stories the other girls shared as the result of unsatisfied men who took their aggressions out on them. Before long, she was standing between his legs. She tried to stall his unwanted advances by sparking up a general conversation with him.

"What is it that you like about me?" she asked while she rubbed on his bald head. She had to show some type of attraction given that he was there for pleasure. *Maybe he would find my intellectual side more stimulating than sex.*

"I'm better at showing than I am telling," he said, rubbing his rough hands up and down the back of her legs. He began to grope her ass. "Let's stop talking. How about we play show, not tell?"

Seconds later, they were embracing each other on the twin-sized mattress. With Seema on top, he lifted her shirt, rubbing her soft, smooth back. He then instructed her to lie on her back so he could be the more dominant one. But the voice inside her head was still playing mind games, and for some reason, she couldn't break free from whatever spirit was constantly telling her not to do it.

No, the voice spoke to her. *Don't let him take it. Fight! Fight for your life!* Mesmerized by her strength as she kept him from mounting her, the man finally gave up and stood to his feet.

"Come on," he complained. "What the hell is the matter with you? I didn't pay for this shit!"

She smiled and shook her head. "I didn't do anything to pay for this either," she countered and sat upright.

He hit her with a closed fist. "You need to be taught a good lesson," he scolded her. "If you were mine, I'd beat you till you were black and blue."

The pain that Seema felt from the blow was hidden behind a rush of adrenaline; she had conquered the inevitable. She couldn't wait to run downstairs and tell the girls about what had just happened. She had fought and won the battle! Earlier that day she was so paranoid and scared about the thought of doing something she had never done before. She watched the livid man rush to put his clothes back on, and the feeling of accomplishment hid behind the modest smile pasted on her face.

"I'll be sure to tell The Broker about this bullshit too!" the man grumbled just loud enough for Seema to hear. At that moment, she didn't care who he told. She had already accepted the fact that she would have to face him eventually. She was prepared for the beating that was guaranteed to be handed down by The Broker. *What's a little pain compared to having your innocence brutally taken?* Her decision was final, and it was a choice that at that very point in time made her comfortable.

"A good beating is what she needs," Seema heard the angry man say. She pressed her ear against the wall, and could hear the commotion clearly.

"I want my fucking money back!" the man complained. "That bitch in there wouldn't put out."

"She wouldn't put out?" It was a woman's surprised voice. "What do you mean, she wouldn't put out? All of our girls here are trained."

"That one in there surely isn't! If you call that trained, then you better fire the teacher and close the school."

"Are you sure that you're not confused, sir?" The Broker's voice came from a distance. He walked over to join the others. "Slow down a bit and tell me what happened?"

"Do any of you speak good English?" the man stood with his hands on his waist. "Open your eyes and read my lips. Nothing happened. Nothing at all!" He yanked his jacket off the hanger before continuing, "Now, hand over my money."

"We're sorry," The Broker said, clearly embarrassed. He gave the man back all of his money. "We truly don't know what got into her tonight, but if you'd like, we can have one of our regulars assist you with anything you need."

"No thank you," he shouted. "I'll pass. That girl in there needs to be taught a lesson. I've never in my life experienced such disrespect. A good beating would be a start."

He snatched the wad of money from The Broker's hand and lit a cigarette on his way out. Once the man was outside of the building, The Broker made sure the door was locked, then he closed the blinds and went straight for Seema.

He attacked Seema, hitting her constantly in the head while she tried to roll her body into a tight ball near the corner of the room. He yanked her hands away from her face and backhanded her, then a bruising left hook caught her flush on the cheek, and she fell over, trying desperately to crawl away from him. But The Broker was way too swift and was already on her again, kicking her in the midsection. Seema cringed in agonizing pain.

"You fucking whore! How dare you betray me," The Broker yelled at her. His face showed no signs of stopping yet. In fact, when he snatched the clock radio from the wall and began looping the cord around his hand like a cowboy, she knew more beatings were coming. And she was right.

Slashing blows with the cord caught her on the lower back, and her frantic screams for help recoiled off the thick white walls. *Fight back. Don't let him beat you like this.* She tried to defend herself, eventually making it to her feet, but when her swing at him barely grazed The Broker's face, his anger boiled over.

He smacked her back to the floor, and she knocked over the lamp on her way down, shattering it. He yanked her pants down.

I wasn't expecting all of this. What happened to the beating I prepared myself for?

When he got them off her, she began to scurry on the floor like a bug afraid of getting squashed, yet she couldn't escape. He ripped her shirt from her body, stripped off her panties, and punched her one final time to ensure that she was too weak to stop what was about to happen next.

Seconds after the blood began pouring from her mouth, he picked her up and laid her flat on the table. He spread her legs high in the air, forcing them apart. Although she put up a frenzied struggle to squeeze her legs together, an elbow crashing down on her abdomen forced her to cave in. He unzipped his pants, pulled out his cock, and forced his way into her, hammering at her immature pussy time after time. The painful look on her face said it all: *another teenage girl raped by the man who owned her.* While she prayed for the nightmarish episode to stop, little did she know that hours after this horrific episode ended, she would have to endure the same exact thing all over again.

The next few times weren't as bad for her. At least he drugged her up with heroin and crack cocaine before viciously tearing into her insides. In the beginning, it was always a fight between Seema and The Broker, but he came out the winner each time. After a while, it became a common occurrence between the two of them. Mixed in with the drugs that she became dependent on and the forced sex several times a day was fear and force of habit. Once he was comfortable with her, and after he was certain that another client would never leave dissatisfied, he allowed her to gather her belongings from the closet where she was living in isolation and rejoin the others downstairs.

"Yes, she did it," The Broker said to himself as he puffed on a cigar late one evening after she had entertained her first customer. "She is now fully trained!"

He sat back in his chair and smiled at his wife, who was busy counting the money at the opposite end of the room.

*   *   *

Monahan was organizing his cluttered desk when he felt a pair of warm and gentle hands cover his eyes from behind.

"Guess who?"

"The lady I often dream of," Monahan responded, smiling. "You love to play games, don't you?"

"At times," the woman's voice said softly. "What good is all work and no play?"

"Anybody who knows me knows that I love to play around," Monahan joked, rubbing the hands of the lady friend standing behind him. "Let's see, in all my fifteen years as an officer of the law, there's only one cop I've ever known who'd dare come to work with manicured nails."

"I see that you pick up on things rather quickly," the woman said, surprised by Monahan's attention to detail. "So, let's see if you're truly as good as you say you are. Take a guess."

Monahan inhaled. "Ahhh, the sweet smell of a woman," he said. "I was taught that a guess is something you do when you aren't sure of something."

"Then try me."

"Let's see, from the smell of that perfume, it could only be one person," Monahan replied, removing the hands blindfolding his eyes. "The lovely Ms. Madeline Harris."

He joyfully spun around in his chair only to see that he was mistaken. Detective Rusco stood there, stunned.

"Wrong answer!" she spurted out in disappointment. "I thought you were better than that."

"Oh, what's up, partner." Monahan tried to cover up his inaccuracy with a high five. "I ever tell you how glad I am to have you as a partner?"

"Yeah, whatever," Rusco sighed in disbelief.

After several weeks of teaming together, she was attracted to Monahan like a magnet.

"What are you doing for lunch today?" she asked. "Wanna run out and grab a few Coney dogs? We have a little time before our two o'clock."

Coney dogs were a typical source of protein consumed by many Michiganders during a lunch break. The loaded hotdog with the works was famous in the Midwest states.

"Naw, I'm good," Monahan declined the request. "I need to look up a few things online, but thanks anyways."

Officer Rusco decided to poke her nose into his business. "Like what, background checks?" she asked. "Is that all you do in your spare time?"

It was something that she had heard he did during his pastime, and a true statement at that. Monahan often explored the criminal records section on the police database looking into the past history of those close to him. He had already done his research on Rusco.

"Hey, don't knock me for wanting to know who's around me at all times," he said, surprised that she had the nerve to bring up such a thing. "Let's just make sure that the next time we're in a jam, you don't decide to pull out that Tazer."

She looked at him in surprise, realizing that even she had fallen victim to his investigations. Years ago, she had received probation for attempting to zap her boyfriend with a stun gun. It was Monahan's way of saying don't fuck with him.

She let him be and left him sitting at his paper-strewn desk. He turned on his computer after deciding to check on a few others he wasn't able to look into the last time he searched the database. The first name he typed in was Gloria Stephens, a young Italian woman he was seeing on the side. It wasn't anything serious, but certainly a physical attraction was brewing. Monahan was picky, and before he would let anyone invade his circle they first had to pass the preliminary background screening. Seconds after he sent the name into cyberspace, the results came back: *No Search Records Found.* Monahan nodded his head in agreement.

The next name he decided to look up was Ed Zucal, Madeline's partner. He typed the weird African name into the computer and sent it off. What came back was hilarious.

He had received a misdemeanor charge at the age of seventeen. The only reason the charge wasn't sealed by the courts was because in Africa, at the time, a person was considered an adult at seventeen, as opposed to eighteen in the United States. Searching a bit further, Monahan found that Zucal was one of two streakers arrested during the '64 World Cup soccer game between Argentina and South Africa. He was booked and released that night, later charged with the misdemeanor crime of disorderly conduct and indecent exposure. Monahan fell over in laughter, wondering how it was that Zucal was able to get a police officer job with the Detroit Police Department with a misdemeanor conviction on his record. Then again, Detroit was a huge metropolitan city with crime numbers steadily rising. *Does Human Resources really give a damn about a man who took his clothes off at a soccer game?* Monahan couldn't stop laughing and decided to share the good news with Madeline. He picked up the phone.

"Homicide," Madeline answered.

"Hey, Maddie," Monahan tried to contain his laughter. "What are you doing for your birthday this year?"

The question threw Madeline off guard. "How am I supposed to know?" she asked him. "That's three months from now. Besides, I don't event want to think about it. I already feel like I'm getting older by the day."

"I was just asking because I plan on providing the entertainment for you," Monahan said, struggling to hold the joke in.

"What are you talking about?" Madeline asked him, totally lost. "Come on, spit it out."

"I'm just saying," Monahan carried on, "instead of Simone or any of your other friends taking you to Henry's, this year I can order you home service."

Henry's was a famous male strip club on the other side of the border. A lot of horny women went there for a fun getaway with the girls.

"And who do you know that could provide such a thing?" Madeline inquired, teasingly. "Certainly it wouldn't be you, unless you've decided to stop guzzling down them MGDs and take your big butt to BTF."

"See, I don't even drink Millers like that anymore," Monahan denied the truth. "And what is BTF anyways?"

"Bally's Total Fitness." Madeline laughed at her own cleverness.

"Funny girl. How about I just bring your partner and let him be the evening's special guest? From what I hear, he has no shame in sharing any of his ass…ets with women."

"What exactly is that supposed to mean?"

It was then that Monahan filled her in on Zucal's crazed side. At first she didn't believe a word that was coming out of his mouth, waiting patiently for him to stop ridiculing her partner so that she could step in.

"Are you serious?" she finally asked him after he finished teasing. "Don't lie, because I'm gonna ask him about it."

"No, don't do that," Monahan pleaded with her. "I don't want him finding out that I looked up his personal history. If the Chief finds out, he'll have my throat. He already warned me about searching on anyone other than suspects. You gotta promise me that you won't tell."

"Only if you promise that you'll stop acting like a little kid with a new toy," Madeline said, waiting for Monahan to give his word. "People knowing that they're being checked is one thing, but doing it behind their back is another."

"All right already," Monahan reacted, showing his cranky side. "Whose side of the bed did you wake up on this morning, anyways?"

"Obviously not yours," Madeline snapped back. Her snippy attitude made her desirable.

"Maybe tomorrow?" Monahan questioned her, playfully.

"Only if you're lucky." Madeline gave Monahan an unexpected answer.

Suddenly, a hungering tension for each other rippled through the phone lines, and the silence was soon breached with a change in topic.

"So, are we ever going to get together and watch a movie one of these nights?" Monahan asked her for the third time in two weeks. He was devoted to getting his friend back, who lately seemed too occupied with work to engage in any fun.

"I have to work the fireworks tomorrow night," Madeline replied. Realizing she had stood Monahan up just a few days ago, she made an attempt to patch things up. "I'll see if Rosemary can watch Amber, and we can do something on Saturday."

"Rosemary?" Monahan asked, surprised. "Rosemary's been watching her an awful lot lately, hasn't she? Whose daughter is she, hers or yours?"

"Excuse me?" Madeline bit back sharply.

Monahan, knowing that he had overstepped his boundaries, quickly apologized.

"My badd!" he told her. "Guess I'm not used to always being placed on the back burner. But I understand, you're busy with your new position."

"It's not even like that," Madeline informed him. "We can go out Saturday night. Let's make it a date."

"Naw, maybe next time," Monahan objected. "Remember, I told you my family is coming down this weekend. Just fit me in your schedule whenever you can."

And that was it. Monahan hung up the phone and continued searching the criminal records section of the police database. Madeline, on the other hand, placed a call to Rosemary, informing her she would be late picking up Amber again that night. She had paperwork that needed to be completed first.

CHAPTER SEVEN

They chased after him as though he was one of "America's Most Wanted" criminals and they were U.S. Marshals, racing through the Eastside neighborhood. He weaved in between houses, parked cars, and through a back alley. With his awareness of the area apparent, and while Ali and his friends struggled to keep pace, it was the man's athletic ability to scale a fence that eventually set him free. Giving up on their pursuit, they watched with their hands on their knees as the long-striding man sprinted down the dirt trail and into the grassy yard of the elementary school.

He continued running for blocks until he had made it to the nearest bus station. The Metrolink that ran at the top of each hour was due to arrive in a little over three minutes. As the killer waited patiently, a man tightly gripping a walking cane sat down next to him.

"We've had a beautiful day today," he said as he lowered the shades over his eyes. "They say it was supposed to rain, but from the sight of things, I don't see that happening."

The killer didn't feel cheery enough to hold a conversation with anyone, especially with a man who looked like he could be a twin with *Bob Barker* from *The Price is Right*.

"Them damn news anchors are always getting it wrong," the man continued. "That's probably the one profession where you can be wrong ninety percent of the time and still keep your job."

Something about the way the man laughed at his own humor sent chills through the killer's skin. It was one of a kind.

"One of the channels said the high was going to be fifty. It sure feels hotter than that to me," the man said, easing out of his jacket. "What do you think, Sonny? These news crews full of crap or what?"

The squeaky sound of the bus coming to a slow stop saved the killer from the meaningless discussion. He climbed aboard and sat near the front. Surprisingly, as the elderly man made his way on board, he took the empty seat next to the killer. After the driver closed the door, the man continued talking, "I prefer to read the weather reports in the paper anyhow," the man said. "They tend to be a bit more accurate."

The killer was growing impatient with the old man. His persistence was bothersome, but the killer tried his best to be respectful.

"Look, sir, I just wanna get home, that's all," the killer said politely. If the man was anywhere near his age range, he would have already told him to *shut the fuck up*.

"Who struck a match under your ass, buddy?" the old man asked, grabbing the killer's attention by tapping him on the leg with his cane.

"Sir, I just want to get home," the killer shouted in annoyance. "I don't feel like talking right now!"

"I don't give a shit what you want," the old man shouted, showering the killer with saliva. "That's the problem with you youngsters these days. You don't respect your elders."

"Hey, Charlie, calm it down, would you?" the driver finally spoke up as he adjusted the rear view mirror. "Why you always gotta mess with people, huh? Sometimes folks just want to be left to themselves. Now leave the man alone."

"And sometimes I just want a little respect," Charlie retorted after nearly coughing up a lung. "I've been riding this bus for five years now—"

"I know, I know, Charlie," the driver said, anticipating his next words, "and you just want to be respected."

"Damn right I do."

Many years ago, Charlie Landrum was arrested and charged with serving alcohol to minors. It didn't sound like a major offense, but in Charlie's case, it was. Charlie was once head of the State Liquor Control Commission and was highly regarded in his line of work. The majority of his career was spent hiring underaged teens to work undercover as moles to go into establishments and buy liquor from vendors. Once the purchase was made, Charlie and his team was responsible for citing the business for serving alcohol to minors, revoking their liquor licenses at the same time.

But karma eventually caught up with Charlie. He became intimate with one of his workers, and it just happened that the girl's father owned one of the businesses that Charlie had closed down. In a retaliatory attempt, the girl's father tried to drag Charlie into the mud with him. Although he was unable to prove that Charlie was intimate with his daughter, he was successful in sticking him with a case of his own, providing liquor to a minor.

The charge was devastating to Charlie's reputation and his career. When the rumors surfaced and the news reporters got a hold of the information, they ran with it. Charlie was eventually given a pink slip from the State of Michigan and received another termination letter from his wife of seven years. Unable to fully bounce back from a tarnished reputation, Charlie worked daily to regain the respect of others as he caught the bus daily to the Hammy's Restaurant where he washed dishes for a living.

"Whatcha think about Tommy Andrews being caught last night?" Charlie asked out loud enough to gain a response. Tommy Andrews was the latest capture from *Michigan's Most Wanted Sex Offenders.*

"Thank goodness they caught him," the driver answered the floating question. "I hear he was hiding out in a motel near Cincinnati."

"That's what the paper says," Charlie replied, "but you turn on the news and they got a different story."

"What do mean?"

"Well, on the ten o'clock news, anchorman Huel Perkins said it was Columbus. Boy, I tell you, if I had a dime for each time the news aired the wrong information, I'd be a rich man by now."

"It doesn't happen that often, does it, Charlie?" the driver asked behind a chuckle.

"It did to me. If the little prick that told my story would've reported the truth, I wouldn't be in the shape that I'm in today."

The killer swung his head around and looked at Charlie in amazement.

"You were screwing a helpless child," the killer reminded him. "How else should it have been reported?"

Charlie was so upset that he started shaking in his seat. *Who was this middle-aged bastard that had the nerve to speak to his elder out of line?*

"Just be glad that you didn't get what you deserved," the killer said, biting his bottom lip in resentment.

"You little punk!"

"Fuck you, old man!"

"That's enough!" the driver finally yelled. "Charlie, this is your stop. Don't get back on my bus tomorrow if you can't control yourself."

"This is my stop too," the killer said after waiting for Charlie to get off first. He handed the driver three dollars for the ride.

"Hey, buddy," the driver yelled at the killer before closing the doors, "don't pay him no mind. He's just an old fart."

*   *   *

He had no idea that he was being followed. As the man took his sweet time crossing the street, little did he know that the killer was close on his heels.

Step. Push. Step. Push. It was the pace that the man had acquired from years of walking with his cane and arthritic knee condition. While he waited for the walk signal at the busy intersection, he took out his flip lighter and lit a cigar. His shift started in twenty minutes. Every day he typically would arrive at work in time to sit in the back alley and puff on a vanilla-flavored tobacco stick.

As he sat out back, the man heard something rattle near the garbage can and figured was the rats that frequently hung out looking for scrapped food. He took a cookie from his pocket and tossed it that way. When it came flying back at him, the man knew that the beast hiding behind the dumpster was much bigger than any rodent.

"Who's there?" the man asked to a silent response. He stood up and walked in that direction. Suddenly, when he was grabbed from behind, the man's heart skipped a beat.

"Boo," Jason said, grabbing both of Charlie's arms and shaking him. "Gotcha!"

"You dumb ass! I could've had a heart attack, for Christ's sake," Charlie said, trying to regain his breath. "What the hell are you doing out here?"

"I had to empty out this tub of lard," the boy said. "Boss said the inspectors might show up today, so he's making us get rid of all the bad stuff. You on the schedule for today?"

"No, I just showed up to serve pancakes," Charlie griped. "Of course I am."

"Then hurry up and come in and help," Jason said as he started to go back indoors. "You're a bitter old man."

Charlie returned to his crate and sat down. He still had five minutes till the start of his shift, and he planned on milking every second. *Damn that kid. If he respected his elders, he'd cover till I decide it's time to come inside.*

As Charlie blew a trail of smoke into the night air, a shadow appeared from behind. Charlie tried to slip out of the tight clinch, but the killer kept his bicep wrapped around Charlie's throat. While the old man struggled to break loose, he was dragged away from the back door and to the side of the dumpster. The killer maliciously strangled the old man by twisting and turning his head like a bottle cap until his neck snapped. In the blink of an eye, the killer had scampered in the direction of the nearest bus stop, hopeful that he could still catch the next Metrolink passing by at the top of the hour.

*   *   *

Known to the Indians as *Wahl-nah-be-zee* (White Swan), Belle Isle Park was once a breeding ground for wild hogs. That was until development and reformation initiatives eventually transformed the island into a popular attraction with state-of-the-art exhibits.

The park was a place where children could visit, swim, eat, and play. Marathons, bike-a-thons, model boat races, concerts, and campouts were some of the regular activities held there. It wasn't abnormal for fisherman to throw out their lines into the river from the distant shore either, or for athletes to train there on a sunny day for an upcoming game. The island was frequently visited, and Detroit's people always went in peace to witness one of Michigan's most noteworthy recreational areas, but years of slow depreciation and subtle misuse eventually caught up with the aging park.

In the late 1970s and early '80s, the park evolved into a popular hangout spot for teen gangs. Local gangs pursued their turf wars, and soon after, the park turned into an out-of-control battleground. The violence made top stories on every station and became such a regular weekend trend that the news programs grew reluctant to report on the notorious crimes. With policeman fearful to enter the park, it wasn't until a few fearless senior citizens and two notable societal figures joined forces, and the park began to show signs of life again.

With civil rights leaders Al Sharpton and Jesse Jackson at the helm of the movement, the campaign to decrease the violence in Detroit gained steam, targeting the infamous island-park. Soon, after the park weeded out the hooligans, derelicts, and drifters, it began reopening its gates to families, friends, and children who had waited years for the park to return to prominence.

With services from organizations such as the Friends of Belle Isle, the efforts to restore the park back to richness had been revitalized. While advocates for Belle Isle continued to fight off the development of gambling casinos, equestrian centers, and other unwarranted structures, it was the Friends of Belle Isle who continued to play a key role in influencing city officials to better maintain the island. As Ali surveyed the tremendous enhancements the park had to offer, he couldn't help but boast about its evolution in his prayer.

"Dear God, first and foremost I want to thank you for the generations that have passed and paved the way for us to host an event at a spectacular place like this. I ask that you bless this food that we are about to eat and let it be nourishment to our bodies. In Jesus' name we pray, AMEN!"

After blessing the feast that had been prepared by several kitchen-go-happy church members, Ali marveled at the foods that included nearly every soul food entree imaginable: fried chicken, black-eyed peas, cornbread, mustard greens, pies, hot sausages, and pork and beef rib tips. As the attendees assessed the full course meals, it was Ali's gurgling stomach that chased away the group of flies that had invaded in groups to get a taste of the zesty foods.

"Boy, this sure looks good," Ali said as he stood in line behind Pastor Wallace with a paper plate in his hand shooing away the pests. "They must have spent hours preparing this yesterday."

"Actually, they were up all night," Pastor Wallace corrected him. A very conservative, clean-shaven, bald-headed man, Pastor Wallace was neatly dressed in a long white shirt, a designer silk tie, and black gabardine dress slacks. He always dressed well regardless of whether he was counseling church members, Brethren Fellowship, or entertaining members at a social event. It was his way of establishing a certain persona.

Scooping some macaroni onto his plate, he continued, "My wife was in the kitchen till three-thirty this morning, so you better leave room on that plate for some of her peach cobbler."

Glancing at the untouched dish sloppily stuffed in an aluminum foil pan, Ali's face tightened at the sickening sight.

"I sure will," he lied. "I'm gonna come back and get some after I've had the chance to eat some ribs. Can't have sweets before the meats."

Ali sat next to members of other churches who had already begun tearing into their meals. Talking with them, they all seemed so happy with the direction in which their respective churches were headed. One member in particular made mention of a new childcare center that was in the works at her church, Greater Metro, a larger place for devotion with members in the thousands. Excited to speak on the member discount she was soon to receive, she explained how she'd now be able to put her five kids into a Christian center without worrying if they were fed, taught, or looked after. Several others had similar stories of new facilities being built, field trips, and donations. They talked for nearly an hour, and while the smooth gospel sounds of Yolanda Adams serenaded the joyful attendees near the picnic area, Ali was already mentally preparing for the picnic's after-party. *All of these fake-ass people out here. I can't wait for this day to hurry up and be over with. I'm going to have fun wasting their money.* Once the music switched artists, and Kirk Franklin blasted from the loud speakers, Ali snapped out of his daze. Nearly everyone capable of advancing to the grass for fun and games did, and a jam-packed evening of activities followed.

A water balloon was provided to each team. As they began dividing into groups of two, Ali sat back and waited patiently for any young women who had not been selected. Checking out the talent from the different churches, he stood by his friend Eric, lusting over the prettiest, sexiest, and best built women the same way he would privately flip through a Victoria Secret's catalog. Once all of the cliques formed, it was Ali who was odd man out. As he started back to the picnic area, he saw her, and from that moment on, he was glad that he had.

She had on a Greater Metro Church of God in Christ white t-shirt, and by the way Nikira Parker knotted up her shirt exposing her flat stomach, you'd assume she carried beverages over her head at a local bar for a living. While she turned down several salivating men surrounding her, Ali inched closer, thinking of what to say to better persuade this woman—stacked like a truckload of melons—to participate. After the young brother from Fruit for Life was turned away, Ali strode to her.

"Afternoon, Sister," he purred. "Is there a reason that you're standing here with that frown on your face? I spent hours putting this event together so everyone could leave here with a smile. From the looks of things, that's not about to happen with you."

"I'm having a good time," she replied, plastering a smile on her face from ear to ear. "I'm just not in the mood to get wet. Tell you the truth, I have a cabaret to go to tomorrow night, and I just got my hair done."

A cabaret was a mature celebration for adults, more famous in the Midwest states, Michigan and Illinois in particular. It was an event that provided working professionals with an opportunity to dress to impress, ballroom, hustle, or salsa dance without worrying about some childish kids behaving inappropriately.

"I don't see you out there," she continued. "Let me guess, you're too cool to catch a water balloon. I get it!"

"That's not it at all," he countered. "I'm gonna participate, but first I need to make sure everyone does. And that includes you."

"What are you, the picnic monitor?" she said, rolling her eyes at him.

"No, I'm Deacon Ali Gaines from Mt. Zion Church," he said, offering his hand. "My buddies and I put this together ourselves. Hopefully, everyone is appreciating the effort that we put into this thing. You know it's difficult for men to put together anything that doesn't involve power tools and instructions."

"A deacon?" she asked, embarrassed. "I never would've—"

"I know," he said with a bit of arrogance. "Most people don't. Do me a favor. Go out there and join in. It's the least you can do, especially after eating up all my food."

She laughed. "I was hungry."

"Well, now you can exercise it off. I've gotta make sure you keep that nice body of yours," he said, slowly lifting his wandering eyes. "Either you come out here with me, or I'm gonna tell Brother Winbush to come and join you."

Ali pointed to the table where an older man sat, gnawing on the core of a slice of watermelon with his gums.

"Since you put it that way, I guess I'll play," she said, taking Ali's hand. "But if you wet my hair, I swear I'll kick your butt, deacon or not."

They walked to the middle of the circle, joining others who had teamed together in hopes of winning the first prize of two concert tickets to the Circle of Glory Musical, a star-studded event expected to fill every seat inside of the DTE Music Theatre. Once the game's organizer instructed everyone to separate five feet from each other, the tossing began, and while several water balloons exploded upon impact, Ali and his partner's stayed intact. Taking a giant step backwards, they all tossed their balloons, back and forth, repeating the same until only two teams remained. Surprisingly, Ali and Nikki were still in the hunt.

"All right ladies and gentlemen," the loud, boisterous, organizer announced. "Let's give it up to both teams for making it this far. What we'll do now is have a face-off. This is for two pairs of tickets to the Circle of Glory concert." She waved the tickets high into the air and at the same time, the teams prepared to let their balloons fly.

He looked over at his friends, and when Ali got their approval, he knew exactly what to do next.

"On three, you will toss your balloons together," she proclaimed. "Whoever doesn't break theirs will be the winner. Ready? One, two, three...!"

The other team members tossed theirs first, each gently guiding and catching the largely filled balloon as though it was a delicate baby. Winding up like a fast pitch softball game, Ali hurled his underhand. With double the speed of its counterparts, the wet balloon smashed against his partner's white shirt. As the other team jumped for joy, declaring themselves victorious at that particular challenge, the young lady on Ali's team quickly scampered back to her car to change her soaked, see-through shirt, which had now made her look like she had just took part in a Hugh Hefner wet T-shirt party. Minutes after they joined together, Ali and his friends shared high-fives with each other, overjoyed by his perfect aim.

The next game was the dunk tank. The rules were as follows: only a pastor or a deacon could sit in the tank. Each member participant would get three baseballs to pitch. If successful in hitting the target, the pastor or deacon would be ejected from his seat and fall into a tank of water three feet deep. After the instructions were clearly explained, Ryann King hurried up front to throw out the first pitch.

He was physically challenged since birth. A rare bone cancer had limited the growth of Ryann's limbs, and the way he flung the ball at his target was like a minor league pitcher who had thrown over a hundred pitches in a game. It was apparent that fatigue was one of the main weaknesses that affected him. Begging his mother for one more chance at nailing the target, he stormed away, crying when she wouldn't agree to wasting her money on the five-dollar fee.

Next up was a little girl with golden-brown curly locks. A very fiery child she was, the eagerness in her showed when she ran up to the basket after handing the helper a twenty-dollar bill and grabbed four balls without any help. As she sprinted up to the throwing line, Pastor Wallace caught a glimpse of the immobilizing brace she wore to support her wrist. While the balls she threw traveled in every direction but straight, the pastor clapped gallantly at the little girl's effort.

Thirty minutes had elapsed, and Pastor Wallace was still dry, no one was able to upend him from his seat. Seeing the line growing from shortest to tallest, the pastor decided to change spots before the adults had the chance to throw. After changing positions in the dunk tank, he handed his replacement, Ali, the unused beach towel, joyful that he didn't have to feel the true temperature of the chilling water.

"If you're lucky like me, you won't be needing this," he said to Ali as they exchanged places. "Good luck in there. The line is getting better with their aim."

It didn't take long for Ali to find out how cold the freezing water was. When Charissa Barnsworth took center stage, it was as though she couldn't miss, pitching the ball like Roger Clemens during the peak of his career, throwing strike after strike. Ali couldn't stay dry to save his life.

Friends since eleventh grade, Cherry and Ali had lost touch once Cherry moved to Nashville, Tennessee. A very giving person in high school, she was very helpful, lending a hand to many horny high school boys. Having had a reputation as the campus whore during her freshman and sophomore years, Cherry was known in circle groups as "the easy one." That's until the day she met Ali through mutual friends.

Taming her like a lioness, Ali was suave enough to convince Cherry to commit to him and him alone. Gravitating towards each other like magnetic forces, they considered themselves casual sex buddies, engaging in the activity in indescribable places: bathrooms, the gym, empty classrooms, they did it everywhere, but nowhere could compare to the night they made love underneath the packed bleachers during a school basketball game.

Solemnly swearing to each other not to tell a living soul, Cherry had bent over on the metal support beams, enticing Ali to cum inside of her to see if he could quickly make her reach a crowning point. To Ali, the rush of something new was invigorating. He had knocked off quite a few girls since Elena, but nothing could compare to the spontaneity of doing it in public. It was such an all-time high that he just had to run back and tell his friends about it. That's when the mutual alliance between the two was ruined. Word got around about what had occurred underneath the bleachers and soon after, Cherry chose to split. With the stigma following her around like a leech, Cherry ultimately chose to focus her time on athletics as opposed to sexual affairs.

Ali remained one of Cherry's biggest fans. An athlete himself, he loved women with athletic prowess. With Cherry's beauty and her ability to compete, he stayed after her, desperately trying to remain her friend, but when she moved away, all hope vanished and they had lost touch. Now, after not seeing each other for nearly ten years, Ali couldn't tell if the pretty, fair-skinned woman in the short, yellow sundress was still upset about what had happened way back when, or if her throwing arm was really that good. Ali couldn't take his eyes off her.

She paid for an amazing dozen balls. And while Cherry stood there with a smirk written on her face, Ali had already figured out why she was so determined to dunk him. The look that she gave him clearly implied that she was still mad.

He could feel her animosity towards him. Still, Ali began to entice her, "You can't hit the target," he shouted out. "Come on, Cherry, why did the Volunteers sign you again?" Seeing that he was challenging her, Cherry picked up a ball and began circling her arm around in a whirlwind so fast that if she were to do the same with the other, gravity would propel her into the air. When she finally let go of the ball, Ali remembered that it was Charissa Barnsworth's pitching on the high school softball team that earned her a scholarship to play on the Tennessee Volunteers girls' softball team. Pulling himself out of the water, Ali smiled at her as she reared back and threw another ball. Each time she threw at her target, Ali had to pull himself out, snickering at her, pleasantly surprised that Cherry was now back in town. Amazingly, she smiled back at him.

They had years of catching up to do. Walking along the riverfront, they filled each other in on their lives since high school. She was a cheerleader for the Tennessee Titans football team, living in Memphis, single and happy, in town to take care of an uncle who was sickly and on his deathbed. He told her of his single status and how he was still looking for Ms. Right, in spite of the fact that no one had come remotely close to claiming the title since Cherry's departure. A mother of two, captivating his interest with pictures, she pulled out one after the other from her pocketbook. Ali had no kids and zero pictures in his wallet to share. Still, Cherry was mesmerized by hearing the different stories he told, one in particular of a distraught woman who claimed he had fathered her child. Even though years ago they had separated on bad terms, if the old cliché was true, time heals a broken heart and the years away from each other seemed in their favor. They stayed and talked for the duration of the picnic. Just before the sun retired, they returned back to the eating area, smiling, laughing and embracing each other as though they had been together all those years. Just as Ali was getting ready to exchange numbers with her, Sister Douglass rushed towards them.

"Mighty close there aren't you, Deacon Gaines?" she said as she stepped in between the two. An old, timeless, white-haired granny, Sister Douglass was alive beyond her allotted years and was always in somebody's business where she had no business. For the last two months she had been really riding Ali, making false accusations to the pastor about him gambling and drinking at the casino, the same one she attended every first of the month. He would listen to her and get pissed whenever she mentioned it. For some reason, it was okay for her to gamble her savings away since she was a senior citizen, and God wouldn't hold anyone over sixty accountable for having a mere pastime. But a deacon gambling, now that was something entirely different. He was supposed to be a minister of the Word who had been blessed to shower down the teachings of righteousness. Sister Douglass knew there was nothing right about Ali's gambling addiction, and she tried to exploit the negative she found in him.

"He sits on the Wheel of Fortune dollar slots all day and even has a membership card to the casino," she would fuss to the pastor one night over dinner. "I'm telling you, something's not right about him. Did you notice that ever since he became a counter, money has been missing? Our people have been putting their hard-earned money into those baskets each week even though they're financially strapped, all in hopes that God will shower them in return with His blessings. And now we have to worry about a thief overseeing the monies. I'm telling you, we need to watch him!"

It was her most absurd statement to date. When she brought it to the pastor's attention, he blew her off. After all, she had slept that same dream of five other church members. Now she held out her wrinkled, cracked hand, mischievously wondering who the hot mama was Ali was toting around on his arm.

"Hello there, sweetie," she continued. "I'm Sister Douglass. And you are?"

Holding back on shaking the old lady's sweaty palms, "I'm Cherry," she said.

"No, ma'am, we don't use our street names when in God's presence," the old woman said, stepping in to condescendingly hug Cherry. She knew Cherry didn't appreciate the gesture so she embraced her as long as she could before Cherry finally broke the clinch. "Baby, what name did your momma give you?"

"Charissa," she said, faintly answering the old nag. She turned her back on the woman, raring to go. "Look Ali, take my number down and call me sometime this week. Maybe we can get together before I go back."

The old woman, determined not to be ignored, remained persistent.

"Call you 'bout what?" the woman asked after snatching the napkin where Cherry wrote her number. "The only thing the deacon needs to call you about is church service."

"She's coming," Ali butted in on the heated exchange. "Isn't that right, Charissa? I can teach you an awful lot during Wednesday night's Bible Study."

Ali winked at her with his left eye.

"Wednesday night's Bible Study starts at 7:00 p.m."

With his back against the wall, Ali had to appear pure and holy as other members of the church had began to linger around the area, throwing their trash away and picking up items off the grass to help preserve Belle Isle Park. Although he desperately wanted to jot down her number, he couldn't take the chance of members from his congregation seeing that. He gave her a location where he could be found, and it was in her court whether or not she wanted to pay him a visit. The picnic was a success.

*   *   *

Pounding against the cathedral ceiling of the chapel, the rain echoed off the newly painted walls. Wednesday night's Bible Study was scheduled to start at 7:00 p.m. sharp. Ali normally wouldn't attend the prayer session, but that week's study he couldn't afford to miss. He was hoping Cherry would be there. Advising her of the church's location, Ali prayed that she didn't skip out on his invitation. With the pastor out of town for the week, Ali had the duty of filling in as interim pastor. As he waited with twenty or so church members for the remaining stragglers to make it indoors, Ali disappointedly flipped to the book of John, where he was prepared to read a few scriptures and act like he gave a damn about God giving up his only son. To his surprise, she came walking through the doors by herself, dripping wet.

She hung her coat in the hallway, shaking raindrops from her long, curly hair, a look of frustration stamped on her face. Ali rose to his feet, excusing himself from the encircled group as he went to assist her.

"Let me help you with that," he said, grabbing her broken umbrella and stuffing it onto the top shelf. "I'm glad you could make it. I was starting to get a bit worried."

"I'm soaked," the woman said, ignoring his statement. Going straight from the hospital visit of her uncle, she had worn a gray button-up suit and black open-toed dress shoes with heels half the height of a polo stick.

"You mind if I change?" she asked, making her way into the restroom. "All I have are some sweats. You'll have to excuse my attire. I hope you don't mind."

When she returned in her workout attire, she reminded him of Serena Williams, who he considered today's sexiest celebrity, body-wise. Although she wore baggy sweatpants, he was still able to see the outline of her firm ass. Bowflex, he said to himself.

Not wanting to seem overly excited, Ali welcomed her into the house of worship, taking her to join the other members who were suspiciously waiting for Bible Study to begin.

He covered exactly what he was supposed to. Following the pastor's notes, Ali managed to get through the lesson, years of ministry school teaching him just enough to build on the confidence of others. Plus, the book of John was one that he knew from start to finish. *For God so loved the world that he gave his only begotten son* was a line he had heard over and over again, and was a scripture he was taught to recite as a youngster before bedtime. Speaking on the unselfishness of Christ, Ali spoke on how he, *Jesus*, had given his life for the sake of others. It was a lesson commonly taught in church homes by pastors, but the way Ali weaved a storyline of sacrifice, suffering, and commitment, everyone listening felt empowered and gained a new respect for this man referred to as the Son of God. Once he finished teaching, Ali answered every question, shedding light on the purpose of such surrendering of oneself, even though he himself considered Christ's sacrifice quite foolish.

After he prayed to conclude the session, many members left in admiration, while one continued to sit. *Cherry!* After walking Mr. and Mrs. Teague to the side door, Ali locked it behind them, did an about-face like a well-trained soldier, and hustled over to where Cherry sat. Taking a seat next to her, he grabbed the Bible she held and tossed it far over his right shoulder without any regard for the sacred text. Looking deep into her powdery blue eyes, Ali thanked Cherry for coming, then he kissed her.

They moved towards the altar, kissing and groping each other like an ecstasy pill ran through their blood. They cleared a space on the floor next to the podium. Just like the old days, spontaneity was on full throttle, and Ali wanted to be on top, rolling her over so that he felt more dominant and in control. Sliding her beautiful hair behind her ear, he kissed her neck, then slid her pants off and tossed them aside.

Kneading his right hand against her inner thigh, he completed a series of motions that left her craving for more. He slid her panties to the side and introduced her to his right thumb, gently inserting his thick, meaty finger beneath her pubic bone. He rocked his hand slowly back and forth with a light pressure, while his other four fingers rested outside in her pussy hair. When he finally familiarized his other fingers with her vagina, the come-here motions he made inside her were near her

G-spot. With a light touch against her clit, she climaxed, shivering and jerking against his hand.

The rain serenaded them with a frenzied whistle that grew louder with every passing moment. While the thud of tree branches crashed against the church's cemented walls, the windows shaking vigorously momentarily interrupted Ali's advances. He was too occupied, though, to allow Mother Nature to ruin his self-indulgence. After all, he was a lovemaking machine, and making out was simply a pastime. After a powerful clap of thunder and a lightning strike caused the lights to flicker, Ali raised himself up and looked out the church windows into the flooding parking lot. The downpour of water streaming like Niagara Falls suddenly bothered his train of thought. Almost about ready to call it a day and go home, he hurried to his feet, pulling up his pants. Moments later, the lights flickered again, then went out completely.

"All of that rain must have blown the power," Ali told Cherry as she slid from his clinch. "If I can see to get to the door, the lights in the parking lot should be enough."

"Wait for me. I can barely see a thing," she said.

"Where the hell are my keys?" Ali patted his pants pocket. "I hope none of the other members took them."

"Same old Gaines," Cherry teased him. "More irresponsible now than ever before. I'd be more than happy to drop you off if you'd like."

"Shit!" he blurted out. "I remember what I did with them. I left 'em in Sanford's glove compartment."

"So, what are you gonna do?"

"I need to call and see if he can drop them off. If I didn't have to get in my house tonight, I'd wait till tomorrow."

Ali dialed his cell phone, hopeful that Cherry had caught the hint that he preferred to stay at her pad. When Stanford picked up the other end, he assumed she hadn't.

"What's good, Stanford?" Ali asked him after the brief letdown. "I think I left my keys in your car."

Cherry could hear Stanford on the other end but couldn't make out the squeaky words.

"Oh you are? Cool. Well, I'll see you in about five then."

"What happened?" Cherry asked as soon as Ali hung up. "Does he have them?"

"Yep, he'll be here in a second."

It took Stanford ten minutes to actually arrive at the church. Once he parked and ran across the wet parking lot, he was at the side door. Ali greeted him there.

"Thanks for coming. You're a life saver."

"Yeah, whatever," Stanford said when he handed over the keys. "Be glad that my sister stays just down the street."

Stanford tilted his head to look around Ali. Cherry stood there, embarrassed. She waved at him.

"Hey, Cherry," Stanford dragged his words like a teasing preschooler. "Good to see you're doing well."

"Hey," she spoke up.

"I just got one question for the both of you before I go. Why the hell is it so dark?"

"The rain blew the lights outs," Ali told him.

"So, just turn on the generator."

"I don't know how," Ali said.

"And how long have you been going here?" Stanford mocked. "Move, I'll do it."

Stanford made his way into the church. He walked past Cherry's half-naked body with a smile on his face. When she dropped her head shamefully, he continued through the chapel doors.

"Maybe I should've grabbed my flashlight," he yelled out while he headed towards the basement. "It's darker than hell down here."

"You sure you know where it is?" Ali joked. "You know you haven't been to church in ages."

It was a true statement and one that Stanford couldn't challenge right then. Ever since the dishonesty that he and the others took part in, he seldom came to church. He just felt as though he couldn't look the other members in the eye. He had thought about coming clean and facing the congregation while they threw stones at him for his contemptuous behavior, but he had embarrassed his family so badly the last time he was the hot topic in the local community that he dared not do it a second time. Stanford felt that a secret worth dying for prevailed over a secret worth told.

"What the hell was that?" Stanford murmured out loud as he reached for the lighter in his coat. Suddenly, as he flicked for a flame, he walked dead into what felt like a sledgehammer.

The crushing blow knocked him to a knee. Blood poured from his head like a broken water faucet and while Stanford tried to cover the gaping wound, he used his free hand to try and get back to his feet. Another blow with double forearms pounded down hard on his back, and he sprawled onto the floor. A swift kick to his stomach made him gasp for air. When the fifth and sixth blows crashed into his body, he could hear the bones of his ribcage shatter like a thin piece of fiberglass.

A rope looped around his skinny neck in a shoestring knot. As the killer yanked, tugged, and wrenched his neck, Stanford grabbed for the rope, trying desperately to relieve the pressure crushing his Adam's apple. His neck stretched taut as it made the struggle to get his fingers underneath the suffocating bind impossible.

"It can't be," he croaked, raising his eyes to meet his attacker's. "Nooo," he puffed out. "We never meant to hurt you."

His words irritated his attacker even more. Pinning his face onto the floor, the attacker threw the rope over the top edge of the guard rail and pulled. As Stanford's head snapped back and lifted into the air like a piñata, saliva oozed from the corners of his mouth. The killer waited for the pronounced vein to appear in the middle of his forehead before letting loose. As the sorrow of Stanford's eyes glared at his killer in the dark, he could only say a quick prayer to himself, asking for the Lord to take his soul.

Ali had excused himself minutes earlier and had taken a short walk to the restroom in the back. Cherry was busy piecing together the clothes that had been torn from her body when she heard the footsteps behind her. Whipping her head around, the impact against her jawbone caused a wad of blood to spurt from her mouth. He didn't want her to see him, but she did. Now she had to be removed as well.

As the killer was certain that there was no other choice than to finish her off, he grabbed her tiny head and twisted her neck like a Phillips screwdriver until several cracks sounded. She slumped onto the floor. When the electricity suddenly came on and he heard Ali calling his friend's name from afar, the killer ran out of the chapel doors. There was no rush. He would get Ali Gaines according to the plan.

Do unto others as you would have them do unto you. He raced to his vehicle. He pulled the stick into gear and burned rubber against the asphalt of the Lord's parking lot.

*   *   *

Things are getting out of control now. The killer was worried as he sipped on a cup of green tea in a Starbucks coffee shop. The local circulator was running late as usual and had yet to drop off the daily papers. Although he hadn't seen one yet, the man was sure that the news of the murders would make headlines in each edition. He wasn't in the greatest of moods. Another person had been killed outside of the master plan, and the burden of it all was tearing at his insides. *The girl wasn't supposed to die.* He beat himself up, over and over again, thinking of a different way he could've handled the situation. *But she saw me. I had no choice.* It was then that the man took out some old pictures that were folded inside his wallet. The one that choked him up the most was a print taken at the San Diego Zoo. Life was perfect then, and the smiles on every face proved it. When he peered into her eyes, he felt instant gratification. He traced her face with his forefinger and smiled, stuffing the wallet back into his pocket. As he waited for the red-haired boy to gather the piles of daily tabloids from his car, he sat, annoyed at an angry woman standing in line who had suddenly began to grill her son for being disobedient.

"Get your ass off that floor," he overheard the woman say. She yanked her son's hooded coat and lifted him to his feet. "I told you about embarrassing me in public. Now get up!" She began wailing on the bottom of his leg like he had stolen something. With other patrons now looking on, she continued with the ass-kicking, paying little attention to the people she felt had no business being in hers anyways.

"Wait till we get in the car," she continued scolding him, pinching on his upper ear with her knuckles. "Just wait."

"I'm sorry, Mom," the boy cried out in return. "I won't do it again. I promise."

"Damn right you won't," she told him after she grabbed her latte and turned for the door. "I'm gonna make sure you don't."

As they rushed for the door, the little boy couldn't keep pace with his mother's steps and fell onto the floor. When she realized she was walking alone, she turned, her fuming eyes not only scaring the boy but everyone in the joint. Each step she took towards him was slow and scary, similar to the abusive madwoman from *Flowers in the Attic*.

He just knew that the boy was about to get a beat down, and he rushed from his seat to help. Once the mother reached the boy and snatched him up with one hand, her free hand caught the midsection of the child's back, and a loud thud echoed in the midst of all the stillness that suddenly pervaded the coffee shop.

She swung again, and the swishing sound of her arm coming down made everyone cringe. Luckily for the boy, the woman was caught in a bear hug and pushed against the wall before she had the chance to strike him again.

"That's enough," a deep voice said as he held onto the woman, who was desperately trying to get at her son like an angry pit bull. "Be lucky that you have him."

"I'll kill 'em! Swear I will." The woman tried to shake loose. "Let me at him."

"Then what?" the man asked her. "You beat him some more? What good would that do?"

"It'll teach him not to mess with me. I brought him here and I'll take him out! I ain't about to have no disrespectful child."

"You just don't know how good you have it," the man said.

"What in the hell is that supposed to mean?"

A short blonde lady wearing a green apron rushed up. "I've already called the police," she said, grabbing the boy and taking him by his collar to the other side of the room. The man focused his eyes into the woman's, and she shamefully looked away, realizing that she'd taken things a bit far.

"Cherish what God has blessed you with," the man said calmly. "At any given moment he can be taken away from you." The man moved to grab his things before the police arrived. When he reached the swinging doors, he glanced over at the stand which was now filled with the day's papers, each one with the church murders in headlines. *I didn't want to kill her.* The killer was distressed as he exited into the cold blustery weather, destined to finish the final two chapters of his true-life story.

CHAPTER EIGHT

Madeline made sure a broomstick was available to jump over at her reception. A historical ceremony that began on plantations, slave weddings were initially prohibited, but the desire of couples to bond for life prevailed, and slaves created their own ceremonies to recognize and honor marriage. For that reason, while the D.J. spun the cultural music of African drums, Madeline prepared herself to jump in honor of and respect for her ancestors, their legacy, and a notion that whoever jumped the highest would ultimately make family decisions. As she gladly lifted her gown to her ankles and leaped over the decorated broomstick, the phone rang and caused her to nearly jump out of her sheets. It was Simone.

*   *   *

"Girl, what are you doing waking me up during the happiest day of my life?" Madeline asked her, rolling over and sitting upright in her bed. "You have perfect timing, you know that?"

"I just wanted to make sure you woke up before you had a little wet dream on yourself," Simone said, talking foul to her best friend. It was common talk. "You dreaming of Johnny again, aren't you? I keep telling you, girl. You better go out and get some and stop that shit!"

"Get me some what?" Madeline came back at her, yawning. "I don't need nothing but Mr. Dil and his friend, Do. That's it!"

"Yeah, keep grinding against that rubber like that and you're gonna get a yeast infection," Simone told her, bursting out in laughter.

Madeline couldn't help but laugh at her friend's raunchy sense of humor.

"Maybe I should throw it away and have you come over and please me," Madeline said. She loved to joke with Simone, and they both knew not to take the other seriously.

"Bitch, I'm strictly dickly. Plus, I got way too much junk in the trunk for you to ever think about handling me."

"Don't you know that's why they made U-Haul trucks?" Madeline roasted her. "They rent them for loads that are too heavy."

"Well, just be sure the one you get comes with a dolly 'cause when I get done throwing all this ass, you better have a lift support somewhere nearby."

Madeline shook her head. "Do you tell all the guys you sleep with the same thing?"

"I don't have to," Simone added. "If he's not built like an ox, I don't want to have nothing to do with him. I'm a lot of woman. It'll literally take a donkey man to please me."

"A what?"

"A donkey man," Simone repeated. "You know. Half man, half donkey. This way you never come up short. Catch my drift?"

She was being way too nasty for an early morning chat, so Madeline decided to change the subject.

"Amber's finally doing well in school now. It took her a while to get used to public school, but now I think she's finally beginning to fit in."

"Goddamn right she's fitting in. I told you she would. She never needed to be in those private school uniforms, anyways."

"I just hope she doesn't get into the wrong sorts of things now," Madeline said, clearly concerned. "I tell you that Rosemary said she's starting to talk about boys now? That bothers me."

"Why would it? She's a little girl. Don't act like we never talked about boys when we were growing up."

"Yeah, but that was different."

"How so?" Simone asked. "One thing that doesn't change with time is curiosity, Boo. She just needs someone to talk to about it. Her mind is spinning the same way ours was back then."

"It just hurts me that she chooses to talk to Rosemary rather than to come to me about these sorts of things. I am her mother, you know. Besides, that's my baby, not hers."

Simone laughed at her. "Do I sense a bit of jealousy here?"

"Come on, Simone. I'm serious," Madeline snapped. "Why hasn't she talked to me about it? Rosemary hasn't even been around that long, and Amber already feels more comfortable talking with her than with me."

"That's probably because she can't understand what the hell Rosemary is saying half the time," Simone blurted out. "She can barely speak a lick of English as it is, so I'm sure the advice she's giving Amber can't be that great."

"She can too speak English. It's just not the greatest we've ever heard."

"Whatever! That woman is straight off the boat, and you know it. I don't even know where you found her at."

"She's a friend of a friend, okay? Plus, she was cheap," Madeline confessed. "I was paying over a hundred dollars a week for a sitter. Now I pay half as much."

"And you get half the vocabulary with it," Simone replied. "You wanted a Molly Maid, and now you got her. She's just a Taliban, that's all."

"A who?"

"A Taliban," Simone repeated. "You heard me loud and clear. All these people unemployed and you go recruiting overseas. You're no better than these assembly plants."

"You're so naïve," Madeline said as she rolled over in her covers. "All I'm saying is that I miss my little girl. I should be first, regardless. She needs to know that she can always come to me. Guess I have to accept the fact that she's growing up."

"Yep, she is," Simone sympathized, "but you can't be Mother Grinch either. That girl is as smart as they come. She knows right from wrong. You've done a fine job raising her. Just continue to be there and everything will work out fine."

Simone was a true friend to Madeline. She always lifted Madeline's spirits and had that unique ability to make the best out of the worst situations.

"So, what time are we going out later today?" Simone asked, holding Madeline to their plans. "You want to do lunch or something later tonight?"

Madeline fumbled with her answer and felt bad that she was about to stand Simone up once again.

"I thought we were going out on Sunday?"

"Don't even try it. Let me guess, you gotta work again? Maddie, you're going to let them work you into the ground, girl. For God's sake, you couldn't even take a vacation without being called back early."

"I know, I know," Madeline said, cutting her off, "but the Chief wants me to work the fireworks tonight."

"There will be three million people down there. What does he expect you to do?"

"Remember that case of the guy who was running a prostitution ring out of his strip club? Well, he's back on the streets. I'll be looking for any young girls who look like easy targets. You can come if you'd like."

"Naw, I'll pass. I figured you'd cancel, so I made sure to have a backup plan. Don't worry about it. I'm good."

A backup plan. I really have been neglecting my friends.

"Who will you be working with, Monahan?" Simone sighed, trying to cover up her disappointment. "Make sure you tell him hello for me."

Madeline could hear it in her voice. Simone was devastated. "I will when I see him. I'll actually be with Zucal tonight. We still can go eat on Sunday, Simone. How about that? We on for Sunday?"

"Yeah, Sunday," Simone said.

"Come on, Simone," Madeline cheered. "We'll go out for sure. A couple of missed meals won't hurt anybody."

Normally Simone would laugh at Madeline's fat jokes, but the one at that particular point in time she didn't find amusing.

"Yeah, see you Sunday."

Madeline could feel the disappointment in her voice as she hung up the phone.

*   *   *

The piercing roar of the million plus attendees, all excited about the announcement of the fireworks show starting in five minutes, caused Madeline to cling tighter to Zucal's arm. Detroit's riverfront played host to the most spectacular blockbuster event of the summer. The annual Marshall Field's and Target fireworks extravaganza attracted more than a million spectators who watched from both sides of the United States/Canada border as the sky was illuminated with an assortment of beautiful colors. Friends and family packed the historic event, which yearly continued to grow and fulfilled the dream of a lifelong friendship between the American and Canadian people. With businesses and civic leaders looking on from skyscrapers, upper-level high-rises, and atop rooftops, it was those on ground level who jam-packed Hart Plaza and the edges of the Detroit Riverfront who continued to make the event an outstanding success.

"I'm glad we decided to come early, Zucal," Madeline said, taking a bite of a corndog she had bought from a street vendor. "This is great. I wish I could've brought Amber with me. She would've enjoyed this."

"This is no place for all these children," Zucal said, grumpily looking at the numerous kids running around, playing, and enjoying themselves. "Amber is right where she needs to be, at home and away from all of this mess."

"You're such a downer," Madeline told him. "One of these days I'm gonna get you to loosen up a bit. You act like a sixty-year-old whose only purpose in life is to bitch about not receiving a Social Security check."

"Thanks for the compliment," he said. "If I could make it to sixty by staying at home and not worrying about one of these thugs packing a pistol, I'd gladly welcome the opportunity."

Minutes later, the astounding sound of ohh's and ahh's coursed through Hart Plaza as firework after firework lit up the sky. Dazzled by the rainbow-colored arrangement bursting in the thin air, Madeline jealously looked at the couples embracing under the bright lights. Suddenly, the overwhelming feeling of loneliness hit her twofold. Standing there, the only person she could think about was Johnny. Fourth of July with him was always special. While most people went to parks and stadiums to watch fireworks year after year, Madeline remembered vividly how she and her deceased husband used to spend Independence Day, in the bedroom, igniting their own sparks. Although she knew she loved Johnny, there was a dying need for her to fulfill her relentless sex craving, which seemed to be driving her up a wall lately. Although convinced that not many men could compare or dish out the same love they had once shared, she realized getting back on the dating scene meant she'd have to be selective about the men she chose to date, making sure each candidate was thoroughly screened. With more and more men on the down-low nowadays, she could take no chance. If she needed help, she knew her good friend Monahan would assist her in checking backgrounds. After all, he had often taken it upon himself to screen her potential friends anyhow. Now, as she looked in envy at the many couples sharing an intimate evening together, she glared at her attractive partner at the lemonade stand.

Tilting her head to get a better peek at Zucal, Madeline looked him up and down, impressed by his tall physique and glistening asphalt-colored skin. She had never really examined her partner like that, until then. Boy, was he sexy!

A real African. She began thinking nasty thoughts to herself. *If it's true what they say then he probably has a cock bigger than his country.* Just as she was nibbling on her bottom lip, Zucal walked up with two fresh cups of lemonade.

"Here you go, Maddie. I thought you could use a little sugar water," he said, handing over her drink.

"Huh?" Madeline said, dazed out.

"I bought you a drink," he repeated himself. "Do you want it or not?"

While Madeline struggled to gather her brainwaves, she couldn't take her wandering eyes off of Zucal's midsection, which always appeared as though had an erection even if simply sitting behind a desk writing reports. Snapping out of it, Madeline graciously took her drink and soon was back watching the other couples

She enjoyed what she considered "people watching." Some days she would go to a mall just to sit and observe the way others behaved. It was probably how she became so expert in understanding others' motives, but unlike other police officers who had become content with neglecting the social aspect of their lives for their careers, Madeline was committed to getting her groove back. Determined to jumpstart the pieces of her long forgotten social life, she smiled at the thought, surveying the large crowd for any potential prospects.

Once the festivities concluded, the crowd began to disperse like snails back to their cars. A few unruly citizens had to be apprehended for not following instructions and becoming belligerent with officers. One in particular thought he was immortal and couldn't be restrained by anyone, but when angry officers with T-shirts reading "Gang Squad" intervened, the man had a change of heart after they ground his face into the cold, wet, pavement. All in all, the Detroit fireworks show was a huge success as always, and children, along with their cheery-eyed parents, had something festive to discuss the next day.

The night was just getting underway for Madeline and Zucal, as they hopped into the unmarked police car, pulling into an overcrowded gas station which appeared to be a hangout spot. Watching from a distance, they observed numerous vehicles entering and leaving, some filling up with gas, others seeking attention with their custom-made wheels. When she noticed a dark blue van pull up to the convenience store, Madeline focused her attention that way. The automobile had overly dark windows causing her to want to cite the driver for having illegal tint, but she decided to pass on issuing such a minor violation. She watched the driver rush to open the back door, and four men dressed as women in flamboyant outfits hopped out and rushed inside.

"I have a gut feeling this is gonna be another freak night," Zucal said, stunned at the spirited crossdressers. "Look at them. It makes no sense how anyone could choose that kind of lifestyle."

"Maybe it wasn't a choice," Madeline said as though she were a politician. "You ever think that maybe they were just born that way?"

"No way, Madeline! God made Adam and Eve. If he wanted it any different, he could've easily created Adam and Steve."

Madeline laughed. "You are so immature about this whole drag queen thing. I think it's kinda sexy to see two men together. It's a turn-on."

"A turn-on?"

"Yes, a turn-on. Who wouldn't want to see two aggressive men going at it like barbarians? I know I would."

"That's because you're a freak," Zucal teased her, tapping her gently on the thigh.

Madeline enjoyed his touch.

"Don't let the cop-thing fool you," Madeline said. "I'm only lady-like outside the bedroom walls."

"Is that so?"

"Yes sirrrrrr," Madeline joked, giving her best Richard Hamilton impersonation. It was a pretty good mockery of the Detroit Piston!

"Well, anyways, those aren't two men getting together. I mean it is, but it isn't. Those people are disguising themselves as women to lure some innocent man into a bedroom."

"How do you know that?" Madeline said. "If that were true, Club Sticks wouldn't be their hangout spot. I bet you won't go nowhere near there on a Thursday night."

Club Sticks, a well-known juke joint in downtown Detroit, graciously accommodated hundreds of trans-sexuals every Thursday night. Efforts had been made by anti-homosexual activists to close the openly gay club, but the large support in the gay community had fought to keep the doors open.

"You got that right," Zucal agreed with her. "You won't catch me near that club. The only sticks I'll be around anytime soon are the ones in my front yard."

Shortly after Madeline expressed her amusement at her partner's ignorance, an off-white Ford Expedition pulled up next to the van. A handful of rough-looking street thugs sauntered into the store, one in particular deciding he was going to confront one of the drag queens. He went straight towards her.

Madeline couldn't make out what was being said, but by the way the man stood with his fists clenched at his side, she knew she had better hurry if she wanted to intervene before a fight broke out.

Madeline rushed to the front door of the store and got there in just enough time to hear the altercation in the making.

"What the hell is this?" the man boasted loud enough for his friends to get a kick out of him. "Ru Paul in the Motor City? What is the D turning into? If I wanted to live around this shit, I would've stayed my black ass in San Francisco."

His buddies burst into laughter, but the drag queen wasn't backing down.

"Yo mama sure wasn't complaining when I was putting this San Francisco treat in her the other night, was she?"

The comeback was so shocking that even Madeline had to crack a smile.

"What you say about my mama?" the man said, throwing his honey bun down on the floor. "What the fuck did you just say?"

Just then, Madeline decided to break up the argument, stepping in between the two and identifying herself. They all chose to disperse like rats and went their separate ways, which gave Madeline and Zucal a chance to grab a few snacks before getting back in the car. The surprise came while they stood in line.

It was like they were straight out of the hit sitcom series from back in the day, *Saved by the Bell*. Four girls, clearly in their teens, dressed in clothing that if their grandparents would have seen the amount of skin they bared, would have resulted in a firm ass-whipping.

Madeline couldn't keep her eyes off the promiscuous teens, and neither could Zucal for that matter, but Madeline's gaze was more motherly. She had a little girl of her own and couldn't imagine ever allowing her Amber to dress in such a way. Even when she reached twenty-one, Amber would know to go home with respectful clothing covering her body.

The night rolled on. Back in their car, Madeline and Zucal continued to patrol the downtown district, looking for anything suspicious. Deciding to turn down one of the busiest streets in Detroit, Zucal made a left down Monroe.

They were met with bumper-to-bumper traffic. If anything negative came out of a discussion about the

City of Detroit, it was downtown's heavy traffic. With cars honking at other drivers for trying to reverse park into tight spaces, Madeline could only marvel at all of the pedestrian traffic going in and out of some of the well-known restaurants still holding it down, like Fishbone's and Pizza Papalis, places where her father used to take her years ago. She waved at the owners as they slowly crept past the front entrances of both establishments.

Late night was upon them, and steamy mist began rising from the potholes in the street. Nothing had popped off yet, and both Madeline and Zucal were getting agitated. Since it seemed that there was nothing to do but waste time as the derelicts and panhandlers took to the streets, Madeline and Zucal chose to pass by a few of Detroit's more popular clubs just to make sure everything was orderly there as well.

In front of the The Woodward, Madeline stuck her head out the window to try to see why the crowd was wrapped around the corner. The bouncer at the door noticed her looking and went over to the car after calling for a guard to replace him.

"What's up, officers?" the buff man said, running up to Madeline's side of the window. "Everything all right tonight?"

"All is good," Madeline said in return. "What do y'all have going on tonight? Looks like an audition to be the next American Idol."

"Naw, it's not like that," the man responded with a smile. "Don't be surprised. It's like this every Thursday night. It's called the 'after work affair'."

"It should be called, the, I-don't-have-a day-job affair," Madeline said, surprised by all the professionally dressed adults waiting their turn to enter the club. "I never understood how people could party during the week and still be able to wake up and go to work the very next morning."

"Welcome to Detroit," the bouncer said, throwing his hands into the air. He was certainly proud to live in the city. "That's how we do it here in the D."

"I guess so," Madeline said. "So there's nothing for us to be worried about tonight?"

"Nope, I got this one here. Besides, it's not that hard to get in touch with you if I need to. The number is still 9-1-1, right?"

Madeline and Zucal drove by a couple of other popular spots on the strip, making sure everything remained peaceful. That night, all of the hot spots appeared to be banging with lines out the door. It was amazing how the bouncer at each spot played the role of crowd control, letting Madeline know that everything was good before she ever had the chance to get out and see for herself. After checking on their last club, Madeline and Zucal continued driving around in circles, patrolling the downtown one-way streets until they were empty. Once three o'clock rolled around, Zucal thought about turning in early.

"It's been a long night," he complained. "Why don't we just phone the Chief and see if we can bring it in?"

Madeline, dozing in and out, became alert when Zucal tapped on her leg.

"Hey, Harris!" he shouted. "I said maybe we should call it a night."

"Oh, Zucal, I'm sorry," she said, yawning. "I don't know why I'm so tired, but I can barely keep my eyes open. You haven't seen anything, have you?"

"No, that's why I say we should phone in and call it a night. The night is over, and I'd like to get at least a couple of hours before turning right back around."

Their shift started at eight o'clock sharp. The Chief
was kind enough to allow them an extra hour as long as
they made it in before nine. The extra hour of sleep
should help with the double they had to work.

"Yeah, it is pretty dead out here." Madeline looked
around. "I say we just leave. There's no need to call him
unless you wanna hear him tell us otherwise."

"Nothing more to be said." Zucal hopped into the left
lane to make a Michigan U-turn. "Remember, if you're
asked, we were out here till four in the morning."

It wasn't until they made a right turn onto a side
street that Madeline suddenly became suspicious. A
teenage girl ran across the street and into the back of a
shabby building.

"What the hell was that all about?" Madeline tapped
on the dashboard for Zucal to pull over. "Did you see
that?"

"Yeah, I saw it. What do you think it is?"

"Whatever it is, it can't be good. Let's go see."

Madeline started to open the door, but Zucal grabbed
her left wrist.

"Hold it, Tiger," he said. "Close the door. Let's wait a
few minutes and see what's going on before we run in
like the Dukes of Hazzard."

"Wait a few minutes?" Madeline slammed the door in
frustration. "We're gonna mess around and be a minute
too late. It's obvious that girl is underage. Let's go in."

Her plea was met with Zucal's silence as he
continued to gaze through his window.

"Look," he said, watching as a short man wearing a
long sleeve dress shirt slipped out into the alley.
Moments later, two women joined him there. One of the
women had on a thick scarf and tinted glasses that hid
her entire face. The other one could care less about who

saw her. As the woman spun around to spit out the butt of her cigarette, Madeline recognized her.

"That's her," she shouted. "That's the chick we interviewed a few weeks ago—Ketaki. I knew she was up to no good."

"Wow, it is her!" Zucal said, stunned, putting his glasses up to his eyes to catch a better glimpse. "But who's the other girl?"

"I can't tell," Madeline said. "I don't recall the Chief mentioning a second woman."

"Naw, me either. Let me call in for backup."

"Backup," Madeline said, stunned. "How can you be so relaxed? There's no telling who's in there. By the time backup arrives, it could be morning."

"Exactly. We don't know who or what's in there. That's why we should wait on backup."

At that time, Zucal picked up the receiver and called in the location.

"By the time they arrive, anything could happen," Madeline barked. "It's clear to me it's some sort of sex party. Let's just go in."

"And what if you're wrong," Zucal asked, defensively.

"Wrong about what?"

"About the club. It may be nothing to it. A young girl running to the back of a club says nothing. Besides, we don't even have a search warrant to raid nobody's place like that."

"A warrant?" Madeline asked, totally surprised by her partner's apprehension. "It's three o'clock in the morning. We have our suspect in visual. What the hell would we need a warrant for?"

"But we still have nothing. We go running up in there and then what?"

"Then we arrest their asses!"

"Come on, Harris. You know it's not that easy."

Madeline, growing intolerant, snarled at her partner, "I can't believe what I'm hearing. You just need to let me know if you got my back or not."

"All right already." Zucal finally accepted the challenge. "But let's at least wait until an additional unit comes. Another five minutes won't hurt."

"Sit here and wait if you like, but I'm going in."

They crept around to the side of the building. Backs pressed against the brick wall, they were kitty-corner to the front door. Madeline pulled her gun first, keeping a firm grip on it with both hands out in front of her. Zucal pulled his as well.

"Wait a second, Harris," Zucal said, momentarily stopping her from storming in. An older black man with short nappy hair was now at the front entrance. He was arguing with someone at the door. "Listen."

"I'm not leaving here without my fucking niece," they overheard the man say. "Where is she? I know she's in there."

"She hasn't been around here in weeks," a man's husky voice said. "Get away from here. You're not welcome."

"I don't give a shit what I am," the man protested. "My niece is in there, and I ain't leaving until she comes out."

"Look, I already told you your niece isn't here. What do you want me to do, snap my fingers?"

"Do you!" the man demanded. "But go and get my fucking niece."

Just then the man tried to rush the door but was prevented from entering. When he was pushed back, he tripped and fell onto the ground.

"Jive mothafucker," the old man spat as he got to his feet and limped away. "I got something for your ass."

Madeline chose to seize the moment. She swung herself out and pointed the barrel of her gun directly at the doorman's chest.

"Detroit Police!" she yelled out. "Put your hands where I can see them."

The young man slowly raised his hands high above his head, and Zucal placed cuffs on his wrists and sat him down on the curb.

"What's going on in there?" Madeline asked him over the music blasting out the door. The man wasn't being cooperative and copped an attitude.

"I know my rights," he said. "I'm not answering shit."

"Oh yeah, well answer your Miranda rights then, punk." Madeline slapped him in the back of the head. Just then, another unit pulled up, and two uniformed officers hopped out.

"Stay here with him, Davis." Madeline instructed one of her colleagues as she and the others geared up. They weren't prepared for what awaited them on the inside.

Inside, the place was a wreck, an abandoned building turned after-hours spot, the joint looked more like a crack house than it did an underground nightclub.

Madeline moved swiftly, stepping over rusty poles and fallen wood slabs, heading towards the thump of the music. Behind an old, burnt, mustard-orange couch that blocked the side doorway, Madeline waited as Zucal and Brady pushed it aside. When she kicked the door open, those inside began trampling over each other, trying desperately to get to the opposite exit. Madeline had to quickly gather herself after glaring into the faces of several young girls struggling to get their clothes back on their exposed bodies as they made their way out the door. In the confusion, additional backup arrived and blocked off the back, trapping a large percentage of young girls and the older men who patronized them.

Just how big could this child prostitution phenomenon really be? Madeline searched high and low for the two women from earlier.

A single shot rang from outside, and people began racing back in. Madeline and Zucal scurried toward the gunfire. When they finally made it to the back exit, Madeline joined in on the foot chase that had just begun, and she recognized the slain victim as the woman who had been brought in earlier for questioning. She hurdled the body that was laid out on the cold concrete and was soon on the heels of the other officers.

They ran after the shooter through the empty streets of downtown Detroit. He sprinted southbound past several police vehicles in pursuit. Madeline cut through a side street to try and gain on the considerable distance between them.

He was fast and agile, and the officers couldn't keep pace with his Maurice Green-like speed. With the streets near empty, seeing the direction he was headed, Madeline was smart enough to know that he would try and get to the one place where there was still a crowd that time of night, the casino.

Madeline curved onto Bagley Avenue, and she could see the glittering lights a quarter of a mile ahead of her. The police sirens were becoming more apparent with every stride, and Madeline realized that her hunch was accurate. Darting down the street the way she was taught by her high school track coach, Madeline pumped her arms and kept her head cocked, hoping that her tiring feet would keep up with the rest of her body. She was careful crossing against a red light and saw a man running with no one chasing. He leaped over the guard rails at the MGM Grand garage and headed up the several flights of parking levels. He opened the door and ran up the escalator, knocking over pedestrians.

"Hold it right there!" Madeline yelled. She yanked open the door to the fourth floor and pulled her pistol. At the sight of the police chase, screams broke out inside of the building, forcing Madeline to stick her gun back in its holster. With everyone ducking and running for cover, Madeline struggled to keep up. Suddenly, as she moved through the rows of coin machines, the suspect turned and opened fire.

She dropped to the ground, crawling underneath a blackjack table. When she felt it was safe, she leaned out and fired back, the bullets ricocheting off the slot machines. He fired again, grazing the wooden table. Madeline waited a second, then shot twice, missing both times. He took off again, making it to a stairwell at the opposite end. She got to her feet and chased him, shuffling down the flight of steps. She was then on the third floor with him. Word must have gotten out by the way people had already begun fleeing the scene.

"Watch it! Move! Watch it!" she repeated, bumping into citizens trying to make it out safely. She jumped over a lady he had thrown to the ground and followed him into an exclusive private room.

"Give it up," she said as she took cover behind a ten-dollar Wheel of Fortune slot machine and crawled to the end of the aisle.

"Not a chance," he said, stepping out and firing repeatedly.

When he began to change clips, Madeline inched out and aimed for his kneecap. She closed her left eye and pulled. The man fell hard onto his back, his gun dislodged, and Madeline ran towards him, kicking the gun away. She held hers against his forehead, daring him to move. Seconds later, when the other officers arrived at the scene, they cuffed the wounded man and took him away.

CHAPTER NINE

Ali Gaines sat on his balcony with a pint of Remy Martin in his lap. He had already downed half of the bottle and was feeling a little queasy when he poured himself another shot. It was his escape from thinking about his two best friends, killed by some madman on a rampage. But who was behind the murders? Who was out to get him? He tried piecing the puzzle together himself.

The first name that came to mind was Elena Sanders. Although she killed herself in the kitchen of her own two-bedroom apartment, Ali knew that a part of her depression was due to what had happened years ago. After the jury had found him not guilty of rape, Ali received several anonymous mail threats. The police tracked the mail back to Elena's father, and the letters stopped soon after he was arrested and sentenced to community service for the death threats. Deep down inside, Ali was more than seventy-five percent sure it was him, but there was still a chance it might be others.

There were also numerous individuals in the congregation paying their weekly tithes and offerings with the expectation that God would return their blessing; Ali had been stealing small amounts of money from them every week. The wrath of God would surely be upon him now! He shook his head, eliminating the silly feelings that it might be someone connected with the church. He swallowed another chest-burning shot.

Days after his seventeenth birthday, he had gotten into a senseless fight at the skating rink with a punk who had cut in line for shoes. The guy, thinking he was tough, challenged Ali when he spat in his face. Ali fumed with anger. Never backing down from a brawl, Ali and company knuckled up with the guy and whipped him kinda the same way a few blacks did Reginald Denny a few years back in the L.A. riots. Eric, Stanford, and Chris jumped in, and they ended up putting the kid in the hospital for a couple of days. Ali remembered that the boy was told he would suffer from chronic migraines as a result of the thrashing, and he wondered if this might be retaliation.

Then there were Ali's sexual partners with whom he had been heavily involved the last two years. It was his way to get what he wanted with no commitment and no repercussions. Anyone of them could be the killer. But he was careful covering his tracks. He would simply contact The Broker and pay to set up whatever sexual services he needed. It was easy, reliable, and worth every dime. Over the past few months, The Broker had been able to provide young girls, a treat that kept his selected customers happy, including Ali. The girls were from abroad. Although Ali understood they were underage, he strongly believed the only thing better than some pussy, was young pussy. For that reason, whenever he would contact The Broker to set a date, he made sure that his picking came from the cream of the crop, a beautiful gal who was young at heart.

He picked up his headset and dialed The Broker. Minutes later, he was headed northbound on the expressway towards the parlor. He swerved onto the service drive and slowly turned onto Michigan Avenue.

What fools, he thought to himself as he passed several strip joints with lines of horny men drooling at the mouth to get in. *They'll waste hundreds just to stare at a dancer. If they were only hip to my world.*

He was soon at the dark intersection and cut his lights before pulling into the parking lot. Several cars were parked in the back corner away from the entrance. Ali decided he'd park there as well. Hurrying across the lot, he pressed the intercom at the front door.

"It's me, Ali," he said into the tiny speaker.

When the door finally buzzed open, Ali carelessly walked towards the front counter. The place was stylishly lit with a red strobe light reflecting off some sort of sparkling disco ball that hung from the ceiling. Out of the corner of his eye, Ali glanced at an older gentleman, probably in his fifties, kissing one of the girls in the hallway. He had to do a double take to make sure the girl with long curly hair wasn't the one he had called for. It wasn't, and when The Broker emerged from a small room behind the service counter, Ali was happy to greet him.

"How have you been, my friend?" Ali asked, shaking The Broker's hand.

"Pretty damn good," he said. "It's nice to see you again."

"Likewise."

"So, what are you in for tonight?"

"It's been such a long week," Ali said with a sigh. "Whatever will take my mind away from all the bullshit."

"I'm sure we can arrange that," The Broker said as he rubbed his fingers together. "How much you got?"

"I got enough." Ali took a knot of money out and placed it on the countertop. "Is she ready for me?"

"Of course. She'll be up any minute now. I'll take you to your room"

Ali was escorted down the hallway to the fourth room on the left, and he closed the door behind him. The room was smaller than the ones he normally used. It came with one chair, a sheetless bed, and a dingy sink. He looked around the teal-colored walls and for a second thought he was in a doctor's office. But even a physician would make sure the table that his patients sat on was at least cushioned. The stiff mattress Ali sat on was like a brick. He started to go and see if The Broker would change his room, but the door creaked open, she entered wearing a silk robe and house shoes, and all thoughts of leaving went away.

Nizama's face was fuller that go 'round, but Ali was too excited to notice her thickened neck and swollen nose. He was there for one thing, sexual pleasure. As she made her way to him, he stood and embraced her with a delicate hug as if he was becoming reacquainted with a former love. In an odd kind of way, he was. Ever since The Broker had begun recruiting young girls, Ali had found pleasure in just one, Nizama. While they stood face to face in the middle of the room, he delicately placed his lips on her cheek.

"It's been a while," he whispered in her ear. "Tell me that you missed me."

"I missed you," she replied in a low voice. The sound of her voice was endearing.

"If that's the case, why'd you get up and suddenly take off that last time?"

"Because I didn't know what to do," she told him with a kiss on the forehead. "I was scared at first, but now I'm all ready for you."

"Oh, are you?"

Ali loved her change in attitude. She was more womanly than her age might indicate.

"Let's stop wasting time and get this over with," she said as she got down on both knees. "What do you say?"

Ali, looking down at her, grabbed her by her hair. "Don't rush me; I'll tell you when it's time."

He yanked her up and rejoined his mouth to hers. He felt her rounded ass, gripping her cheeks with the palms of his hands. He pulled her hips in close and began bouncing her pelvis off his in a slow grind. He clearly wanted to have sex, and Nizama backed off.

"What the hell are you doing?" Ali asked.

"I'm just following the boss's orders. I'm only supposed to please you, and that's it."

"What do you think this is!" he snapped at her. "Get your ass over here."

"I'm sorry!"

"Get over here!"

"This was just supposed to be a blow," she cried out, completely surprised. "I can't have sex right now. Please understand. I'll do anything else you want."

As she gently rubbed the upper edge of her rib cage, Ali moved towards her. "What? Are you crazy? Not with the amount of money I just spent."

"Wait, I can't," she said fearfully, walking backwards.

"Get your ass back over here!"

Ali grabbed her arm and jerked her towards him. He threw her against the bed and pulled her robe off. She was carrying more weight than he had remembered, but at that moment in particular, he could care less about the baby fat. He climbed on top of her and rammed his index and middle fingers into her vagina like a forklift. He reminded her that screaming did no good, and she heeded his advice. No one would save her anyhow. They never did when she called.

Moments later, Ali was in, humping her wildly while tears escaped her eyes. When he was tired of fucking her in the conventional missionary position, he pulled out and made her stand with both hands gripping the chair. He wanted her from behind. As he began to fuck her doggystyle, the sudden tightness of her stomach cramping made her scream.

"No! Please don't do this to me! I'm pregnant! I'm pregnant! Please don't! I'm pregnant!"

Ali pulled away and backed against the wall. "What's that you said?"

She stared at him remorsefully, and by the way her eyes had begun to overflow, she didn't need to repeat herself a second time. Ali had heard her loud and clear.

*　　*　　*

"She's fucking pregnant!" Ali jumped down The Broker's throat. "Next time I call, I don't want to be disappointed. Cuz if I am—"

"What?" The Broker asked, not taking kindly to threats.

"Just have me one ready and able," Ali asked. "No need to fuss over spilled milk. You just make it up to me next time."

"I will," The Broker agreed, handing Ali his money back. "Next time, I'll give you two for the price of one. You have my word."

"Sounds good to me." Ali headed for the door, but The Broker stopped him just before he reached the exit.

"Hold it! I got it," The Broker said with a grin on his face. "It's perfect."

"What are you talking about?"

"I'll make it up to you sooner than you think." He hid a conspicuous grin below his well-clipped mustache. "What are you doing next Friday?"

"Nothing planned," Ali said after glancing at his Palm pilot. "What, you want me to come back next week?"

"Nope," The Broker told him. "I have a suite reserved for the Tigers' game, and I'll be hosting a few of my noteworthy acquaintances."

"You know I don't like to mix my biscuits with gravy," Ali said. "Can I trust your so called friends?"

"Trust me, Ali. They will worry the same about you," The Broker said, pulling out a parking pass and handing it over to Ali."

"Five dollars off?" Ali shook his head. "Your cheap ass won't even let me have the freebie."

"It's for me and the girls, Ali," The Broker laughed at him. "You expect me to pay for parking and walk across the street with five girls attached to my arm?"

"You're a corrupt fucker, you know that?" Ali snatched his ticket along with the discounted parking pass.

"And you're going to hell," The Broker snarled.

Ali took his keys from his pocket and adjusted his thick winter jacket.

"If I go to hell first," Ali said, jangling the key to his Ford The Broker's way, "I'll be sure the devil saves a spot next to his bed for you."

Ali flipped out his Razor and placed it up to his ear. "Robert Thompson," he said into the phone's voice recorder as he made his way out of the door. He couldn't wait for Rob to answer so that he could tell him what he would be doing when Friday rolled around.

*   *   *

Minutes later, Nizama was creeping back to the basement when she overheard The Broker talking loudly.

"Damn it! You take her to have it taken care of tomorrow morning," he said, lashing out at his wife. When she informed him that the doctor's office was closed on President's Day, he barked even louder.

"I don't give a shit whose day it is!" he yelled at her. "I'm giving you till Friday to have this fixed, or else!"

Nizama hurried down the hall and was soon in the corner of the basement floor. She balled herself up in the corner and cried for the rest of the night, realizing that Friday was only two days away.

That next evening, they waited patiently for the lights to turn off upstairs, figuring the nighttime was as best chance as any to make a run for it. While Seema played with the remaining noodles in her bowl of soup, Nizama sat on the bottom step of the basement, gently caressing her shifting stomach.

"Everything's going to be just fine, Saleem," she said as she tried calming her kicking fetus. She had already given the unborn a name, knowing in her heart of hearts that she was carrying a little boy. "Mommy loves you, and I will make sure nothing happens to you."

Nizama stretched against the step for added support. She had made up her mind that she was keeping her child. They had a plan and no one was going to force them into doing anything else. When she felt comfortable again she continued singing the same tune she had been singing for most of the day.

Mommy loves you, yes I do
Mommy loves you, yes I do
Your Momma loves you, yes I do
I am your Momma and I love you

Seema stared at Nizama as she swayed to the sounds of her own beat. She could tell that Nizama was in love with her unborn by the way her face glowed whenever she felt him move.

"Would you like to touch him?" Nizama asked her, wiping the tear that fell from her eye with her shirt collar. "He won't hurt you. I promise you he won't."

Seema edged her way over to where Nizama sat and placed her hand on her curved stomach.

"Wow," Seema exclaimed. "You can't tell from a distance, but now that I actually feel it, there is something in there."

"I know there is," Nizama acknowledged. "I'm four months now, I think."

She rubbed her stomach. *I am your Momma and I love you.*

"Hey, have you ever heard of a trimester?" she asked.

Seema shook her head from side to side.

"When I was nine my mother told me that all women have three trimesters during a pregnancy," Nizama said proudly, showing that she had had some bit of education, though it wasn't classroom taught.

"During the first one, your face breaks out and you get bumps all over your face. Momma said your nipples will start to harden like dried clay too. The second is when you start craving for food. Everything looks good to eat. French fries, ice cream, pretzels, whatever you can stuff your face with is what you eat. But the last one, now, that's the one I'm scared of."

Nizama's faced tightened as she cringed. She continued, "From what I hear your nose will widen from cheek to cheek. And your neck gets dark like a plum. I can't afford for my nose to get any bigger than it is now."

"So how do you know which one you're in?" Seema curiously asked.

"I don't know exactly, but about a month ago you could have bit down hard on either one of my nipples, and I wouldn't have felt a thing."

Hours later, the bright yellow light underneath the door darkened. Seema and Nizama looked at each, understanding that what they were about to do had not been tried by any of the other girls before. They waited until the others were sleeping before tiptoeing to the top of the basement steps. Simultaneously, they placed their ears against the wooden door. When neither of them heard a sound, Seema pushed the door open and Nizama stepped her foot inside of the house first.

It was dark. The snores of The Broker drifted down the long hallway. The girls chose to go in the opposite direction. Nizama's shoes squeaked with every footstep, so she took them off and held them in her hands before The Broker or his wife awoke. As they cautiously walked around the corner, Seema made sure to stay close on Nizama's hip until they were at the front door. Once there, Nizama unlocked all three locks and they were soon outside, running down the street.

"Run, Nizama. Run!" Seema said, desperately trying to motivate her fatigued friend. "You gotta keep going. We've got to make it to the tire."

The tire was the one thing Nizama often told the others about. Like the Sears Tower in Chicago, the tire was by far the tallest structure in the area. Every time The Broker would allow her to sit on the porch, she would stare at it hovering over all the other buildings. If there was any chance of getting to a place where people could help, the tire was it.

"I can't go anymore." Nizama gave up, slowing her sprint to a walk. She placed both hands onto her waist. "These extra pounds aren't helping. How far have we run anyways?"

"Only about a mile," Seema told her. "We've gotta get to the tire, then we can rest."

"You're just gonna have to leave me behind then," Nizama said. "My feet are hurting. They feel more swollen now than ever, like I'm walking on a tennis ball."

About a quarter of a mile down the road, a dullish yellow porch light flicked on.

"There," Nizama said, pointing to the ranch-style brick home. "Thank God! Let's go and get some help."

"I don't think that's a good idea," Seema said. "Let's just keep going. We need to get where people can see us."

"They already saw us," Nizama said, pointing at the window facing the street. Two beady eyes peered at them from behind the blinds.

"Let's say that our car broke down. We can ask them to take us to the closest police station."

"I don't know about that," Seema argued. "That house looks scary."

The house was isolated in the middle of nowhere. A two-story bungalow, the closest dwelling was a small gas station about a mile up the road.

"Let's just walk slowly then," Seema voiced. "We can walk on the side of the road, and that way, no one will see us. Are you even sure we're going the right way?"

"I don't know. The only sign I saw was Greenfield Avenue. Do you see anything else?"

"I don't," Seema said. "So let's keep going until we find something."

"I swear I can't," Nizama cried out. "There's no way I can go any further. I'll drop."

Nizama looked teary-eyed into Seema's. "Please, Seema, please."

They walked hand in hand to the front door. Before they had the chance to ring the doorbell, a rough voice greeted them.

"Come in," the voice instructed. Seema looked over at Nizama in fear, and Nizama returned the favor. Courageously, Nizama opened the door.

From out of nowhere, they were snatched by their shirt collars and yanked into the house. While their frantic screams were drowned by the crickets chirping in the night, they were tossed onto the hardwood floor of the dining room. Seema snapped her head around first, only to be met by a fist against her chin. She fell out. Knowing that the man would be going for Nizama next, Seema raised up, grabbed onto the man's leg, and bit through his khaki pants. He kicked her off him and backhanded her an additional time for her heroic attempt. He went towards Nizama.

"No, I'm pregnant, I'm pregnant," she cried out in distress. "Please don't harm me."

Unfortunately, the man didn't mutter a single word as he continued in her direction, striking her on the forearm as she tried to defend herself. Grabbing her by the hair, he pulled her from where she had scurried like a roach to the other side of the room next to Seema. He made them sit with their backs against the wall.

"I don't want to hurt you," he said in a low tone. He picked up the phone and dialed, keeping a close eye on the two girls sitting in front of him with their hands on their knees. "Just do as I say, and I won't harm you."

"Eight hundred," the man spoke into the receiver. "Nothing more, nothing less."

He hung up the phone and waited, staring at the two little girls while they continued to ask question after question.

"Who was that?" Nizama asked, paranoid. "Dear God, don't tell me you called The Broker. He'll kill us."

The man just stood there and looked at them.

"What are you going to do with us?" Seema decided to give it a try. "Can you call the police? We've been taken away from our families and are being forced to have sex."

The man smirked, looking at them as though he already knew that bit of information. For the next fifteen minutes he watched them like a guard dog whose owner had given the attack command if it sensed the slightest movement. When the doorbell eventually rang, the man yelled for The Broker to enter and reclaim his two girls.

He had prepared the room in advance. As The Broker and his wife suspended the girls' arms high into the air with rope, he kicked the wooden pallets from underneath their feet. While they hung, The Broker stripped them naked, and the girls wailed tears of pain as the rope dug deep into their wrists. The Broker decided Seema would be first. The beating he had in store for her would be much more delicate than the one he had planned for Nizama.

He grabbed the branch from the table. It was a prickly stick that he'd retrieved earlier from a tree in the woods. With a tremendous amount of force, he swung and struck Seema on her lower back.

"Awwweee," she screamed out. Tears flooded her eyes like a river. "No, please."

He paid her no mind, whipping her as though she were a useless slave. For ten minutes, he cursed her, spat on her, and struck her countless times, all over her body. When her bare skin turned the color of a grapefruit pink, he struck her more. It wasn't until he felt she had had enough that he motioned for his wife to take her down. It was now Nizama's turn.

This was her second time to betray him, and betrayal to The Broker was the worst form of deception. As Nizama hung suspended in the air, she stared at him remorsefully, trusting that he would spare her life. However, her pitiful look didn't matter; The Broker was uncompromising.

He whispered to his wife to leave the room, and to take Seema with her. Once they were gone, he walked over and stood in front of Nizama, gazing at her naked body. Her developing baby was on the left side of her stomach now and was moving like a tidal wave. He smacked her with his forearm in the midsection.

"You bitch!" he raged at her in broken English. "Who the hell do you think I am?"

"No!" Nizama winced in pain. "Please, my baby. Don't hurt my baby."

The Broker responded to her plea with another swipe at her stomach, this time pounding her twice with the broken switch he had picked up off the ground.

"I'm gonna show your ungrateful ass once and for all," he shouted as he connected with her ribcage once more. She cringed.

Did he not care that she was pregnant?

"You disloyal bitch!" he roared, taking the switch and lashing it across her breasts. "All that I've done for you and this is how you repay me?"

He heaved the stick onto the ground and snatched the extension cord from the counter.

"You're gonna get what you deserve, I promise."

He took the thick orange cord and struck her on her hind legs. It wasn't till her hamstrings were covered with welts that he looked for another place on her body to scar. He saw the tight knot moving around in her stomach like Jello and he went for the baby. She had defied him by not getting it taken care of like he had commanded. Now she had to suffer the consequences. He would take care of it himself.

At times, people cry from inflicted pain or from the loss of a loved one. Maybe out of fear or humiliation. The Broker drove the bottleneck from his pop bottle into Nizama's exposed vagina, and she cried from all of the above. Her stomach felt like a bomb exploding within, and she could only close her eyes until finally, when the pain was unbearable, she passed out.

When morning came, she woke up on the basement floor in a pool of blood, still bleeding uncontrollably. With the other girls looking on in disbelief, it was Seema who tried to build her friend's confidence that her unborn child was just fine. But Nizama knew differently. She knew her body. With the constant cramps stabbing at the left side of her abdomen, she knew that something was terribly wrong. Her son hadn't moved the entire morning. That in itself was unusual.

By the time twelve o'clock came, Nizama had cried herself out. Her face had turned a ghostly white, and her strength was failing fast. Seema held her hand, and the coldness that had invaded Nizama's fingertips worried her. She had to get her friend some help. As Seema nervously puffed on a cigarette she had stolen from a patron, she thought of what she could do to help Nizama. Just like a student that stumbles across the answer to a question he clearly knew, it clicked. She had an idea. Not only was she going to get Nizama the medical attention she needed, but also save her own life and others in the process.

"Oh, please let this work," she prayed softly as she emptied the tobacco from two cigarettes onto the floor. "I'm gonna get you some help, Nizama. I promise. Just hold on a little bit longer if you can."

CHAPTER TEN

She couldn't believe he had prepared all of this without her knowing. She had heard about the romantic resort in Chicago, but being there in person was breathtaking. The perfect honeymoon spot was far beyond her wildest dream. With room amenities including a private swimming pool, Jacuzzi, steam room, and fireplace, she figured her new husband had to have spent a fortune. Deciding to pay him back for every dollar spent, she stepped into the bathroom to prepare for a night of unforgettable sex. Returning in a red silk peignoir, she climbed beneath the sheets, closed her eyes, and spread her legs wide. On her back, Madeline anticipated the romance with a vagina so moist that if he were to enter her now, he'd drown in a pool of her flooding waters. Unsure if he knew how to immerse himself into a love nest so cultivating, she soaked up some of the moisture with a pillow clamped between her legs, but the streaming flow continued to pour out like a volcano until it reached the point of uneasiness.

*   *   *

Madeline opened her eyes and woke from her dream. She lifted her head off her desk and ran towards the women's locker room to slow a menstrual cycle that she had not been appropriately prepared for.

"Murder! At a church?" Madeline asked Jenny Davis after taking a pad out of her locker. Jenny, a tall, skinny blonde from the Narcotics Division was known as the chatterbox of the Bureau. Whenever a breaking story aired, Jenny was sure to know first and made certain everyone else knew as well. It was her way of kissing ass to gain recognition in the department. So far it had worked for her. Jenny was highly thought of by her male counterparts and moving up the promotion ladder fast. With the force's demos being at an eleven to one, male to female, who wouldn't think highly of a blue-eyed, six foot, conversational blonde?

"Yes, murder," Jenny confirmed. "What is the world coming to?"

"A war zone, that's what," Madeline answered. "I don't see how anyone could have the balls to kill someone in the house of the Lord. It's the most absurd thing I've ever heard of!"

"Tell me about it," Jenny said. "Guess there's no begging forgiveness for a crime like that."

"Yeah, right," Madeline snickered. "Forgiveness."

She finished dressing, rushing to stay a step ahead of the day's busy schedule. The first order of business was a nine o'clock interrogation she needed to complete before tackling the streets.

She walked into the room and took a seat across from the man dressed in an orange sweatsuit, his face desperately in need of a shave. Madeline placed a mini-recorder in the center of the table and lit a cigarette, taking a long drag before starting.

"So, are you ready to talk?" Madeline asked blowing out a long trail of smoke. "Don't just sit there and act like you don't know nothing. You're up for murder. Murder! Unless you wanna be buried underneath the Jackson State Prison, I'd suggest you start talking."

"I don't know nothing," the man said in a deep, low voice. "Even if I did, why would I tell you?"

"You're right!" Madeline said. "You don't have to tell me shit. But better me than Tyrone. You sure you want the boys upstate examining you and not me?"

"Go fuck yourself."

"You first," Madeline answered back. "Where are you from, anyways?"

"Blow me county, bitch!"

"Now, that's not the way you're supposed to answer a lady. Think you outta try it again?"

"Screw you!"

"Not very nice," Madeline said. "Did your mother ever teach you any manners?"

"Fuck off," the man blurted out. "You don't scare me one bit. I know how you pigs are. And it won't work with me."

Madeline reached over, grabbed her recorder, and stuck it in her shirt pocket before getting up from the table. "Fine with me." As soon as she started to walk away, the man stopped her just short of the door.

"Where are you going?" he said as Madeline turned the doorknob. "Okay. All right."

"Come again?" Madeline said, standing with her back towards him.

"I'll talk," he said. "Don't leave me in here by myself."

"So, now you wanna talk to this bitch cop?"

"Look, I said I'll talk."

"Good," Madeline replied, retaking her seat. "Now, what do you say we try this a second time? I'm Detective Harris."

She cordially reached her hand out to greet him. The nod of his head told her that was the best response she would get.

"What were you doing at the after-hours club last night?"

"What do you think?" he grumped. "I was doing the same thing everybody else was doing. Looking for some ass."

"Can you tell me how you heard about the spot?"

"Through a friend."

"And who is that?" Madeline asked, growing frustrated that she had to pry for information from a guy possibly facing life without parole.

"You're the cop, not me. Aren't these questions you should have the answers to already?"

As soon as he said that, Madeline swiped the recorder with her hand and it went flying across the room.

"Look! I don't have time for your bullshit. Either you're gonna talk or not. Stop wasting my fucking time!"

At that moment, the man realized that Madeline was the little hope for any sympathy that he would receive from the justice system, and decided to cooperate.

"What do you want to know?" he said, pouting like a teenager. "I was there to get my niece back and that's it. Those creeps brainwashed her."

"Is that why you shot her?"

"No," he said, rocking side to side in his aluminum chair. "I was trying to touch The Broker, but I ain't tripping 'cause I was gonna get all three of them eventually."

"You got names for me?" Madeline asked.

"She was an accident," the man said, ignoring Madeline's question, "and that's the truth. I didn't mean for her to die. Not yet."

"Names?" Madeline demanded. "Names, you got names of the other two women for me?"

The man looked at her guardedly through his snake eyes. "All I know is The Broker and that's it!"

"Then who was the bullet intended for?"

"Didn't I say I was trying to touch The Broker," the man said with humor at Madeline's lack of knowledge of street talk. "For you in the suburbs, that means I was shooting at The Broker. If I can get that bullet back, I'd jam it so far in his fucking chest he'd think he was having heart surgery."

"Tell me a little more about your experience with The Broker."

"The asshole rapes innocent girls!" The man pounded his fists hard into the table. "And my niece is one of them. She was so far out there at one time that the only person she could turn to was him."

"Out there? What do you mean? In the streets?"

"In the streets and everything else," the man admitted. "My family had disowned her. My brother cursed her. And her mother...let's just say she never stopped doping since dope found her. The bastard took advantage of that. When I heard Kim was down there giving up ass for a few measly bucks, I had no other choice than to go and bring her home."

He stared at Madeline with anger cooking in his eyes. "What other choice did I have? Kim is the baby in the family."

Madeline felt sympathy for the man. If someone would have been outrageous enough to use her daughter Amber in a sex ring, she would have quickly transformed into Lucy Liu from Quentin Tarantino's *Kill Bill*, and gone to get her daughter back.

"How do you know The Broker is responsible for all of this?" Madeline asked. "Couldn't the practice of hiring street girls for sex be widespread? I don't see how you could pinpoint him?"

"Word travels. And people talk. When you start hearing your buddies brag about different girls they're knocking off, of course you wanna know. The dotted line to street whores isn't hard to connect. I just wish someone would have warned me that my fucking niece was one of them."

"So, that's why you went down there? To get revenge?"

The man's eyes began to fill, and Madeline shoved a box of Kleenex his way.

"Come on, don't start crying on me now. Did you go for revenge?"

"Revenge is an understatement," he said. "I went to get my family back. Now I have to pay the consequences, huh?"

He dropped his chin onto his chest before continuing. "I've never been to jail, Detective. I won't be able to make it in there with those animals. I know I won't. There's no way. What am I to do, Detective Harris?"

"You'll be just fine," Madeline reassured him, paying no attention to his desperate cry. "Pray about it."

Just then, before Madeline could get out anymore questions, a knock on the door interrupted their conversation. The Chief and Zucal stood side by side in the hallway.

"Madeline," the Chief spoke first, "I apologize for interrupting your chat, but I need for you to get over to Mt. Zion Church immediately. A double homicide took place there last night, and I want to see if there's anything you can find out."

"But sir, I'm still working on the child trafficking case. I actually got some good leads to work off."

"I understand, Harris," the Chief said, cutting her off. "This one is dear to me. I'm a member of the church where the murder happened. The victim was active there. So I'd appreciate it if you and Ed would get over there and complete an investigation."

"No problem, sir. We'll take care of it," Madeline said, simultaneously looking at Zucal for concurrence. "Any word on the woman who was killed last night?"

"You mean to tell me you haven't heard?" Zucal said, excited. "I forget you've been out of the loop for most of the morning. Coroner's confirmed our suspicion and identified her as Ketaki Majhi. We got her, Maddie. Finally, things are looking up for us. Now we just need The Broker."

"Yeah, and whoever this third woman is," Madeline said.

"Don't go get your panties in a knot, Zucal," the Chief warned. "All we did was catch a bee in a honey field. We still have a lot of work to do on this case."

"I'll be ready in about thirty minutes," Madeline told them both. "I need just a few more minutes with this guy and I'll have the information that will lead us to him."

"Before you go and do all that, I need you to get over to the church first," the Chief persisted. "After that, I don't care if you spend the rest of the day questioning this clown. But I need you over there, now!"

"Chief, I just need thirty minutes with him." Madeline pleaded for him to change his mind. "I got him right where I want. If he's willing to talk, by all means, let us listen."

"I said, when you get back," the Chief snapped. "Whose department is this, mine or yours, Harris?"

"Yes sir." Madeline caved in to his direct order. "Can I at least have two minutes to grab a coffee? I haven't slept in forty eight hours."

"Of course, Harris. Who cares that Detroit ranks in the top three cities for having the highest murder rate in the world? Why should that be any of our concern? We're just the police."

"Come on," Madeline muttered to her partner. "I'll drive."

*　　*　　*

The entrance to the church's parking lot was blocked off with yellow tape. Cries of outrage from spectators behind a barricade across the street rang a depressing melody in Madeline's ears. She hurried inside and braced herself for the inevitable. A year in Homicide had provided a great deal of preparation for viewing deceased bodies, but as she stood over that one in particular, she shook her head in amazement. He was young, handsome, and mature looking. Stanford wore an elegant bracelet with a charm of Jesus Christ hanging from his slim wrist. Minutes later, a crowd control officer approached and tapped Madeline on the shoulder.

"Sorry to interrupt, Detective Harris," the rookie officer said, shaking nervously after acting on impulses. "I wasn't going to let them in, but they demanded to speak to someone in charge. I hope you don't mind, but I gave them your name."

"Wait, slow down a bit," Madeline said as she grabbed the stuttering officer by the shoulders. "Who are you talking about?"

"The gentlemen in the church," the officer added, pointing towards the door leading into the chapel. "They said they'll wait as long as it takes."

After Madeline made a mental note to get in the patrol officer's ass later for allowing a pedestrian not in uniform onto the crime scene, she called for Zucal, and they headed into the church. Two men dressed in black cashmere suits were sitting near the altar. At the sight of them, Madeline tensed up. She could tell by their pious appearance that they were extremely religious. Although she had been, for the most part, a "good girl" since the passing of her late husband, the lifestyle she had lived prior to his death is what worried her. The things she did as a teen would have sent John the Baptist himself to hell just for watching. As the two men of good spirits stood to greet the police, she couldn't muster up enough pride to look them in their eyes. Lowering her head, her eyes took in the expensive shoes on one of the gentleman's feet. She admired the illustrious lifestyle he had to have been living at the moment; alligators were definitely not a trademark of a lower-class Detroiter.

"What can we do for you?" Madeline said as she shook hands with both Ali and Eric.

The men introduced themselves and then pointed towards an empty row. "You mind if we sit? We don't plan on taking up too much of your time."

Madeline and Zucal sat down next to them. It was Ali who was eager to start the conversation.

"I believe we have some information that can help you with this case," Ali said, looking over Zucal's shoulder to make sure they were alone. "The man lying in the other room is a close friend of ours. We feel that we owe it to him to come forward."

"Go ahead, continue on," Zucal told him. "Take your time and start from the beginning. You've got our attention."

For the next fifty minutes, Ali walked them through every intimate detail of their lives, from childhood to adult, enlightening Madeline and Zucal about their mischievous childhood years and the haunting cloud that was hovering over their heads, compliments of Elena Sanders. They told them everything—how the group of four met, where they went to school, both public and ministry. Ali proudly discussed how he had turned his life around to become a servant of God but failed to mention the part about purposely taking the church's money, soliciting prostitutes, and committing almost every other sin mentioned in the Bible.

To Madeline, the story seemed surreal. Childhood friends, all members of the same church, and one of them a deacon; it didn't make sense. She continued to listen to the fable of their upbringing, questioning the truth and the integrity of the two gentlemen sitting before her.

"Wow," Madeline finally said after Ali finished the chronicle. "So, who do you think might be behind this?"

"I'm not sure." Ali shook his head. "My only guess is her father. He never could stand me, even after I turned my life around."

"For what you did to his daughter?" Madeline asked.

"No, Detective," Ali quickly corrected her, "for what he assumes I did to his daughter. It has to be him. That's the only person it could be."

"Why do you say that?" Zucal asked. "No disrespect, but both of you look relatively young. Early thirties?"

They both nodded. "Barely," Ali spoke up. "They groom us young now."

"I know when I was your age, I was a wild man. Wasn't too much of anything I wouldn't do." Zucal glanced over at Madeline, who struggled to keep from laughing.

"I had it all, the girls, a nice ride, a crib. I was living like the Huxtables. You mean to tell us there's no one else but this gal that you could've rubbed the wrong way since high school?"

"I'm a deacon," Ali finally spoke up. "I can only speak for myself in saying I denounced that lifestyle years ago. Plus, I believe that my faith in God would help me hurdle any obstacle, including this one. That's why we came down, to tell you what we know. Now that we've done that, it's up to you to follow through. I trust that you will."

"Of course." Madeline thanked both Ali and Eric for taking time out of their day to come down. "If you should think of anything else, don't hesitate to give us a call." Madeline handed her card to Ali. He took a second studying it.

"Ms. Harris, if you don't mind my asking, do you have a church home?" Ali held her hand after the handshake. Her response was muted, so he asked her again. "Well, Ms. Harris, do you?"

Here we go. Why me? I'm not ready for this. Not now. But I can't lie either. Not in a church. To a deacon?

"No, I don't," Madeline admitted. "Last time I was in a church was for a funeral. I'm sorry to say, deacon, but with work and a kid, Sundays are the only time for peace in my life."

Ali looked at her as if what she had just said was the most treacherous thing to fall upon the human ear.

"Then I want to invite you both to service this Sunday. It's the first Sunday of the month, and I'll be speaking in for the pastor. Promise me that you'll join in worship. If God can guarantee you eight hours a day, five days a week to do your job, you can certainly give back two hours on the seventh for him to do his."

Zucal declined the invitation, but with the guilt cascading down on her, Madeline accepted. She made a note that on Saturday she would call her best friend Simone and coerce her into going, in addition to picking up a Sunday dress for Amber, since she didn't have one. It would be her little girl's very first time going to church, and if she was going to go, she would look good. With her heart skipping beats, Madeline stared out of the chapel windows as the two young, handsome men hopped into a brand new rosemary-painted Mercedes and carelessly veered onto the Southfield service drive as though the luxurious vehicle they drove was a Tonka Toy.

Later that evening at the office, Madeline decided to browse the net for any archived stories about Elena Sanders before entertaining her witness again. With the new age of technology, stories both ancient and recent could now be viewed by using the proper search engine. After typing in Elena Sanders, she hit Enter. What appeared next definitely caught her interest.

Twelve different links of news articles covering the trials of the four friends provided more than enough reading material. Propping her chair up, Madeline sat most of that evening reading all of the articles, most of which were written by Shane O' Bryan of the Detroit Free Press. One thing Madeline noticed right away in O'Bryan's articles was, he shared an almost committed interest in reporting all of the obscurities he found in the cases. It was almost as if he took it personally, denouncing the teens for the accused rape of Elena Sanders. Even in his post trial write-up he had expressed his disagreement with the jury's decision, emphasizing a true deficiency in the court system, *moral principles*. Despite the fact that the general public grew to accept the boys back into society, his subtle condemnation of the four was clear in his columns.

"What are you looking at, Harris?" Zucal asked as he stood over her. "You have any idea what time it is? Now I understand why you can't get those bags out from under your eyes. You don't get any sleep."

"Look at this," Madeline said, tracing the screen with her finger. "She was a wreck. Her mother gave birth to her at the age of fourteen then sold her off for a few hundred dollars when times got rough."

She continued scrolling the page. "She was the youngest in a Miami prostitution ring that got broken up several years ago. Reports say she was only nine at the time."

"My God, Maddie," Zucal said in dismay. "Nine? What could anyone possibly want with a nine-year-old?"

"Sick!" Madeline muttered underneath her breath. "And check this, twelve years later she still ranks as the youngest to ever have been involved in such a thing."

"What else does it say about her?"

"Her last name wasn't always Sanders either. It appears she was adopted by a family out of the Dade County Family Courts and brought to Michigan when she turned thirteen. That's it!"

Madeline sat at the edge of her seat. "She was kicked out of a private school in the Upper Peninsula and when her father relocated the family to the Metro area, she enrolled in high school. From the looks of things, either she couldn't get rid of her promiscuity, or the four boys raped the shit out of her. I'd put my money on a little of both."

Zucal push rolled a chair from a separate cubicle and took a seat next to Madeline. She clicked on a different article.

"Look here," Madeline continued. "This one says that a contributing factor in her death was severe depression. From the sounds of her upbringing, who could blame her? I know I don't. Her childhood was screwed from the beginning."

"If depression is what killed her, someone should've given her a thicker backbone." Zucal said. "Don't make any excuses for her."

"I'm not making excuses," Madeline snapped back. "But you live according to the conditions that you're awarded. It just happened to be that hers were made from brass."

"I'm with you Maddie, I'm with you." Zucal calmed her with a gentle pat on her shoulder. "Don't get so wound up. Does it go on to say anything else about her death?"

Madeline shot out of her chair and stood, staring at the computer screen.

"My God! It wasn't depression."

She clicked the *next* icon at the bottom of the page. "She died from a self-inflicted gunshot wound."

"She killed herself," Zucal said softly.

"Poor thing," Madeline sympathized. "Says she leaves behind loved ones, but the article doesn't go into any further details."

"Probably the foster parents," Zucal said.

"Yeah, probably so. Such a shame," Madeline said after she finished printing off the remaining articles she needed and powered the computer off. Once she collected all of the articles, she snapped them with the three-hole punch and placed them into a binder. Back at her desk, she rushed to catch up on her work.

"So what you are going to do, Maddie? You gonna sit here for the rest of the night and work?" Zucal asked.

"I think so. At least for a couple of hours. I'm up to my head in paperwork. I haven't had the chance to do a thing, let alone write these reports. And you know how the Chief is. He won't understand that we've been in the streets. All he cares about is making sure our reports are tight."

"You can do that this weekend," Zucal added. "Come on, let's get outta here. Leave your car, I'll drop you off at home."

"Naw, I'll pass," Madeline said, stroking the knots out of her neck with her knuckles. "I'm off on Sunday, so I'm gonna make sure to leave it free. I've got some catching up to do with old friends."

Madeline had arranged an outing with her good friend Monahan. The State Fair was in town, and the two of them taking Amber was at the top of her list.

"So, I take it that you were full of shit when you told that deacon earlier today that you'd be attending his church."

"No, I'm going," Madeline said. "I don't know if I'm gonna stay the entire time, but I'll make an appearance. It's just so hard to stay awake after the choir sings."

Madeline stuck out her arms like Frankenstein. "Especially if the speaker is talking slooowww like a zommmbiiee."

Zucal flashed a friendly smile. "It's not a concert you're going to, Maddie."

"Yeah, but it's not a funeral either. Some of these churches should require their members to dress in all black. That way it'll match the way these pastors preach. I hope this one on Sunday is the exception."

"You'll have a nice time," Zucal told her. He took a moment to survey the office. Everyone had gone for the evening. Either they were out in the streets or done with the day's work. "Look around, everybody's gone. Maybe they're not as stupid as we are."

"Or not as dedicated," she said. "You can go if you'd like. I'm a big girl."

"No way, Maddie," Zucal lifted his feet, crossing and placing them on her cluttered desk. "If you're staying, so am I."

Spending time with her partner made time pass by quickly. Before she knew it, the clock on the wall read two minutes before the ten o'clock hour. Madeline hadn't gotten as much paperwork done as she had planned. In fact, the conversation she was currently having with Zucal took precedent and was much more stimulating than putting ink to a sheet of paper. It had been a while since she had the chance to open up and talk to someone. Although, at any given moment she was able to freely communicate with her buddy Monahan, there were certain matters she never discussed with him, matters like the one she had been talking on for the past hour with her now interesting partner.

"So, is that why you haven't found love?" Zucal asked her. "Because you're afraid?"

"I lost everything when he passed," Madcline said, opening up to him. "He was my foundation. I didn't have a backup plan for the 'what if' factor. Then, once the 'what if' became a reality, I was devastated. And I haven't been able to bounce back since."

"That's sad," he said, "but sooner or later you're gonna have to unleash this guilt trip of yours and give yourself to someone again. Do you think he would want otherwise?"

"I know Johnny would only want the best for Amber and me," she said with a smile. "He was a great man, Ed."

"And there are other great men out here too," he countered. "I'm not taking anything away from Johnny, because he probably was one hell of a man. All I'm saying is, give love another try. Let yourself go for once. You'll find happiness in it if you do."

"Sure I will," Madeline replied. "That's not what Oprah believes. She said a woman can find happiness within herself. As long as she understands and knows herself, then having a man would only be a secondary."

"Funny you're taking advice from a woman who has been on the dating scene for twenty years."

"She's happy."

"Trust me, and so is Stedman," Zucal said. "What man wouldn't want the richest woman in the world and not have to commit? I know I would."

"And that's why you're single just like me."

Madeline and Zucal shared a laugh together. They enjoyed each other's company. Never did either of them perceive the other could be such fun. They were still on the topic of relationships when minutes later the question came from out of nowhere and completely caught Madeline off guard.

"So, what does it take for a guy like me to get a date with a gal like you?" Zucal said, momentarily acknowledgeing the importance of her answer. "I'm dead serious. What would I have to do for just one outing? If you don't like, then I'll never ask again."

The question made Madeline uncomfortable. Sure, Ed was handsome and had the body of an Olympic athlete, but she had rules when it came to dating. Number one: *Never date a colleague.*

"Well, Ed, I don't know," she said, a bit bewildered. "I normally don't date anyone on the force. It makes life easier that way."

"We won't call it a date if that's the case." He stayed persistent. "So how about it, Maddie? We just go hang out for an evening. If you enjoy yourself, we go hang out again, and again, and again after that, if you'd like."

"I would if I could," she said, quickly thinking of an excuse, "but I can barely find time to spend with my little girl, let alone go out on the town."

"We'll make the time. Whenever possible. As long as I have your yes, then I can fit myself into your schedule. Step out on the limb, Maddie. Find your happiness. It's out here. You can't be afraid of it."

He was right, and deep inside, Madeline knew it. It had been nearly two years since the last time she was out on a date, and Mr. Washington, the principal, was a complete disaster. From that experience she had learned that she couldn't afford to waste time dating when it could be spent with friends and family. Time was too valuable for that! But looking at Zucal's sexy-ass body, temptation got the best of her.

"I guess we can go out once," Madeline said, finally giving in. "It will have to be after I've had the chance to spend some time with Amber, though. My daughter comes first!"

"I understand, I understand," Zucal happily replied. "As long as I know that we have a date on the horizon, I'm good to go."

"A date?" she teased. "I thought we agreed that it would be called an outing."

"Yeah, whatever! Call it what you want. This will be one outing you'll never forget."

Zucal leaned forward and planted a delicate kiss on Madeline's mouth. His soft, full lips matched hers perfectly, and when they separated, it was like a sparkle had been lit in Madeline's eyes the way they shined.

Damn, he's a hell of a kisser.

The spine-tingling moment was interrupted by her cell phone.

"Harris," she said. "What do you need?"

Suddenly, the way her voice went up a notch, whoever was on the other end of the receiver could not have re-layed a favorable message.

"You've got to be kidding me," she said, clearly disturbed by whatever piece of information she had just received. "He killed himself?"

CHAPTER ELEVEN

He was frustrated, annoyed, and bothered that each one of the girls continued to complain that Nizama was suffering badly. He could give a shit, paying no attention to the crabby girls who often bitched about everything under the sun anyhow. He'd been in that same position numerous times, and every girl he had injured had always healed on her own. They never needed medical treatment. So why should this one be any different from the norm? But with the constant whining of the girls a steady buzz in his ear, he had no choice except to check on her condition. Once he snatched open the door to the basement, what met him at first sight was gorier than a *Final Destination* movie.

A line of blood drippings ran from the edge of the concrete floor near the bottom step and ended where Nizama sat by the furnace. She was curled in a tight ball like a snail inside its shell. Her eyes were swollen as if she had been tortured all night. Her pants were soiled with wetness; the saturation of blood filtering onto the floor in a dark red circle of thick clots. At the pathetic sight of the helpless girl, The Broker went over and picked her up. As they headed back up the stairwell, he strapped her arm around his thick neck for added support.

Her eyes rolled back in her head, and The Broker rushed to get her into his van. When he opened the door, she flopped into the passenger's seat and fell over, limp, banging her head hard against the glove compartment, nearly causing the airbag to deploy. He jumped in and strapped on his seatbelt. *Where should I drop her?* He was afraid if he wasn't careful, she would tell everything and lead the police back to his place of business. *A wooded area maybe. God knows Michigan has a million of those. Or maybe a dumpster? No one would ever find her there.* His mind raced back and forth like a ping-pong ball. Nizama's weakened body collapsed onto his lap. *What the hell?* He shoved her back onto her own seat and decided to check on her. Her eyes were completely shut, and her mouth was as still as a standing pond. He grabbed her by the wrist and with two fingers checked for a pulse. He couldn't find one. He tried shaking her, but the effort was no good. Outraged, he struck the steering wheel twice with his fist. He was livid that just that fast Nizama had died before his very eyes.

He decided to drop her off at Henry Ford Hospital in a remote location of downtown Detroit. It wasn't the main hospital but one of those overnight urgent care clinics where people could get in and out in a hurry and not worry about an overflow of people visiting emergency. He parked in front of the entrance and lifted her into a wheelchair that an orderly brought to the car.

"Is this your daughter?" the enthusiastic red-haired youngster asked as he helped lift Nizama. "What's wrong with her? Is she dead?"

"No, she's just sleeping," The Broker told the boy. "And she's not my daughter. Look, I need you to do me a favor. Take her in while I find a parking spot."

"You got it," the boy said, grabbing the ten-dollar bill The Broker held out to him. "What's her name, sir?"

"Nizama," The Broker said, climbing back into the car. "Now hurry off and get her in. I'm right behind you. Be there in a second."

The Broker turned towards Nizama and said, "Well, you've got what you wished for. You're home now. Hope that it's better than this hellhole." The Broker drove off fast, whipping the van around the corner. He continued straight past the hospital's parking lot, making a hard right onto the busy city street.

*   *   *

It was three o'clock in the morning, and The Broker was on the Lodge Freeway driving past the Bagley Avenue exit when he thought about stopping at the newly built MGM Grand Casino to find a replacement for Nizama. Hosting an extravagant party in the very near future, he needed to find a girl quickly and get her trained. Usually it would take a week or two to strike enough fear into the girls he brought in. Time was short, and he would have to do it in three days max. Each minute that passed was crucial, and the casino was the one place many attractive young women would be at that time of night. With nearly every club in the downtown district closing at two, a flood of partyers would continue their late night excursions by gambling, socializing, or filling their bellies at one of the sumptuous buffets open twenty-four hours. He had promised his guest a girl like Nizama, and didn't dare show up with a girl twice her age. At the casino, he might get lucky and find a girl, maybe fifteen or sixteen, who by chance had gotten by with flashing a fake ID to one of the clueless security guards. It was a long shot. In two days, he was expected to host a party for a customer who always came to his parties with thousands to spend. Ali Gaines was his favorite, and he would not let him down a second time.

The Broker decided to pass up the casino and continued on the expressway for the next mile until it ended. He stopped at a red light on Jefferson Avenue, and in his periphery, he saw her, captivating him as she stood on the corner with one leg out, her hands on her hips, and a cigarette hanging out the side of her mouth. The girl with boots laced up to her knees and denim jeans that fit her ass tighter than thermal underwear was the one, and The Broker had to have her.

He looped back around the block, cautiously driving down the empty one-way street. He had a lot to lose if caught picking up a whore. After the ring he ran years back was busted, he ended up doing minimum time thanks to a judge on the Court of Appeals he'd paid off under the table. But if he were to get busted again, the magistrate wouldn't be as understanding as she was last time when she issued his prior slap-on-the-hand sentence.

Dimming the lights, The Broker lowered the passenger's side window when he crept up to where the girl stood.

"How much?" he asked her, studying her youthful frame like a textbook. Her body was tight, with hardened nipples poking against her tight shirt like needles. She had much more to offer than his other girls.

"Come on, sweetie, how much you want?" he continued, rushing her for an answer. "You gonna give me a price or what?"

"Calm down, hon!" she told him, walking up to the vehicle and sticking her head inside. "These are my streets and I know when the smell of a pig is around."

She glanced around just to make sure that there weren't any police in the area.

"And as long as you don't smell like pork, we have nothing to worry about."

"Of course not," The Broker answered. "How old are you? You don't look old enough to be in these streets.

Shouldn't you be at home and in bed with a Tickle Me Elmo?"

"I'm old enough to please you," the young girl said with confidence. At such a young age, she was poised.

"Why don't you get in, and I'll take you for a ride?" The Broker said as he reached over to unlock the door.

"Sorry, cutie, but I'm the only one who gives rides around here," she said, tantalizing The Broker with charm. "Really, though, what is it that you're looking for, daddy?"

"A good time. You think you can help me with that?"

"I probably can, but for a nominal fee," she said, businesslike. "All depends on what you want."

"How about some head?" he asked her. "What will some good dome cost?"

"Since it's late, I'll give you a discount," she said. "How about one twenty-five?"

"That's highway robbery," he screeched, frowning up at her. "You're too young to rob people like that."

"When I'm done, if you still feel like you've been robbed, then I'll let you shoot me in the mouth."

Her nastiness was more than he had bargained for. Not even Nizama could compare to this witty teen whore.

"All right, hop in," he instructed her and leaned over to open the door.

She slammed it. "Not here. Meet me over there in two minutes."

She pointed to an empty, badly lit, parking lot. "You must be a rookie," she told him. "I'm gonna have fun with you."

As the teen walked seductively to the tan van, The Broker opened the door for her and she climbed in.

*   *   *

Monahan rushed to start the engine. Not only would the man be going to jail that night for solicitation of a prostitute, but his face would be blasted on television sets across the state as Michigan's newest sex offender. As Monahan and his partner, Rusco, geared up to take the man down, they were amazed to watch as he suddenly delivered a quick, chopping, blow that caught the girl right on her chin.

"Go, Mono, go!" Rusco yelled for Monahan to put the car in gear. "Get over there, now!"

As Monahan fishtailed against the wet asphalt as he pulled out, from out of nowhere, a truck sent them flying across to the other side of the road. Their car spun around in a circle like a wrecked race car before coming to a screeching halt. Checking to make sure Rusco was all right, Monahan hopped out and ran around to the other side to help unbuckle her seatbelt. Afterwards, they got out, and stood in the middle of the street, pissed that the tan van was pulling onto the 94 expressway headed east, and nobody was following them!

*   *   *

She was dragged down the stairs and tossed onto the cold floor. The Broker was gracious enough to throw the girl a pillow and a blanket for the night, the broken seals in the downstairs window causing a moderate chill to seep through. As she bundled herself for the lonely night, she could hear the chattering teeth of other girls.

"Hello," she squeaked. "Who's there?"

"Hey," someone from across the room said, "just relax, girlie. The first night's always the roughest."

"What do you mean, relax?" she said, crawling on all fours to the nearest wall. "Where am I?"

"In hell," another voice shrieked. "Welcome to your *Nightmare on Elm Street.*"

"Be quiet, Tee. Why you always gotta be so damn evil?" a third voice spoke up. "You weren't as talkative when it was your ass three weeks ago. You were just as afraid as any other bitch would be."

"Go fuck yourself!" Tee said. "I'm just being real. There's no need to sugarcoat things. This is hell, like it or not."

"Well, you don't need to get her any more scared than she is now," the first girl said as she shuffled herself in the new girl's direction. "What's your name, girlie?"

The frightened teen didn't answer. She was still too leery of things and wasn't in the mood for making new friends. Not now. *What was going on? Was this really hell?* Those questions the girl wanted answers to, especially before speaking out in vain, but the woman's deep scratchy voice asking her a second time encouraged her to speak up.

"They call me Niecy," she answered. The fear of the unknown was enough to make her submit. She waited for an answer back, jumping after feeling a gentle tapping on her leg.

"Niecy," the girl said. "That's a pretty name. Never heard that one before. I'm Seema. I know that you're scared now, but it will take some getting used to. You'll be okay eventually. Trust me."

"Where am I?" Niecy screeched. "What do you mean getting used to? I'm not getting used to shit. I wanna get outta here!" She stood to her feet and stretched her arms like a blind man looking for the way to go.

"Come on and sit down," Seema said, pulling her back to the floor. "There's no way out. We've all tried.

This place is like prison. Only way out is up the stairs and through the guard men at the door."

"Go and take a chance," one of the other girls butted in from a distance. "It's about time for someone else to lose their life trying to escape. Go ahead. Give it a try."

"I said shut up!" Seema demanded. "Say another word and it's on."

A sudden hush swept through the room like a moment of silence after a tragedy. After losing Nizama, Seema had become the new girl in charge of the others. If they didn't do as she said, she would tell The Broker, and he would make sure they listened to her.

"You're one of us now," Seema continued. "Let me guess, he promised you work and school as well?"

"Huh?" the girl said, confused.

"Did he promise you schooling?"

"I don't understand."

"The Broker," Seema said. "Did he and his wife make you a promise that you could work and go to school? He did that to all of us."

"No," she told Seema. "I'm from Flint. I was living with my aunt until I got tired of her strict ways, so I hit the streets again. This was just my second night."

"Well, I guess welcome to Hollywood," Seema kidded, trying to make light of the situation they were in.

"Sure, thanks," the girl said with a smile. "So, what does he plan to do with us? We can't stay down here all night. Can we?"

"Shit yeah," a voice blurted out from across the room. "More like all of your life. This is your house now, bitch. When you get done fucking, you come home and go straight to your room."

"Quiet!" Seema yelled. "Why don't you stop? Please, she's just a kid."

"And so was I," the girl said. "But they don't give a fuck. All they see is a piece of ass. Young, old, black, purple, or pink, if you look halfway decent, prepare to be the fuck of some weirdo's fantasy."

The door at the top of the stairs creaked open. A short, burly muscleman without a shirt stood in the middle of the doorway and yelled, "Enough talking down there. You ladies get to sleep. You need to be on your P's and Q's tomorrow evening."

He shoved an additional girl down the stairs, and before he could close the door, Seema was able to see her clearly. It was at that moment that Seema's face flushed with disbelief. *Another girl thrown into the pits of the underground sex trade.* As the girl stumbled her way down the stairwell, Seema was shocked to see a petite Caucasian girl who could not have weighed more than a hundred pounds soaking wet.

"How old are you?" Seema asked the petrified girl who couldn't stop herself from shaking. Seema took her in her arms to console her.

"I'm twelve years old." The girl cried as tears rolled off her fat baby cheeks. The door slammed shut, and Seema could only shake her head at the fact that another young girl would soon have her innocence brutally taken by some creep who could care less about anything other than getting his rocks off and returning home to his loved ones.

*   *   *

The killer stood directly behind Eric in line at the grocery store. He had carefully watched his every move that morning. It sickened him, the way he casually strolled up and down each aisle as though life was perfect.

Nothing's perfect! Especially now.

The killer contemplated ending it there, grabbing Eric Thompson from behind and slicing his throat while the entire store screamed in horror. But that would be too easy and careless. Plus, he had one more life to end. Being careful was a necessity. As Eric paid the cashier for his basket full of groceries, the killer put the magazine down and followed him out into the parking lot.

Look at him. The killer watched Eric unload the bags into his Chevy Blazer. *I could run him down and keep on going. No one would ever know.*

He was just about to act on the urge when an armored truck pulled in front of the grocery store and two men with handguns hopped out carrying bags of money into the store.

"Shit!" the killer yelled at the missed opportunity. He grabbed his cell phone and called a number. A woman's voice picked up the other end.

"Hey," the killer said, frustrated. "I'll be about another half an hour."

He ended the conversation and followed Eric as he pulled out onto the busy intersection. The streets were jammed with cars going in both directions. The annual Woodward Dream Cruise was going on, and while people slowly drove their antique vehicles up and down the street, the killer worked hard to stay within visual distance of the Blazer.

Eric turned onto a side street, and the killer made the left with him. After watching Eric come and go home from work for the past week, the neighborhood was familiar to him. Now, as Eric turned into his circular driveway, the killer passed by, reverse parking in the same spot he had for the last seven days.

Game one of the Detroit Tigers baseball series was starting in five minutes, and Eric had to hurry if he wanted to catch the first pitch. He unloaded all of the groceries into the house and took a seat on the recliner. Midway through the bottom of the second inning, the knock came at the door.

As soon as Eric opened it, the killer struck him on the head with his pistol, entering the house as Eric fell backwards. Blood dripped from the corner of his eyelid as the killer continued to bash his head with his gun. Somehow in the midst of getting pummeled, Eric was able to wrap his arms around the killer's legs. He lifted and hoisted the killer off his feet. They were then both on the ground, and the fight was even once again.

Eric went for the killer's throat, wrapping his giant hands around his neck and squeezing it as though it was a lemon. The killer grabbed Eric's wrist and pried his hands away, headbutting Eric in the nose with his forehead. He clawed Eric's face like a tiger, digging his sharp fingernails deep into the pits of his victim's eyes. When Eric clamped down on his arm with his teeth, the killer screamed out in pain.

Eric delivered a fierce elbow just above the killer's left ear that made him wobbly. He outweighed his attacker by sixty pounds and took advantage of the weight differential by smothering him like a pinned wrestler. After draining the killer's power, Eric grabbed his head like a medicine ball and banged it hard against the wooden floor. He continued to bang the back of the killer's head like a drum and didn't stop until the killer lay motionless. He got off him and called the police.

"911," the operator spoke. "What's your emergency?"

Eric, with his back to the killer, answered her. "Somebody broke into my house," he responded to the dispatcher.

"Is the intruder still there, sir?"

"Yeah, I fought him off. He's lying on the floor."

When Eric turned to look at his attacker, a burning sensation suddenly penetrated his chest. A second and third shot near his heart caused Eric to drop to both knees.

"Sir, sir," the receptionist said in a fright. "Sir, are you okay?"

The killer slowly rose to his feet. He walked over and stood over Eric, pulling the trigger once more.

"All units, shots fired at 596 Evergreen Street," the receptionist sent the alert out. "Sir, sir, are you still there? Paramedics are on the way."

CHAPTER TWELVE

"Push, Madeline, push!"

Soon after he said this, Madeline bore down hard on the hospital bed for one final thrust. If it didn't happen now, it wouldn't, and the emergency doctors who had come into the room had already made preparations to take her upstairs for an emergency C-section. She looked into Johnny's teary eyes for support, and the whisper rolling off his lips was all the encouragement she needed.

"You can do this, Maddie," he whispered in her ear. "You can do it. I know you can."

With a kiss on the forehead, Madeline slowly pinned her chin into her chest and closed her eyes. As she tightened every muscle in her body and pushed, the determination of this woman warrior exerted itself. After the doctor handed over her beautiful creation, Madeline instantly bonded with the child. Everyone but her had believed that she wouldn't make it past the third month, let alone to term. *The power of a woman!*

*   *   *

The shove against her leg eventually woke Madeline up, and she opened her eyes to see that she was the only one in the church still sitting.

Service had started precisely at ten-thirty. Madeline was able to persuade Simone to attend with her. All she had to do was promise to take her to *The Woodward*, one of the most delicious restaurants in Detroit, after service. The negotiation with Amber didn't come easily. Even though Madeline could have simply forced Amber to go along, she ended up leaving her behind. After all, she was with her best friend, Simone, and the things they talked about when in each other's company should never fall upon the ears of children, let alone Amber's.

Struggling to keep her eyes open, Madeline became wide-eyed and stood as the church members graciously welcomed the guest speaker for the evening, Deacon Ali Gaines. After a short introduction, everyone took a seat and the deacon began his sermon. Surprisingly enough, the day's lesson focused on the Ten Commandments. Though he touched on all ten, the ones he seemed to focus on were, "Thou Shall Not Kill! Cheat! Steal! Nor Covet Thy Neighbor's Wife!" Once he finished, everyone in the church was aroused and convinced that this Deacon Gaines was a saint. Nearly everyone, that is.

After service, Madeline and Simone went for dinner then concluded the evening with a movie. Monahan was at the house entertaining Amber. Madeline had decided to give Rosemary the night off since she had been with Amber the last four nights in a row. Balancing her daytime job with watching Amber, Madeline felt Rosemary would appreciate the time away. So she went with her backup sitter, Monahan. Even though Madeline trusted him with her daughter, she was still respectful enough not to tie up his entire Sunday evening. Once she dropped Simone off at home, Madeline decided to call her own to let Monahan know she was on her way back.

"Hey, Mono," she said when he picked up after the second ring. "How's it going?"

"It was fine until you called," he said with an attitude. "I just got her to sleep, and you wanna ring the phone now. You had all evening to call if you wanted to check up on her. I don't know why you always do this. It's not like she's in the company of a stranger."

"I know she's not," Madeline said. "Did she wake up? How was I supposed to know that she turned in early? It's usually after nine before she falls asleep."

"See, and that's why she's as restless as she is," Monahan told her. "She should never be up past eight. It's a written rule that little kids should get at least ten hours of sleep per night."

"Well, when you decide to have one, you will need to take your own advice into consideration," Madeline said with a hint of sarcasm. "Would you like for me to pick something up? I'm about ten minutes away. Should be there shortly."

"Naw, I'm good," Monahan said. "It's been a long one. She gave me a run for my money today. That girl of yours has way too much energy. I'll just probably have a glass of wine if it's okay with you."

"That's fine, but wait for me," she told him. "And what do you mean a run for your money? The work that you do for me is volunteer."

"Well, soon all this community service is gonna start coming with a price," he informed her. "And I might install back payments with that."

"You'd do that to me, Mono? I am a single mother with a low-paying job," she reminded him. "Unless you plan on marrying me and making our income one, then a kiss on the cheek and a thank you will have to do."

"I couldn't marry you," he said sternly. "You still like little boys. Once you decide that a real man is what you need, the few of us out here will be taken already."

"What do you mean, I like little boys?"

"Don't play me like I'm stupid," he said. "It's all around the force, Maddie. You and Zucal? I still don't know why you chose to tell Jenny. That was stupid! You already know how she is."

"I didn't tell her a thing," Madeline barked. "That bitch is gonna get enough of starting rumors. I can't wait to get back in that fucking office."

"Now don't go jumpin' through hoops," he said with a chuckle. "I was only playing with you. Don't nobody know anything except for me."

"Oh yeah, and what do you know?"

"I know that you've been seeing him for the last couple weeks. You actually starting to like this guy now?"

"Why?" she answered. "Does it make a difference? You act like I'm not supposed to date anyone. Enough with that shit! I have a life too!"

"That's not it at all," Monahan cleared up the misunderstanding. "All I'm saying is that if you continue to go out with losers, you'll eventually end up regretting it."

"And what makes you think he's a loser?"

"Because, he's not me."

"So what are you saying, Mono? I should date you now?"

"Why not?" he told her. "We have a lot in common. We always have fun when we're together. And Amber loves me to death. I think that says a lot."

"Mono, have you been drinking again? I told you that you outta slow it down a bit."

"You know what the funny thing is, Maddie? I'm as sober as a drunk in his last week of rehab."

Monahan was being sincere. They had been friends for quite some time now and never entertained the thought of dating. They had cuddled up on the couch with each other at night, watched their favorite shows, and taken Amber to the park or zoo, things tight-knit families did together. But never had he pushed the issue of dating until now. Yeah, there was an obvious attraction on both sides. However, because they were such good buddies, acting on impulses could very well result in a fatal friendship.

"You ever heard of the phrase, *carpe diem*?" Monahan asked.

"Never," Madeline replied. "What the hell is that? Sounds like a new pair of fashion jeans."

"Not denim, silly," Monahan couldn't stop himself from laughing at her. "*Diem. Carpe diem.* It's a phrase from a Latin poem."

"So, what does it mean?"

"It means, *'seize the day.'* Madeline, I can't just be friends with you anymore knowing that I have feelings that go above and beyond a friendship level."

Madeline was completely caught off guard by that. She had considered crossing that line with him but valued their friendship too much. Every time she would tell Simone about her affection for him, Simone would encourage her to go for it.

"Life's too short, girl. You better stop passing time being miserable when you could very well be happy," Simone would say, scolding her best friend. "He is a hell of a man."

"I know he is," Madeline would respond.

"So, if you know it, then what's the problem?"

"I can't cross that line. I would lose a very good friend if I did."

"Girl, fuck that line," Simone would retort. "That line is the reason why people can't be happy now. Lines can be erased, Maddie. I suggest you bend your skinny ass over and piss on it until it becomes invisible."

With Monahan confirming what Madeline had felt for such a long time, she was at a loss for words.

"What do you expect me to say, Mono? We've been friends for so long. I know how relationships go. If ours doesn't work out, friendship afterwards is nearly impossible. I don't know if I can chance losing one of my best friends."

"You can't go into it thinking that it won't work. That's setting us up for failure. We don't need to rush into this. All I want you to do is *carpe diem*, before it's too late."

"Too late for what?" Madeline asked. "If it's truly meant to be, it will be."

"I'm a hot commodity," Monahan bragged. "I won't be on the scene much longer. Eventually, Cinderella will find her Prince Charming, and if you're not careful, I might just go with her."

Madeline held the phone away from her ear and looked at it as though she couldn't believe what she had just heard.

"Then when I decide that I want you, I'll simply take you from her," she affirmed with confidence.

"You think it's that easy, huh? You can just take me from whoever I'm with?"

"I know it is," she said before hanging up the phone. "You love me. I know you do. And I love you too, Mono."

She whipped her vehicle around and fastened her seatbelt, continuing down the darkened path headed home. As she pulled into her driveway, she realized that she was singing along with one of her favorite old school hits, "We Can't Be Friends," by Grammy recording artist Deborah Cox and R.L. She let the tune play out, then put the car into park and smiled. She walked the short distance up the walkway and opened the door to her home where her most valued friend waited anxiously on the couch with a bottle of chilled red wine for her arrival.

*   *   *

That next morning, Madeline was closing out her paperwork on her only reliable witness, who had taken his life by plunging thirty feet to his death in the county jail. Zucal was standing at her desk, raring to go.

"You ready?" he asked.

"Ready for what?"

"Chief wants us in the field today. He claims we've been hiding out the last couple of days."

"Hiding out, my ass," Madeline complained. "I've been bustin' my butt trying to catch up. Why is he always riding us?"

"Who knows," Zucal said. "But we better get a move on it. He was pretty upset this morning."

"What's his problem?"

"Don't know. The publicity probably. Mayor's office called down and wanted answers again. Guess he didn't have any."

"They're always butting in," Madeline said. "Shouldn't he be used to that by now?"

"You would think." Zucal pulled her chair out from behind her desk. "Come on, let's get going."

It was a rainy Monday morning, and traffic on the 275 Expressway was thick as usual. Looking out of the passenger side window, Madeline could see the Six Mile exit in the far distance. However, the bumper-to-bumper traffic and paramedics passing on the shoulder convinced her that they would be held up for a while. When the flow started moving again, it only took minutes to get to the exit. The hour of lost time would have to be made up later.

Mapquest had the house twenty-three miles west of Detroit in a suburb known as Livonia. Madeline was apprehensive about the attitudes of the city's residents after remembering the statistics she had read, realizing she had just entered into one of the more racially segregated cities in the state. The wicked looks she received from other drivers as they waited for the light to turn green proved her source to be accurate, which made her love for residing in the heart of the city of Detroit that much more special.

The house was located off a busy cross street. As Zucal pulled into the Woodbridge housing complex, Madeline adjusted her vest to make sure it was properly in place. They parked under the carport and walked up the arching walkway to the front door of the Sanders residence. After ringing the bell once, the door was yanked open and a black man wearing a fitted cap bolted between them like a bowling ball.

"Freeze!" Madeline yelled, chasing the man as he ran in between parked cars and jumped over a brick wall in the back of the complex.

"Foot chase in progress," she said into her receiver. "Woodbridge Apartments."

When Madeline and Zucal cleared the wall, they were met by acres of dry land. The man had separated a considerable distance now and was moving at high speed. Knowing that she wouldn't be able to catch him on foot, Madeline drew her gun and aimed at the back of his leg. She was just about to squeeze the trigger on her gun when Zucal grabbed hold of it.

"No," he said, pushing her arms down. "We already got enough heat on us as is. No need for more."

"What are you doing?" she yelled at him. "I had a shot."

"I don't care. Look around you. There's nowhere for him to go."

They stayed in pursuit of the man, closing a bit of the distance when he got caught on a fence he had to hurdle to get into a schoolyard. There were several kids playing at recess, and as the man hurried through the play area, the teachers scrambled to get to their students. There was one little girl who had isolated herself from the group and was swinging upside down on the monkey bars. The man went straight towards her.

"Chelsea!" the teacher screamed in panic. "Chelsea, watch out!"

The man cuffed Chelsea under his arms and snatched her down. Her foot was tangled under the bars, and she screamed in pain when her ankle twisted. As Madeline and Zucal approached with their guns drawn, the man held Chelsea up as a shield, backing his way into the school building.

Ms. Lacey was teaching her mathematics class when the man rushed into the room carrying Chelsea on his hip. The kids in the classroom began screaming and crying in fear.

"Get out of here!" the man yelled at the panic-stricken children. "You too. Get the fuck out!"

They scrambled like mice out the door. The man grabbed another child with his free hand, a boy with big hazel eyes.

"Not so fast." He yanked the boy by his jacket collar. "You're staying here with me."

"No," the boy cried out, trying to shake himself loose. The man tightened his grip, nearly choking him.

"I said you're staying with me." He jerked his jacket like a slingshot and the boy fell onto the ground.

"How about me?" Ms. Lacey negotiated. "Take me instead."

"Get the fuck outta here before I hurt them."

Ms. Lacey hurried to get the remaining kids out of the classroom. Madeline and Zucal now stood outside the door.

"It's over with," Madeline yelled out. "Let's end this without anybody getting hurt."

She didn't get a response from the man, so Zucal pounded on the wooden door. "Come on, buddy. Let's not do anything stupid."

For the next ten minutes they tried negotiating the release of the children. They would offer concessions and seek demands from the man, but would get no answer in return. The kids were awfully quiet, which was a real concern for Madeline. Outside the door, Madeline and Zucal decided they were going in. *Whatever was to happen, they would soon find out.*

Zucal kicked the door in, and Madeline went first. She swung her gun around like she was one of *Charlie's Angels*, controlled and experienced. With her finger gently touching the trigger, she looked for all three of them. Moans from one of the tables focused her attention on the teacher's desk. Both kids' mouths were bound by tape, their hands tied to each other. Madeline released the bind that held them together while Zucal went over to close the classroom window. In the midst of the chaos, the man had escaped them both.

*　　*　　*

"You have to turn yourself in," she said, as she adjusted his necktie. "You can't continue to walk around as if everything is okay. God only forgives those who can confess to their wrongdoings. If you expect to get to heaven, then you must turn yourself in. It's the right thing to do"

"I will," he told her. "I just have one more thing to take care of."

The killer grabbed his cufflinks and inserted them into his dress shirt. He looked at himself for the last time, knowing he would probably never be in normal clothes again. Where he was going there was one outfit, and in prison he would have to get used to the orange-colored jumpsuit. Before he left, they prayed together, asking God to forgive them both. Once finished, he yelled out, "Lock up!" and then he left. Never hesitating at the door, he closed it behind him, feeling strongly that he had no other choice than to hand over his soul to the justice system. What else could really hurt him? He was content with himself, content with what he had done thus far. But before he would turn himself in to the police, he had one more task to complete. Ali Gaines was the only one left. He just prayed that God would eventually find it in his heart to forgive him for what he was about to do next.

*   *   *

Madeline was looking through the requested court files on Elena Sanders when she felt a tap on her shoulder. It was Monahan.

"Hey, Mono," she said. "Where are you off to in such a rush? Last time I saw you this excited you picked me up from the airport. Do you want me to go away again so that you can miss me?"

"No, smart ass," he countered. "I'm actually on my way out to look at a body."

"Yeah? What you got?"

"Don't know. Got the call this morning from the hospital. A Jane Doe was brought in late last night and dropped off. Witness said a man in a tan van handed her off like dirty laundry."

"Any specifics?"

"Just that she was pregnant and beaten beyond repair. They prepped me beforehand. From what I got, this one's not for the faint of heart."

Madeline shook her head, disgusted by the news.

"Funny thing is," he said, "I was on watch last night, and a tan van snatched a girl right from under my eyes. Can't be that big of a coincidence. Isn't everyday you see a tan van driving down the streets out here."

"Ain't that the truth," she replied. "Look, I heard about the accident. You okay?"

"I'm good. My back is a little stiff, but all is well. Rusco needed the day off, though. She's a little more banged up than I am."

"She okay?"

"Just a little sore. Her neck is bothering her, so she's taking the rest of the week to get better."

Madeline smirked, "Not as tough as you thought. I never missed a day because of a little soreness."

Monahan couldn't dispute that. Only time Madeline missed days away from work was once after a short struggle with a prior boyfriend who tried to take her out. In the midst of the fight, she had received a huge gash on her forearm. The time she needed to recover was more than justified.

"Come and take a ride with me," Monahan said.

"I really can't. I have so much to do. I still have to go through all these files. We've finally been able to nail down the killer. Now we just gotta find him."

"Yeah, who's the suspect?"

She inched closer. "Get this. It's been the girl's father the entire time," Madeline said. "He's gone overboard with the protective father cliché."

"I guess he has," Monahan agreed. "Why don't you take a little break? Come and take a ride. For old times sake."

"Sorry, Mono, I'm gonna have to pass. Look at all this work I need to finish."

She pointed to her disorganized desk, which was cluttered with papers stacked high. The puppy-dog look Monahan shot her forced her to reconsider.

"How long are you going to be?" she asked him. "I can't be out all day. I still have to sit my turn on watch."

"They don't have patrol on that?" Monahan asked, aware that the Sanders house was now under around-the-clock surveillance.

"Chief said since he got away from us, we're responsible for bringing him in."

"That prick," Monahan said. "Will he ever stop riding you so hard?"

"It's a question I've been asking myself since I started," Madeline said as they headed for the door. "Ride me, baby, ride me."

The waiting area in the hospital was filled to capacity. As several angry people waited their turn to be seen, Madeline and Monahan were taken straight back. They passed along a bright white hallway where Colleen Thomas had been awaiting their arrival.

Colleen was the Chief Medical Examiner of the hospital morgue. She was a heavyset brunette with shoulder-length hair. Her scrubs were a dingy gray, making her body appear wider than it truly was. As she led them through the double doors, her rubber-soled shoes squeaked against the hospital linoleum.

There were only three bodies in the room, each one draped with a sheet. When Madeline walked over to the wrong one and exposed it, Colleen quickly got an attitude with her.

"Don't touch," she told Madeline as though she were a child in an antique store. "I haven't had the chance to clean that one up yet."

"Sorry," Madeline apologized to her. "I thought it was—"

"Please, don't think," she said. "That's for me to do. I've been doing this for thirty-something years. I think I know what I'm doing."

"No one said you didn't," Madeline countered.

Monahan, noticing the sparks between the two women, jumped in before the cat claws came out.

"I take it this is she?" he interrupted, walking over to the shortest body.

When Colleen removed the sheet from the girl's body, Monahan's eyes quickly became fixed on the slash markings scattered across her skin.

"Damn," he said in disgust. "You were right. This is a sight."

"I tried to prep you," Colleen told him, "but I don't think you can ever be prepared. I've been here for years, and my stomach still turns when they're brought in."

"What happened to her?" Monahan asked as he examined her bruises. "Looks like she was in World War I."

"That's an understatement," Madeline said in distress. She recognized the young girl. "Fuck, Mono, we brought her in a while ago. She was found at a truck stop, victim of a gang rape."

"Anything we can run with?" he asked her.

"Not really. Her guardian came to get her and that was the end of it." Madeline looked down at her pretty face. "Somebody killed another baby. This shit is getting tired."

Madeline showed her weakness as she had an emotional moment, turning her back to collect herself.

"You must have one of your own?" Colleen asked.

"I do," Madeline said. "Just a few years younger."

Madeline wiped her runny nose before continuing. "I don't know what I'd do if someone were to ever hurt Amber."

"Sweetie, these girls come from broken homes. Most of their parents are strung out to the point where the only option they have is to turn to the streets. Once they do that, they end up in here sooner or later. Be glad that you provide a stable home and are there to help coach your own."

In some way, the woman was right. Madeline had always maintained a roof over her family's head. As a single mother she had done a damn good job in providing Amber with a solid foundation to build on. But the part about coaching was an overstatement. Since being promoted to Homicide, Madeline had to rely heavily on the babysitter to coach Amber about life's lessons. Looking down at the slaughtered girl, Madeline felt as though she owed it to herself to put the pieces back together with her child.

"Have you determined a cause of death?" Madeline finally asked, rising above the personal guilt.

"Internal bleeding," Dr. Thomas answered. "We ruled it a traumatized death. She was carrying twins. Whoever did this had intentions of killing them. A real Dr. Kevorkian."

"Hold it a second," Monahan interrupted. "I thought this was a murder?"

"Kinda sorta," the woman said. "Let me show you."

The woman folded up the sheet to the girl's waist. Madeline cringed at the sight, but Monahan maintained his poise. The girl's vagina looked like thick lava. The blood that coated her was chunky, almost salsa-like.

"What happened to her?" Madeline asked, clearly disturbed by the sight. "Sweet Jesus!"

"As you both can see," the woman said, "she was assaulted with some sort of foreign object. My guess is a bottle."

"A bottle?" Monahan asked.

"Yeah, let me show you."

Dr. Thomas gave them a run down of her findings. She had a lot of knowledge that came from years of inspecting dead bodies. Being as descriptive as possible, she showed Madeline and Monahan the exact angle at which penetration was made possible. Surprisingly enough, she wasn't finished yet.

"The reason I say a bottle is because of this," she continued by showing them the outer part of the girl's vagina. "See these pink marks? This is normally caused from extensive ripping. Normally, you'll see this on a sexually assaulted victim whose attacker was too big. But it wouldn't be this atrocious."

"I think I've seen enough," Madeline said. She walked away, and Monahan, still putting the pieces together behind the heinous sex crime, stayed put.

Madeline took a seat in the corner of the room next to three bags of clothing, each bag labeled with the name of the deceased that had come in overnight. As she looked at the clothes hanging out of each bag, the Jane Doe bag with a pair of jeans covered in bloodstains caught her attention.

She slid the jeans over with her foot, careful not to alert Colleen Thomas, who was too busy talking with Monahan to pay her any mind. Colleen had already checked her earlier about putting her hands on things that didn't belong to her. She didn't need the Grinch catching her doing something else now. After inspecting the little girl's size eight stretch jeans with a flower design going up the right pants leg, Madeline had to exhale a deep breath. Amber had that same exact pair.

Next, she slid the little girl's stained pink shirt towards her. It was a cute little pink polo with a pocket on the front. After Madeline inspected the blood blotches on it, she was quick to throw it back in the bag before

Colleen could turn around. And that's when it happened. As Madeline stuffed the shirt back into the clothes bag, a piece of cigarette paper fluttered out, landing on the floor next to her. When she went to pick it up, Colleen snarled at her again.

"What are you doing?" she asked from a distance. "I thought I told you to leave stuff alone."

"I was tying my shoes," Madeline lied, palming the paper.

"Then why is the bag open? Why don't you come over here where I can keep a closer eye on you?"

Monahan felt the tension and knew that it wouldn't be much longer before Madeline snapped back. She had a short fuse for disrespectful people, and Monahan knew it. When he saw her face tighten, Monahan knew he had better jump in.

"Why don't we just go?" he suggested. "I believe we have everything we need now. Thanks for taking time out for us today, Doc. Is that her bag?"

"Yes, that's it. The one by your nosy little partner." Dr. Thomas grabbed the girl's clothes and handed them to Monahan. When blood was found on clothing, the articles went to the DNA unit at the precinct for testing. Monahan was gracious enough to take it back himself.

He followed as Madeline rushed out the door, acknowledging Colleen with a wicked smile on the way out. Once they made it back to the car, Madeline took the cigarette paper out of her pocket. The message written in black eyeliner caused her mouth to drop.

"What's that you got?" Monahan asked, keeping one eye on the road and the other on Madeline's stunned look.

"It's some sort of message," she said, reading the note. "Mono, I think somebody's in trouble."

"Let me see that." He snatched the piece of paper from Madeline and held it out in front of him with one hand.

"635 Greenfield...Behind Big Tire...Please Help Me! Seema."

"What do you suppose it means?" Monahan asked, obviously concerned.

"I haven't the slightest clue," Madeline admitted. "Behind big tire. It doesn't make sense."

Madeline kept repeating the words until finally it registered.

"The tire!" Madeline yelled. "Think about it Mono. It makes sense. The tire. Greenfield. Shit, Mono! Shit!"

"Calm down," he said. "What the hell is wrong with you?"

"That's it," she continued. "What's the one thing you see if you travel east heading into Detroit?"

"Huh?"

Madeline's spirits continued to rise as though she had just collided with fate. "Think about it, Mono. What do you see off the freeway as you head into the city?"

"I don't know. Construction barriers?"

"No, dingbat. The tire. You see the big tire."

"Oh shit! The Uniroyal tire," Monahan answered, becoming excited now as well. "Shit, Maddie, I think you may be onto something here."

"Darn right I am." She licked her lips in anticipation. "I pray this leads us to the asshole."

Monahan knew exactly who she was talking about. "The Broker?" he said, just to make sure they were on the same page. "You thinking what I'm thinking?"

"Damn right I am," she admitted. "That girl was part of his sex ring. Whoever this Seema is, she's reaching out for help. Let's go before it's too late!"

Hold tight, Seema. Hold tight for me, little one.

The ride down the expressway way was a bumpy one. Michigan was known for its meteor-sized potholes, but thanks in part to the four days of constant rain, the roads that day were more damaged than ever. While Monahan played a game of Road Rally, Madeline called Zucal to fill him in.

"What's up, Maddie?"

"Hey. I've got some good news. This could possibly be the break of all breaks. Remember the teenage girl we brought in for an interview months ago?"

"Who?" Zucal asked. "We bring girls in everyday. I struggle to remember yesterday, let alone months ago."

"The one from the truck stop," Madeline reminded him. "We found her out in the woods. Remember now?"

"How could I forget?" he recollected. "We brought her in for questioning. The poor girl was scared for her life."

"She had a right to be," Madeline said. "She lost hers last night."

A silence swept through the phone before Zucal continued. "She lost it," he said, choked for words. "Damn, that's a shame."

"Tell me about it. Anyways, she was carrying some sort of note with her."

Madeline filled him in on her hunch—that there might be other girls involved who were reaching out for help. *Seema.* When she finished, she told Zucal to request backup and meet them at a remote location about a half-mile from the tire.

Time to gear up and take this mothafucker down once and for all! Madeline checked the chamber on her 9mm automatic.

"Monahan," she yelled at her good friend. "Can you drive any slower? Floor it!"

Half an hour later, they were gathered in the parking lot of a Blockbuster video store. Madeline took her time prepping the team with everything she knew. She was expecting to see her partner in the group, but he hadn't shown up yet. It wasn't until the officers were about to load up that Zucal came swooping around the corner. He pulled up next to where Madeline stood with her arms folded.

"Sorry I'm late," he said. "But the Chief called me on a tip that came in. The tan van from last night was spotted downtown. He wants us over there immediately."

"But I got a better lead to work off," Madeline griped. She found it strange for the Chief to call off a raid in the middle of the operation. "He can't do this. Not now."

"Don't do this, Maddie," Zucal complained. "Come on."

"I don't give a shit," she shouted. "He's always doing this. I'll take the heat for it this time."

Madeline finished instructing the few officers that had come out in support, completely ignoring Zucal and his orders. She'd had enough of the Chief challenging every decision she made. She was prepared to fight fire with fire and to allow the chips to fall where they may. If he was going to discipline her for making a judgment call, then so be it. At least the time off would be gratifying, knowing she had rescued a girl, or many, from a known violent leader in the sex trade.

"Keep your eyes open and be safe," she finished, opening the passenger's side door to Monahan's car. When Monahan didn't get in on the other side, Madeline grew impatient.

"Let's go!" she yelled at him. "I don't have time for this shit, Mono. Come on and let's roll."

Monahan just stood there like a statue. Emotions were high, and he knew his best friend would calm down in a second. All she needed was time to think about the end result of her action. If Madeline's plan didn't pan out, the Chief would have her neck. And the fact that they both believed he was out to get her anyways was enough to make her change her mind.

She punched the dashboard with her right fist. No one said a word as they all hopped in their vehicles and headed downtown. Madeline raised the music up on Monahan's stereo. She didn't feel like riding with Zucal, nor did she feel like talking with Mono. All she wanted at that point and time was to move her head to the beat and vibe with Detroit's own Slim Shady as he rapped about everybody in the world turning against him.

*   *   *

The residence overlooked the riverfront in a high rise apartment complex in the downtown area. Two unmarked vehicles were already parked at the end of the block, opposite the end where Monahan and Madeline pulled to a slow stop. It was when they had to lower the music that Madeline finally broke her silence.

"I don't see why he always gotta do this to me," Madeline cried out. "I never thought I'd say it, but I miss Sex Crimes. You think Marcellus would take me back?"

Marcellus was the head of the Sex Crimes Unit. He always held in high regard the work Madeline had done when she was under his command. From certificates to formal recognition, she had always felt appreciated and welcomed for the services she gave to that department. She had been entertaining the thought of returning to her old division but never acted on impulses. Now, with her micromanaging boss riding her ass, she contemplated whether or not Homicide truly had a place for her any longer.

"I'll take you back in a heartbeat," Monahan didn't hesitate. "And so would he. But we both know you better than that. You'd never give in to a challenge. You're a scrapper, Maddie, and for this one you're gonna have to fight several rounds before you get recognized as a force to be reckoned with."

The tan van was parked slanted in the driveway. The lights on the house were dim, and no one had been seen roaming inside. With nothing happening, Madeline took the chance to make sure everyone was ready just in case.

"Are we all set?" she asked into the receiver after changing the frequency to Channel Four.

"Good here," she heard Officer Milton come on. He flashed his lights twice signaling his location.

"Here too," another officer on the other side of the park came on. It was when Zucal made his broadcast that things got a little personal.

"I've been set for a while now Maddie," he said in a soft voice.

His stupidity was not called for, especially then, and was completely embarrassing. *He just ruined the one chance he had at any kind of date.* She chose not to respond to his asshole choice of humor.

It wasn't long before the lights came on inside the loft. The shadow of a man about six feet tall moved behind the thick curtains. Minutes later he was standing in the driveway, a "hoody" covering his head, looking around as though he knew he was being watched. He hurried to get behind the wheel, reversing out onto the narrow street. Madeline could see his eyes continuously check the rear view mirror for his followers. Realizing they had been spotted, Monahan sped across the intersection once the man raced through a blinking yellow light.

"Here we go," Monahan said, in full pursuit. The other officers fell in line, and it looked like a California

Highway Patrol speed chase. As Monahan turned his sirens on, he could see the driver look out of his rear view mirror one last time. Surprisingly enough, he slowly pulled over to the side of the road. *The Broker would never give up so easily.* Madeline and Monahan glanced at each other in confusion.

"What the hell?" Madeline said. Monahan came to a complete stop behind the van.

"Bait!" Monahan snarled. "We were thrown some bait, and we bit on it like fools."

Madeline got out of the car and slammed the door behind her. "How in the world could he have us watching the wrong fucking van?" she grumbled out loud, cursing the Chief. "This was a complete waste. I knew we should have gone with my first instinct."

We will get to you soon, Seema. Madeline asked the driver for his license and registration. *It's only a matter of time. I promise.*

*   *   *

"All units in the vicinity of Schoolcraft and the 96 Expressway, please respond to a standoff in progress."

The call came in thirty minutes after Madeline and Monahan had the man's car towed for driving on a suspended license. As the rain fell in full fury, Monahan hydroplaned across lanes and was quickly on the Southfield Freeway. The address was the Sanders residence. Mr. Sanders was spotted returning to his home, and when officers approached for the takedown, he was quick enough to lock himself inside. So far, it was unknown if others were in the house with him.

Monahan pulled onto the quiet street with the other three units trailing. The responding officers had done a good job in blocking off the area and keeping the neighborhood watchers inside their homes. Racing out of the car first, Madeline went straight towards the officer in charge.

"What we got?" she asked him as she slipped her vest over her head.

"One inside. Wife at work. Kids in Florida," he said, quickly giving Madeline the rundown. He was Officer Terrance Scruggs, a senior in the Gang Squad Division. Madeline had crossed paths with him on a few occasions at work but never knew what role he played with the division until then. He had recently transferred from Albany, New York's South Station.

"Any contact made with him?"

"Not yet. We have officers working on the lines now."

"Good. Then we wait," Madeline said, completely taking over the crime scene. "What I need is two on top, three on each side, and four in the back. Make sure you let them know that I am in charge and nobody moves without my command."

The officer looked warily into Madeline's eyes. Since his transfer he had only heard good things about Detective Harris. For all he knew, she could have already been on the level of Captain or Commander.

"You go it," he said. He scampered off to let the others know he was no longer in control.

For the next hour Madeline attempted to reach Mr. Sanders by phone. Each time the phone would ring relentlessly until an operator's voice came on the line stating nobody was picking up and the call would drop.

"I say we go in there," she said as she pressed redial once more. "He's not coming out. All he's doing is buying time. For what, who knows?"

"There you go again," Zucal said. "You always want to go in blind. What happens if he's waiting for us with a semi in his hand, then what?"

"Then we act like we're the fucking police," Madeline retorted, growing impatient with her partner. "This is what we get a paycheck for every week."

Monahan tried holding back his laughter at his friend's snappy attitude.

Out of the clear blue sky, an officer posted on top of the neighbor's roof spoke out, "Suspect within visual," he radioed. "Clear shot. Waiting on a proceed command. Detective Harris, waiting on a proceed command."

Madeline realized she had a decision to make. She could authorize the sniper to end it then, that way killing two birds with one stone. She'd get the killer as well as have time to go and rescue Seema. But did she have enough evidence to authorize a shot on this man? With his fate resting on a single word from her, the man's life was spared by her reluctance.

"Negative," she shouted into the receiver. "That's a negative. Do not shoot."

She looked upwards at the officer peering through his scope with one eye. When he lowered his weapon, Madeline called for the barrage team to come over. Within minutes, they had huddled and broken apart. Madeline said a quick prayer. *Dear God, let me have made the right choice.* She then positioned herself for a forced entry.

Two smoke bombs went through the windows first. After allowing a moment for the vapors to seep through the house, Officer Johnson led the attack. He pounded on the door twice, identifying himself as an officer with the Detroit Police Department. When he counted to three, the battering ram crashed through the door and seven members of the Tactics Team invaded the premises.

Mr. Sanders was hiding on the floor in a pushup position behind the couch. When the officers hurried past him he took the opportunity to make a dash for the front door.

He moved quickly through the front yard, dodging officers like structures in an obstacle course. When he planted his left foot and made a hard cut, Zucal went diving on the ground past him. Sanders turned to his right, and a shoulder caught him in the stomach and sent him tumbling in the dirt. When he finally shook the stars circling over his head, he was able to see the face of the woman who brought him down. Madeline had already begun wiping the dirt off her clothes. He was handcuffed and taken away.

With the sunlight beginning to fade, Madeline wanted to pass on searching the Sanders residence. In fact, the quicker she could wrap things up there, the faster she would be able to close a three-month-old case. She knew the investigation was needed, though. Hard facts were better than subjective ones, and Madeline realized in order for that one to stick, she needed hardcore evidence.

After ransacking the house for clues, she authorized his computer to be taken, along with a mini voice recorder, and a pocketbook of phone numbers and addresses. There was nothing else in the house that might prove useful in convicting Mr. Sanders. Madeline was prepared to rely heavily on facts she had accumulated thus far and if anything panned out from the items collected, that would be an added bonus. As the remaining officers began leaving the scene, a stunning discovery in a *Time* magazine complicated matters.

A ticket dangling sideways from the magazine caught her attention. When she snatched it from the magazine, the findings were beyond belief.

A roundtrip ticket on American Airlines for Rick Sanders was printed on a computer generated voucher. The departure date was five months ago, the return, just last week. Mr. Sanders had just gotten back from his retirement home in Florida where he went yearly to escape the treacherous Michigan winter! Madeline was taken aback.

"Goddammit!" she spat as she flung the ticket far across the room like a Frisbee, realizing there was no way Sanders could be the killer.

Who was behind the killings? From a case nearing its final stage to a case busted wide open again, Madeline angrily walked back to the car and cursed the fact that she had no suspects.

*   *   *

The Detroit Tigers were struggling, chasing the worst record of any baseball team in Major League history. Even with the acquisition of one of the premiere catchers in all of baseball, the Tigers continued to lose nearly every series, and lately, it seemed every game. But sports analysts anticipated a bright future for the young team, claiming that they were a few veteran signings away from turning things around. But they would have to go through the growing pains of losing and upgrading certain positions first. If Alan Trammell and others continued to build a dynasty by going out and getting top players like their catcher, Pudge Rodriguez, the team had no choice but to be successful.

Comerica Park replaced Tiger Stadium, which after many years was now a tourist attraction. The priceless stadium was located right in the center of Downtown Detroit, across the street from the Fox Theatre. With baseball fans licking their chops for a winning season, and the support that came from the city and its citizens, the club had no excuse for its record. As the night's theme, "Take your family to the park night" was prompted by the clubs marketing team, the idea was enough to encourage fans to go out and take their loved ones, only to have watched a struggling team put forth a valiant effort.

Corporate suites for the season ranged in price from five thousand to five hundred thousand dollars. With the money that The Broker made from the sex trade, the bottom line financial impact was nominal. As he glared out of the 800-square-foot suite, he smiled at all who packed the house below, anticipating the doors to open and his guests to arrive, knowing that none of them would leave disappointed.

The game was scheduled to start soon. It was six o'clock when his first guest of the evening arrived. He was Charlie Starks, Director of Manufacturing Operations for a small plant in Kalamazoo, Michigan.

"Make yourself at home, Charlie," The Broker told him. "The girls are running a little late but should be here shortly. Can I get you something to drink?"

The Broker cracked open the cabinet and filled two glasses with vodka and cranberry juice. After handing Charlie his, a second knock at the door made them both turn towards it. The Broker placed his glass on the countertop and went to see who was there.

"Ali!" he exclaimed with a big hug and smile. "Good to see you, old pal. I take it you came by yourself?"

"Yeah, I needed to come alone. Been a little paranoid lately. I got a strange feeling I'm being followed?"

"Fucker's intuition?"

"Maybe."

"Living this kind of lifestyle, Ali, you gotta be prepared for everything that comes with it," The Broker told him. "But tonight you can relax. I owe you one, and I promise to clear your mind from all the bullshit."

He took Ali's coat and hung it in the closet.

"Is this it?" Ali asked, always wary of others invited.

"I'm expecting two more. Don't worry, I trust these guys with my life, the same way I do you."

The Broker poured an extra glass and introduced Ali to Charlie. They chatted for the next ten minutes, and Ali was comfortable having Charlie there. Sometimes, guys had a tendency to put their trust in people they had just met, and Ali fell into that web. When the other two finally showed up, Ali drifted their way.

Sam Collins was a married hockey player for the Red Wings practice squad. He had recently become involved in the sex trade, thanks to his best friend, Jimmie. Both had families at home, and reputations to keep. Jimmie finally had a free moment to escape the demands of his everyday job. He had contacted The Broker weeks ago and let him know that he was burned out, both at home and on the clock. Running for the state governor's position was no easy profession.

Ali looked at his watch, getting a little nervous now. He had promised the pastor at his church that he would fill in as the transient speaker for Bible Study at 8:30 P.M. He tried to get out of it, but there was no way. He had been neglecting the church for the past month, and the pastor made it mandatory for him to attend that night. Ali chased time and wanted to hurry before it was too late.

"What's taking them so long?" he asked The Broker, irritated. "I told you that I had somewhere to be by eight."

"They'll be here in a second," The Broker told him. "I just got the call. They're taking the elevator up now."

"Good, 'cause I don't have time to waste."

*   *   *

Her body was worth a million and one words. As she entered the suite and walked past him, Ali slowly licked his full lips in admiration. *A teenage girl with the body of a goddess!* As he struggled to keep his manhood from rising, he couldn't shake the thoughts of taking this girl in particular as his sex slave, to do whatever he desired with her.

Time wouldn't stop and it was now a little past seven. Ali had done well mixing and mingling with the six girls whose primary purpose was to provide entertainment. But he had already identified the one he wanted, and since The Broker owed him, he was first to have the girl of his picking. After whispering in The Broker's ear, the girl was instructed to get up and follow Ali into the back room of the suite.

"What's your name?" he asked her as he moved her hair behind her ears. "I'm not here to hurt you. Just want to have a little fun, that's all."

The girl answered him in low tone, "Seema."

"That's very pretty," Ali told her. "Now, Seema, everything will be just fine as long as you do as I say. You do understand?"

She nodded, and Ali kissed her, engulfing her lips like he was giving her mouth to mouth resuscitation. She panicked and backed off. He was amused by her teasing and pinned her against the wall, rubbed his hand between her thighs, and cupped her clit in the palm of his hand. When he immobilized her, she tried to squirm away but he pushed her onto the bed.

"I told you not to fuck with me," he cursed her. "I'll be done in a second, and you can go back to where you came from."

She pushed herself away from him and crawled backwards towards the headboard. He walked around and snatched her to her feet, ripping her shirt down the middle. Ali licked around her tiny breasts like an ice cream cone and was soon nibbling on her immature nipples with his teeth. He forced his hand down her panties and began to insert his middle finger into her tight cunt. When he tried to get all four fingers in, the pain she felt at that moment caused her to scream in pain.

"What the hell is going on in here?" The Broker asked after he burst into the room.

"Another one of your sloppy girls," Ali replied angrily, slapping Seema with the back of his hand. When she fell into the corner, The Broker leaped over and grabbed Ali.

"I got it from here," he told Ali. "Nobody hits my girls but me. I'll take care of it. Go and take a walk, and I'll have it all taken care of in fifteen minutes."

"I don't have time for this shit." Ali lunged at Seema, but The Broker was strong enough to restrain him. "I'm giving you ten minutes to fix her up. When I get back, she better be ready."

Ali stormed out of the room and walked straight through the front door. Once he was out of the suite, The Broker turned towards Seema in a frenzy, his teeth clenched in a boiling rage. He grabbed a clothes hanger from behind the door and walked towards Seema with a malevolent smile on his face. She prepared herself to be beaten again.

*   *   *

Ali hurried past them with his head down. Detective Rusco was the last to make it off the elevator and took it upon herself to press the stop button on the elevator. Madeline had placed the call earlier in the day for her to check on the house at *635 Greenfield, Behind Big Tire*. It took every bit of fiber in Madeline to swallow her pride and make the call. She did it discretely, and Rusco was more than willing to get involved. She ended up following the tan van to the stadium, keeping a close eye on the women as the driver parked in the parking garage. She notified Madeline of the exact whereabouts, and they came over at once.

Now that the police force had made it to the fourth level and had begun to secure the area, Ali lost himself in the growing line of spectators watching as the boys in blue prepared for the raid. He had ordered a popcorn just prior to all the concession stands closing down. Waiting with others in the thrills of excitement, Ali put a handful in his mouth, grateful that by the narrowest of margin he had made it out of the room seconds before being detected.

Madeline and Monahan were at the front of the line. As soon as the battering ram hit the door, screams of terror rang out from the five girls. When Sam Collins tried to run, Monahan lunged at him, taking him down harder than any hockey crosscheck. At the sight of Sam being wrestled to the ground, Jimmie and Charlie Starks raised their hands high in the air and allowed the arresting officers to cuff their wrists.

Madeline moved towards the bedroom door and banged on it with the base of her hand. When she didn't get a response, she motioned for the officers to use the battering ram. The heavy steel slammed into the door, an awful noise screeched, and the hinges went flying.

Madeline fell onto her back in excruciating pain, the bullet hitting her in the shoulder inches away from the vest that protected her body. As other officers returned fire with The Broker, Monahan was able to pull Madeline out of harm's way. When the smoke cleared, Seema crawled out from underneath the bed, and Madeline, growing weaker by the second, closed her eyes to the biggest smile a civilian had ever given her for doing her job.

"Thank you," Seema said gratefully, sidestepping The Broker's bullet-riddled corpse to honor Madeline with a kiss on the forehead as paramedics carried her away. Madeline smiled at the teenage girl, then closed her eyes. She was out cold.

CHAPTER THIRTEEN

The killer slipped into the elevator and pressed the button for the main floor. He was careful enough not to allow his colleagues to see him. He had arrived at the stadium minutes before the officers had and positioned himself out of harm's way. Though he stood mixed in with other bystanders watching the game, the killer kept a close eye on the score as well as the suite. When Ali Gaines stormed out of the room in a fury, the killer stood so close behind him in the concession stand that he could smell the sour scent of cologne on his skin. As the doors to the elevator opened, the door to the staircase released simultaneously, and the killer moved stride for stride behind Ali.

He was growing frustrated with Ali not knowing where he was walking. Like a chicken with its head cut off, Ali roamed the parking lot looking for the section where he had parked his car. While the killer sat on edge in his, he was able to quickly reflect on the past and the road that led to this furtive breaking point.

Ever since joining the police force, Deputy Chief Cromwell had excelled in his career. Going through the ranks in record time, he was successful in several divisions and recognized by his superiors as a high performer. But one thing that came along with a successful career in law enforcement was a tremendous amount of hours on the clock. When he made the choice of career over family, Cromwell not only neglected a wonderful partner in marriage, but also a troubled teenage daughter who found comfort on the streets as opposed to in the household. Sweet little Chrissie Valentine had fallen in love with a man three times her age, and ever since leaving the confines of a comfortable home, the brutal path of a young teen striving for her independence ended with a dotted line to near disaster.

She was sold by her lover to a man and a woman for five hundred dollars. Enduring several beatings and the torture of having sex with numerous men on a daily basis, Chrissie eventually ran away from the strip club where the scandal took place. She tipped her father to the location, and after raiding the club, the police brought down The Broker along with several members of Detroit's first sex scandal.

But jail time wasn't enough for Cromwell. He sought blood. After all, it was his only daughter who was raped, drugged, and beaten. Taking the matter into his own hands, he sought everyone involved in the scandal, and even worse, everyone who had taken a piece of his little angel's innocence.

After finishing the investigation, interviewing witnesses and girls in the club, and after a heart-to-heart with his daughter, the Chief was stunned to find out that the crew of boys who made the news a few years back by getting off on rape charges were back to their old tricks. This time was different, though. They had fucked the wrong girl, at the wrong time, and with the wrong father. Needless to say, revenge was a dish best served cold, and the Chief made sure he would be the personal butler for each of the young men involved, regardless of who he had to kill in the process. As he awaited his final payback, the Chief cracked a smile at knowing his daughter's predators were no longer the fierce animals half the city thought them to be.

*　　*　　*

"Answer the phone would you?" Ali spat into the headset. "Come on. Where are you? I need to let you know I'm running late?"

He frantically tried to reach his pastor. If he didn't get in touch with him soon, his entire lifestyle would crumble. The pastor had already threatened to take his position with the church for failing to involve himself in activities lately. It was the one piece of advice Pastor Bailey had given him from the start of his devious scheme. Don't be late and do as I say, period. Ali rushed to uphold his promise to fill in as the guest speaker and continued to dial Pastor Bailey's phone to let him know that he was only a few minutes behind schedule. When the line continued to ring, he slammed his phone down on the passenger seat and the battery went flying against the windshield. Ali looked at his watch and hoped that the members of the church hadn't left yet.

He was running ten minutes late and was driving at ridiculous speeds down the drizzly streets. He had made a promise and needed to keep his end of it. If not, people would start getting suspicious of him, if they hadn't already. With larger amounts of money missing, Ali was taking a bigger gamble than ever before. And anyone who knew the art of gambling knew that you had better quit while ahead. Only, it didn't matter to Ali. Yeah, large amounts were missing but besides the pastor, there was no one who could substantiate for certain that it was him. And with Pastor Bailey in his corner, Ali knew that he was covered. When he finally made it to the church parking lot, surprisingly enough, there was only one car near the back entrance. He parked next to the vehicle and hurried inside.

Ali walked briskly through the long hallway and was soon at the chapel doors pulling them open. Hurrying down to the altar, he was happy to see Pastor Bailey praying on both knees near the pulpit. Courteous enough to make sure the pastor finished, Ali greeted him with fervor.

"Sorry I'm late," Ali said as he adjusted his necktie. "Where is everyone? I thought you were out."

"I sent them home already," the pastor responded in a mellow tone. "We need to talk, Ali."

Something about the way he said it made the hairs stand on the back of Ali's neck.

"Ali, God doesn't take kindly to thieves. I know that I've taught you a lot of bad things in the past, but there comes a time when you can do bad for only so long."

Pastor Bailey looked him directly in the eyes. "I've known you for many years now."

"Yes, you have," Ali said slyly, wondering where he was taking this. "You've seen me grow up. Shit, you've seen us all grow up. You were our role model."

"I know I was, but when I lost my little brother, everything got put back into perspective. Ali, we can't do this anymore."

"So, what are you saying?" Ali asked him. "You're not telling me that you're about to come clean, are you? There's no way that can happen."

"Not in a hundred years," Pastor Bailey relaxed him. "There's no way I could tell God's people how I gave you a deaconship, knowing your true intention. You think what they did to Jesus was bad? I'd hate to see their reaction to me telling them that. But I think we both owe it to Chris not to continue with this charade."

Ali took a moment to regroup. "Boy, I miss him," he continued. "He used to tell me that you can be anything you want as long as you strive to get it. Guess we didn't have to strive that hard, huh?"

"Well, I'm the sole person to blame for that," Pastor Bailey said, dropping his head. "I'm the one that pulled you guys into this from the start. I introduced you to sex and everything else you know."

"But you changed your ways. You don't do any of that shit anymore."

"Yeah, but I let you keep doing it and never stopped you, even after my own brother got killed. I allowed it to continue."

"You can't control another's actions."

"You're right, I can't. But when others take it upon themselves to investigate matters is when things get sticky."

The pastor dropped an envelope in Ali's hands. When he pulled out the black and whites, Ali was stunned to see a picture of himself arriving at The Broker's parlor. He quickly glanced at another picture of him at the bank withdrawing money.

"What the hell?"

"One of our elderly sisters has been following you for weeks." The pastor turned his back and took two long steps. "Instead of making a big deal about the situation, I told her that I'd handle matters. Ali, for the sake of us both, you need to find another church home."

"But my mom is a member here and has been for the past twenty years."

"This isn't a game, Ali. This is real shit. She was angry and was considering getting the police involved. Thank God I was able to talk her out of it. But you can't show up here on Sunday, I'm telling you."

"All right, I understand where you're coming from. So, what do we do now?"

"Nothing," Pastor Bailey told him. "We continue to live life as though none of this ever happened."

"Thanks for everything, Mike," Ali said and stuck out his hand.

Mike Bailey smacked his hand away and pulled him in for an embrace. "It's Pastor Bailey to you."

After a tight hug, Ali turned and slowly began his trek back up the walkway. The doors to the chapel swung open like a battle scene from *Scarface* and bullets went flying in every direction. Chief Cromwell had heard it all.

As the Chief filled Mike Bailey's chest with lead, Ali dropped to the floor and crawled under the pews. Cromwell planned to end it now. As he went to refill his clip, Ali stood to his feet and reached for the gun on his belt. While they stood as though it was a face-off from an old Western, a shot rang out behind Ali. He felt the burning sensation erupt in his skull and landed awkwardly after twisting his way to the ground. He saw the face of his killer, a woman with a basket of fruit on her head and shaking hands holding a single-shot pistol.

"Ready?" Sister Douglass and the Chief prepared to head to the downtown precinct to turn themselves in. "It's all over now. The circle has finally been broken."

CHAPTER FOURTEEN

It took two weeks before Madeline was released from the hospital; thank God the bullet which lodged in her shoulder hadn't come close to striking any main arteries. For fourteen long days she had taken time to recuperate and break from the burdens that went with being a Detroit police officer. Although it wasn't the type of relaxing one would find on an exotic island getaway, she found tranquility in being there, especially with her two best friends by her bedside.

Monahan and Simone had both gone to visit her daily, spending a great deal of time talking and catching up, as good friends normally do. On different occasions, Madeline would openly express how horribly she felt for allowing her job to come between her and her friends.

"It's a shame how tragedy is the only thing that brings folks back together," she said. Both Monahan and Simone paid her little mind, hearing her words travel from one ear and out the other. They were overwhelmed knowing that Madeline was going to be okay, and being there with her was the only thing either of them truly cared about.

As Madeline traveled home with Simone, she stared happily out of the passenger's side window, thinking of nothing but reuniting with Amber and seeing her daughter for the first time since being admitted. She wouldn't allow Amber to see her while she was sick and bedridden, even though the youngster had begged to do so. Allowing such wouldn't have been good since Amber often awoke in the middle of the night from nightmares. Rosemary was gracious enough to accept the responsibility of watching Amber during the two-week span she was hospitalized. *Rosemary's not so bad, after all.* She remembered a proverb her mother liked to repeat. "Most people aren't lucky to have good people in their circle that will be there for them in time of need." It was at that moment that Madeline felt like she had a pretty good circle of friends.

As they pulled onto her cul-de-sac, Madeline glanced over at Simone and smiled. She didn't say a single word to her humorous friend who sang along with the radio as though she were Whitney in her heyday. Once she got out of the car and thanked Simone, Madeline decided to dial Monahan during the short walk to the front door.

Before she had the chance to dial his number, her phone began to ring. *Was it coincidental that they were thinking of each other at the same time?* Madeline looked at the number flash across the screen. Stopping momentarily, she allowed the phone to ring once more before gladly pressing the talk button.

"Hey, sweetie," Madeline said. "What's going on? I know that you're coming to see me today? We can go and get a movie. The new *Scary Movie 3* is out on DVD."

"Madeline, where are you?" he shouted through the phone. The urgency in his crackling voice frightened her.

"I just pulled up to the house," she said cautiously. "Why, what's the matter?"

"Amber. Where is Amber?" he yelled.

"She's upstairs sleeping. Rosemary's in the house babysitting. You already know that."

"Madeline," he continued in a panic, "go and check on her. Rosemary's a fake!"

"What?"

"A fake, Madeline! Rosemary is not who you think she is!" Monahan shouted. "I was looking up The Broker on the database and stumbled across a partner of his, his wife. Her name is Nungi."

"What does that have to do with Amber?" Madeline asked, completely bewildered now.

"Madeline, Rosemary is an alias. The woman's real name is Nungi."

Madeline gasped for air.

"Madeline," he continued, "Nungi is part of the sex trade. She's wanted in several different countries."

It was like she had hit a brick wall. As her cell phone slowly rolled off her fingertips and broke into pieces against the concrete porch, Madeline rushed to the front door of her home. Fumbling through her purse, she found her keys at the bottom of the handbag and was now in the house headed for Amber's room.

She nearly ran through the bedroom door as if it wasn't there, bursting it open with her good shoulder. When Madeline saw Amber's blankets neatly folded on the floor next to the bed, she checked the closet.

"Amber!" Madeline screamed, racing back down the hallway. She felt a sudden rush of paranoia and screamed for her daughter once more. "Amber!"

While she desperately searched the rest of the house, Madeline could feel her exploding heart beating faster with every breath. *Where are you Amber? Dear God, help me. Where are you, honey?*

Nothing ever really seems to come to an end. Madeline shot back out the front door and was in her car, her hands shaking on the steering wheel, her foot pressed firmly against the gas pedal. She was going to save her baby girl. The only problem was, she had no idea where she was going.

Coming in 2008

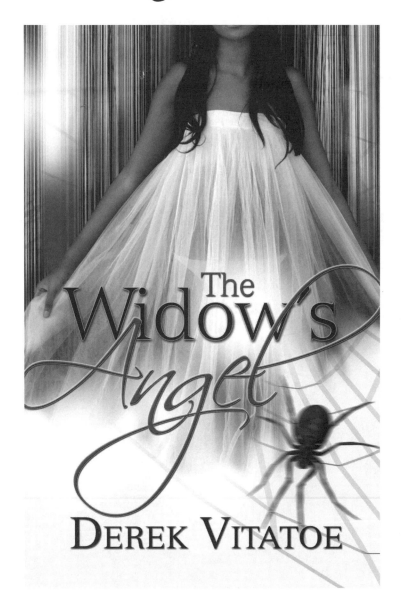

The Widow's Angel

DEREK VITATOE

The Soul of Urban Literature

Name: _____

Address: _____

City/State: _____

Zip: _____

QTY	TITLE	PRICE
	Deacon's Circle	$16
	Shipping & Handling $4.00/book	$

TOTAL $_____

Mail payment and order form to:
Nyack Books
P.O. Box 980586
Ypsilanti, MI 48198